EAST SIDE
STORIES

To Barlara, Elek and hily.

[signature]

3382-WEIS

EAST SIDE STORIES

Tales of Jewish Life in the Lower East Side of New York in the 1930's

Sidney Weissman

3382-WEIS

To order additional copies of this book, contact:
Xlibris Corporation
1-888-7-XLIBRIS
www.Xlibris.com
Orders@Xlibris.com

CONTENTS

This book is dedicated to my wife, Inez,
whose idea this book was,
to my children, Nancy, Richard and Paul,
and to my grandchildren, Lexi, Rebecca,
Jesse and Madeline.

ACKNOWLEDGMENTS

My deepest thanks to Rick Grossman
for his computer expertise,
and to Michael Peters
for his help in production and editing.

Special thanks to Mims Strauss for her help, too.

Sidney Weissman, the author,
can be reached via email
at stantonbooks@post.com

PROLOGUE

"East Side Stories" are the fictional accounts of the lives of Jewish immigrants, their sons and daughters, their families, who lived in the Lower East Side of New York City in the time of the Great Depression during the 1930's. It has been estimated that a half million Jews lived packed together in an area of approximately nine blocks by eleven blocks which also included schools, businesses of all kinds, synagogues, theaters, libraries, dispensaries, some institutional buildings among which were the Educational Alliance and the Henry Street Settlement, a few small parks. And, of course, the tenements rising five stories high, two toilets on each floor servicing six flats.

The original older immigrants spoke Yiddish, their young sons and daughters who had come over to America with their parents or grandparents knew Yiddish yet spoke English. Those born in America spoke primarily English, some knew little of Yiddish because speaking English was the thing to do, it signified being a "Yankee" and that was what they greatly desired—to leave the traces of that foreign Old Country behind. The younger children spoke to their grandparents in broken Yiddish and English.

Education was the goal. To be a somebody, to seek personal freedom, to rise above what their families had been and encountered back there in Europe, to remove that trace of Old World oppression, of being beaten down, of being caged in ghettoes or designated areas by Russian, Polish, East European governments. And free education was what these sons and daughters received in New York City—in the night schools which taught English, in the public schools and high schools, in the free city colleges.

But life was harsh, desperate, during those times. Living was a constant battle, nothing was easy. There were no jobs, banks had failed. They lived in America where there was everything, and they had nothing. They lived from day to day, hoping for a better day. A job, any job, was a prize to hold and keep.

Yet they laughed. At the Charlie Chaplin comedies. At the Marx Brothers movies, in the times when they had saved up enough money to attend the Yiddish theater on Second Avenue where they laughed and cried. But laughter they sought, to escape the world.

They observed the Jewish holidays, some more than others. The older people were more observant; for the younger, more Americanized, there was Rosh Hashanah and Yom Kippur, the days of awe, where it was decided, on high, who was to live and who was to die. And there was Passover when the ancient exodus from Egypt was celebrated and every boy was bought a new suit and shoes, every girl a new dress and shoes, and mama and poppa wore their best finery. But purchasing new clothing had been in the good times, before the Depression, when there had been money.

This, then, is the background of the East Side Stories.

THE ACTOR

He showed us the old photograph taken by a professional photographer many years ago, forty years or so, when he had been in his late thirties. He passed the framed picture to my mother who looked at it, marveled silently as she shook her head and said to him, "Velvel, you were so young, so handsome!" and Velvel, the actor, smiled, the kitchen light splashed gleams on the top of his bald head, on the gray fringe of hair below the baldness circling his head. His round face, apple-cheeked, had grown wider with the smile.

My mother passed the framed picture to my father who as he held it, stared at it and said, "A regular Rudolph Valentino, a movie star."

Velvel's smile slowly disappeared. A faraway look came into his eyes and he began to sing, "*Voos iz gevayn iz givayn und schoin nishtoo*, What was, was, and is no more." My mother said to him, "*Ai*, Velvel, you're still a good-looking man."

"No," he replied. "Seventy-six. An old man."

My father had finished with the framed picture and I reached for it. My father handed it to me and holding it carefully I looked at the posed eight by ten sepia-colored photograph. I could see someone much younger than the Velvel who now sat near me. In the picture someone sat posed theatrically, his chin on his hand, a full head of dark wavy hair, staring into the camera. I looked from the photograph to Velvel who sat across from me at the kitchen table in our tenement flat. There, somewhere beneath the pile of sagging flesh that time had plastered on his face, beneath the drooping jowls, maybe, perhaps, I could imagine that younger man. At least there seemed to be a trace of it there, somewhere. Most of the

hair was gone, lost to baldness, and what remained had long ago
lost its color. Age had been layered again and again on his face, his
body had gone to fat. Now he was short and round all over, round
face, round body. Time had scratched its wounds into the flesh of
his face, had furrowed his brow, put deep lines down from the
corners of his mouth, had gnarled his hands.

"*Ai,*" my father said. "We all grow old." Then as an afterthought,
"It's a heavy life, heavy."

Velvel was a neighbor who lived on the floor above us in a
small flat in the tenement on the Lower East Side of New York. He
lived alone, his wife had died years ago. Now and then, when he
was lonely I suppose, he came to visit us, to spend a few evening
hours with us. He had very little family left, there was a daughter
who lived far away in a place called Cleveland.

Cleveland? I had thought to myself when I had first heard
Velvel mention it, Cleveland? That's far, far away. What Jew lives
outside of New York City? I knew the general direction of Cleveland, somewhere in Ohio, but Ohio was far away, almost as far as
Europe as far as I was concerned, what did I know? I was almost
fourteen, I had only been to Connecticut twice, during two summers before the Crash and the Depression, when we had rented a
room in Silberstein's farm somewhere in that state and even Connecticut then and now was far away, a different country, and I had
always wondered how Mr. Silberstein had come to Connecticut.

My mother served tea and some cake. Velvel had taken a cube
of sugar, vised it between his upper and lower false front teeth and
noisily sipped his tea through it. The steamy liquid had sent visible swirls of heat into the air and around his face. He held the
glass as all the Russian Jews I knew, with his thumb on the rim of
the glass, his other fingers of his right hand tightly holding up
bottom of the hot glass.

Velvel had told us of those other days in the Jewish theater.
Among others, he had played with Boris Thomashefsky, with Molly
Picon, Aaron Lebedeff, Ludwig Satz, Maurice Schwartz. I had once
gone to one of the theaters on Second Avenue where I had seen

Molly Picon in the role of a knickered boy, or tomboy, I forget which, she was wearing a cap and had done a cartwheel on the stage. Velvel had played practically all the Jewish theaters that lined Second Avenue from above East Houston Street to 12th Street as well as outlying theaters in some of the other boroughs of the city. He had played serious roles, comedy roles, he had played young men, old men, at times he had played old women, his voice even now imitated them perfectly. Moisheh, he would say in a tremulous high-pitched voice, *Derlohng, mir iss teppel*, Give me the pot. He had sung in musicals, he had gone on tour with the best of them, even to South America where there were Jewish communities.

He could sing. And when he did, he entranced us. After he had had his tea and cake, to entertain us, he would sing old Yiddish songs, some in a strong voice, other songs in other voices than his own.

He had told us about Cafe Royale on Second Avenue where all the Jewish actors congregated. The men came in their wide-brimmed fedora hats, the brim turned down on one side of the hat, turned up on the other side, when the usual custom was to have the brim down at front of the hat. Some of the actors would wear their topcoats or overcoats draped across their shoulders. One or two wore flowing capes, a few came clutching beautiful canes.

They came to the cafe, sat at the tables, boasted to each other, embellished the boasts. They lied to each other about their roles, the applause of their audiences, the raves they had gotten, the packed theaters. Everybody there knew that everybody else was lying but everybody listened to those lies as if they were truths, everybody played the game.

Velvel would tell us about the times, on festive occasions, when they went to dine at Moscowitz and Lupowitz, the meat restaurant on lower Second Avenue, or to Gluckstern's on Delancey Street near the approach to the bridge where only seltzer was served instead of water, or when they went to Ratner's, also on Delancey

Street, for dairy foods. Velvel's face would light up when he spoke of those gone, past days.

My mother would occasionally invite Velvel to our flat, sometimes when someone, a relative perhaps, would also be visiting us. Velvel would put on his performance, reciting roles from years ago as if they were yesterday, becoming the part, shrinking into himself with old age, seeming to become taller as he played a youth. He was a magician with words, with tones, with inflections, with the movement of his face, the flick of his hands.

That night, sitting at the table, hunched, with a large towel draped over his head and shoulders like a shawl, he regaled us with his women's roles. An animation suddenly came into Velvel's face, his body, his gestures, he became lost in his parts. I understood Yiddish too and I laughed along with my mother and father.

When he left, after the tea and cake, after the performance he had put on for us, my mother said to my father, "A shame, he's all alone. His daughter lives so far away."

"*Nu,*" my father replied philosophically. "What can you do? That's the way it is."

Although it was never mentioned my parents knew that Velvel was on Home Relief, the city's welfare program, where he received a voucher that was never enough for his food. The voucher was brought to the neighborhood grocery store and he would draw against it. Although it was not allowed, he would sometimes ask the grocer, whom he knew, for some small amount of cash so that he could buy a few penny cigarettes at the candy store. My mother always felt that Velvel was not getting enough to eat and at times, when she had some surplus food, she would put it in a paper bag and give it surreptitiously to him. He would always pretend not to want to take the bag but in the end he did.

Our cousin, Yonkel, came to visit us one early evening. He was a thin man, not too tall with a handsome handlebar mustache, pure white, except across the bottom above the lip, where the mustache had become stained with nicotine. He was a ferocious smoker, he had learned it when he had been caught in a round-up in his *shtetl* in Russia by the Cossacks and impressed in the Russian army for many years. He smoked like a fiend, one cigarette after another and he held the stub of a cigarette in a peculiar fashion, cupping it in his hand, lit end near his palm, held by his thumb and two middle fingers, smoking it down until it was practically ash. He too drank tea like Velvel, Russian-style, the cube of sugar between his teeth. Almost immediately he and Velvel got along famously.

"Do me a favor. Please sing," my mother said to Velvel, pronouncing the Russian words, "*Ochi Tchornaya*, Dark Eyes."

"Ah!" Velvel said. He put down his glass of tea, and began to sing the song. Yonkel, my mother and father, all began swaying to its rhythm, my mother's eyes closed in some old remembrance of a distant place.

When Velvel was finished the three of them applauded him loudly. Velvel smiled, nodded his head a few times to acknowledge the applause.

"*Ai*, the Old Country," my mother said. "Sometimes it was good."

"It never was good," Yonkel said vehemently. "What was so good about it? They hated us, they rounded us up like cattle for the army, you call that good? No," he said emphatically. "It was bad, terrible. You like that song, you think it's a nice song? Good. So it's a song, just that. They got plenty of songs here, believe me. You think some things were nice back then, they never were. Never. You liked the *shtetl*? Me, I never liked it. You know what? It's just that you were younger, we all were younger, we want to be young again. Tell me, who doesn't?"

My mother sighed. "The song... the song . . ." she said wistfully.

"Songs I got plenty," Velvel said and he began to sing, "*Ich Chub Dir Tzoo Feel Lieb*, I Love You Much Too Much." My mother began to listen attentively, she lost her wistfulness, finally near the end of the song she joined in with Velvel and when they finished we all applauded.

"Another glass tea?" my mother asked. Without waiting for a reply she went to the stove, took the boiling kettle of water in her right hand, picked up the small teapot with the tea essence in her other hand, and approached the table.

As she poured, my father asked Velvel, "And how are things going? Did you find some work?"

Velvel shrugged. "Nothing yet," he replied. "Maybe soon. Who knows?" He put on a smile and said in a happy voice that was an actor's, "Maybe tomorrow."

"Maybe," my mother said. "I hope so."

"We'll see," Velvel said, picking up a cube of sugar from the dish in the center of the table.

"To find something today is like finding diamonds." Yonkel said as he sipped his tea.

After our cousin Yonkel and Velvel had both gone, my father said to my mother, "Yonkel, he looks all right. But Velvel, well, I don't think he looks so good."

My mother, at the sink, said, "He's sick. His stomach, I think. He goes to the dispensary, they give him some medicine. Maybe they can cure him."

"Maybe," my father said.

And I said, "He's a good actor, he can make you think he's anybody, he can make you think he's okay when he's not."

"Yeah, yeah," my mother said as she finished wiping the dishes. Pointing to me, she said, "Go to bed, it's getting late. You got school tomorrow."

We didn't see Velvel for over two weeks. Several times my mother knocked on the door of his flat, hoping to invite him to our house for tea, but he wasn't in. My mother was worried about him, was he sick? Had he been taken to the hospital? She asked some of the other neighbors if they had heard anything about Velvel. Nobody had. It was as if he had moved away during the night.

One evening we heard a knocking at the door. When my mother went to answer it, there stood Velvel. He entered into the kitchen and blurted out, almost boyishly, "I'll be on the radio, that program, the *shpiel*, the play, you listen to it. So they called me. I went there, and they took me."

"Oh, I'm so glad!" my mother said. "Sit down, sit down," she motioned toward a chair in the kitchen and asked, "Some tea?"

"Yeah," he said grinning. To my father and me he said, "I play four parts. They needed somebody to play four parts. One of them is a lawyer."

"A lawyer?" I said.

"Sure. There has to be a doctor or a lawyer or an accountant in it. There has to be a no-goodnick and somebody who has made something out of himself. And, of course, there's love," Velvel said.

"*Ai, die lieber,* love," my mother said.

"The girl who wants to marry the wrong man, or who wants to marry the good man but he's too poor and her parents want her to marry a rich man, an old man. It's a *gantzeh megillah,* a whole long story."

"You signed a contract?" my father asked. "How many plays are you going to do?"

"Well," Velvel replied. "It's just for this one, right now. We'll see how things work themselves out."

"Where have you been?" my mother asked as she poured the tea. "I tried at your door but there was no answer."

"Out," Velvel said. "Busy. To the radio station. To here, to there. You know."

He had his tea, his piece of cake. Several times he stopped sipping his tea or eating his cake to put his hand to his stomach, they were small hidden gestures, noticed by nobody but me. He said nothing about what was apparently his pain, the normal conversation went on, he sang a song for us, then he left.

When he was gone I said to my parents, "He's sick."

"Sick? What do you mean?" my father asked.

"Did you see how he put his hand to his stomach?" I said as my parents stared at me, shook their heads. "I did. I sat near him. A few times he held his stomach, like it hurt."

"No," my father said shaking his head. "He can't be sick. He wouldn't take that job on the radio if he was sick."

"I'll see," my mother said. "I'll go see him tomorrow and talk to him."

But the next day he was gone again when my mother knocked at his door. She tried several times that day but there was no answer. We didn't see him again until early one Sunday morning when he came to our flat. All of us were still in bed and I ran to the door. When I opened the door, Velvel stood there, all dressed up in his wide-brimmed fedora hat, the brim down on one side. He was wearing a coat, his arms in the sleeves. He looked like someone different from the person who visited us, sat at our table, drank tea and told stories. There was a different air about him, he looked like an actor, he seemed taller than usual.

My mother was at my side, her bathrobe wrapped around her, my father followed her and both of them exclaimed, "Velvel!"

"I can't believe it!" my mother said.

"You're a different Velvel," my father blurted out.

"Come in," my mother said stepping slightly away from the door.

"I can't," Velvel said. "I got to be at the radio station right away. I just thought I would say hello to you."

"Go, Velvel," my father said. "We'll listen to you on the radio. Good luck."

"Yes. Sure. Of course, of course," Velvel said.

He said his goodbye and was gone. At the door, still open, my parents looked at each other in awed stares. I watched as Velvel sprightly walked to the staircase and disappeared down the steps. Still staring at the empty staircase, I slowly shut the door.

My father was shaking his head. "Here, he's just a neighbor, like one of us. Now, he's an actor. I can't believe it!"

Later, they listened to the radio while I half-listened as I did my homework. The play was on, the voices flowed from the radio, the only character we knew was Velvel was the lawyer, but the voice was different, younger, much younger, we wouldn't have recognized it if Velvel hadn't told us in advance. And now and then my mother and father would attempt to identify Velvel in his three other parts, but they couldn't, they really didn't know for sure, he used his many other voices, those we were not acquainted with. And in the play, despite all the obstacles, the heroine was reunited with her true love, all was well, the play was over.

"Can you believe it?" my mother said to my father. "Velvel's so good, except for the lawyer, I didn't know which of the others was him."

"He's an actor, a good one," my father said. "So he knows how to act, so he's what they tell him to be."

Later, as I stood in the brisk fall air on the stoop of the tenement, I saw a taxi come to a stop in front of our building. The driver left the wheel, opened the door to the passenger compartment, and inside, on the seat, I could see a form huddled there.

The taxi driver said to the form inside the vehicle, "We're here, mister." Inside, the form groaned, I noticed the fedora hat sitting awry on the form's head and quickly I ran to the taxi as the driver turned and said to me, "You know him?" I glanced inside and it was Velvel and I nodded to the driver. "He looks like he's sick," the driver said.

I reached into the passenger compartment, put my arm around Velvel, said to him, "You're home," and with great difficulty I helped him out of the cab. As I had begun helping him his hat had come off his head. I grabbed the hat and clutched it while I was helping Velvel. Outside, in the street, leaning heavily against me, his face pale, his hands shaking, Velvel laboriously dug into his pocket, clawed out some money, handed it to me and I paid the driver.

"Come on," I said to him as the taxi drove away. "I'll help you up."

A small crowd had formed around the two of us, there was a loud buzz of conversation and someone said, "He's sick. I'll call an ambulance."

"No, no," Velvel said weakly, his eyes closed. "Let me go upstairs. I want to go up."

Two men came to help me, we practically carried Velvel to his flat. He was moaning intermittently as we crawled up the stairs. At Velvel's door, the three of us who had helped him stopped to catch our breaths and Velvel turned slowly to me, his eyes open now and said weakly, "Well, how was it, the *shpiel*, the play?"

"My mother and father loved it. They said it was wonderful,

just wonderful," I replied.

He attempted a smile. "Good," he said, breathing heavily, and almost whispering, said, "I wanted it to be good."

ORCHARD STREET

He was twelve years old and he needed a new shirt and tie for the holidays. He himself had saved the money to buy the shirt, he had diligently, over weeks and weeks, saved up thirty cents, twenty-five cents which would go towards the purchase of a tie. He turned from Delancey Street into Orchard Street, looking uptown to the next cross street, Rivington, and below that to Stanton Street. Both sides of the street were lined with pushcarts, each cart an open table on two large wagon wheels at its rear, the back end held two curved wooden handles for pushing the cart when the day was done and the cart trundled back to its stable.

These carts were filled with merchandise of all description, uncounted items; in the street from Delancey to Rivington were those that sold items of clothing, shirts, sweaters, ties, leather goods, small articles of dress for women, shoes, used articles, some housewares. Below Rivington Street towards Stanton Street, then down further to East Houston Street, the character of merchandise, imperceptibly at first, began to change, towels, linens, fruits, vegetables, items of canned goods. And all over the streets there was the unabated noise, the yells of the pushcart peddlers shouting out their wares, their prices.

"I got the best shirts!" a man's voice blasted out urging the passersby to his pushcart. "Bargains! Bargains!"

"*Intervesch!*" yelled another, "*Fahr de menner! Koift! Zaynor! Koift!*" And in accented English, "Underwear! For men! Look! Look! Buy!"

Across the teeming sidewalks on both sides of the street were the stores, most of them selling more substantial merchandise, blankets, leather jackets, household goods. Away from the sidewalks, away from the pushcarts, was a flowing mass of humanity which moved in both directions, jostling, looking, shopping, talking, all of it a massive hive of noise.

On the street itself, a man darted between people. Strapped to his back was a large metal tank, a piped faucet was strung around the lower part of his chest. He boomed out, "*Kvass! Kvass!* Drink a *kvass!* Two cents! Two cents!"

The boy had heard that *kvass* was a Russian drink of some sort, made of stale bread and sugar and water, slightly fermented in some fashion. He had never drunk it, he didn't know what its taste was. Somebody now stopped for a drink of *kvass*, the vendor quickly filled a glass with liquid from the tank, he had already taken the two cents, and as he waited for the glass to be returned by the customer, his eyes darted and he shouted out, "*Kvass!* Buy a drink!"

The boy walked on, shoving his way through the crowd. It was a sunny day, still early spring, a hint of winter remained in the chill in the air. Women, their shopping bags looped around their arms, still wore their winter coats. One of them at the edge of a pushcart was wrapping a corset across her coated body to see if it would fit. Satisfied that it would, she folded it lengthwise and said to the peddler, a woman, "The gorset, how much?"

The vendor pointed to a wooden sign nailed to the side of the pushcart and said, "A dollar."

"What?" the other woman said. "A dollar? It's a used one. That's too much. No."

"Used, schmused," the peddler said. "It's a good gorset, no? It's a bargain. New, it cost—"

"I'll give you fifty cents," the other woman said.

"Fifty cents?" the peddler said incredulously, her voice rising. "What do I do here, stay here in the heat and the cold for nothing? Do I work for nothing?" She was studying the other woman's face and now said in a normal tone of voice, "All right, all right. For you, eighty-five cents."

"I'll give you sixty-five. Not a penny more."

"No, no," the peddler said. "I can't do it, I can't. Go," she said. "Go someplace else, buy yourself a gorset someplace else. Go. See what they'll charge you. Go. Go in good health."

The other woman had turned to leave but now she stopped, turned back and said with a heavy sigh, "Seventy-five cents. I can't pay no more than that. Make it seventy-five cents."

The peddler stared at the woman's face for a moment. Then she said as she dropped her hands helplessly to her sides, "All right. Just for you." Her face began to smile as she took the carefully counted coins from her customer and she said in a conspiratorial tone of voice, "Just for you. But you don't tell nobody else. It's just for you, you hear?" She raised her forefinger, waggled it in front of both of their faces and said, "Just for you."

The boy walked on. There was a pushcart spread with bric-a-brac, used items, some drinking glasses that didn't match, a few orange Waterman fountain pens, heaps of dishes, assorted single pieces of silverware, false teeth, eyeglasses, some children's' toys, metal-handled holders for containing tall glasses for hot tea, small cast-offs of all kinds, forgotten mementos of peoples' lives. Someone was testing a pair of metal-rimmed spectacles, holding the eyeglasses in front of that day's edition of the Jewish newspaper, the "Forward."

The boy, fingering the three dimes in his pocket, stopped before a pushcart where ties were being sold. On the cart, between the piece of wood nailed to each end of it, was strung a display of ties that fluttered and flapped in the wind. On the flat bed of the cart itself, divided into three sections, was a display of ties, each section having a hand-lettered sign, one 25cents, another 39 cents, the last 50 cents. The boy stared at the 25 cent section.

He knew he couldn't buy any of those others, those high prices were much too much, what was the use? He picked up a tie, held it, examined its back to see whether its inner strip of white reinforced cloth showed. He suddenly decided he didn't want that tie, it had lost its appeal to him. He put it down and picked up another one.

"Nice ties, good ties," the peddler, a man, said to him. "You can't buy a better one for the price. My price is the best. You want that one?"

"I don't know," the boy said. "I'm looking."

"So look around in good health," the man said. "Twenty-five cents, it's a real bargain, I can tell you."

The man busied himself with another customer, all the while his eyes darting to all those who had stopped at his pushcart, sensing which one to approach to clinch a sale. He was shouting out in a singsong chant, "Ties! Cheap! Get your ties here for *yontiff*, the holidays. Cheap!"

The boy then saw the tie, its fabric dappled in many colors. That was what he had seen, a tie colored in similar fashion, not exactly the same, but similar, in Phil Kronfeld's window of his haberdashery store on Delancey Street, a few blocks from the Bowery, where it was said the gangsters bought their clothing. So it had been priced at $2.95 in the window, so what? the boy asked himself. So they got the money, they can afford it, I can't. He stared down at the tie in his hand, held it up against his shirt and looked down at it. It was the current style, he wanted it.

The peddler had appeared at his side and was saying, "You like it? Take it. For twenty-five cents it's a real bargain. It sells for a dollar, at least, in the stores. Go, look. You'll see."

"I'll take it," the boy said. Reaching into his pocket, firmly grasping the three dimes, he gave them to the man along with the tie. The man folded the tie with an expert flip, placed it in a small bag, gave it to the boy, and digging into his short money apron came up with a nickel and gave it to the boy.

As the boy took the coin, the man said, "Go in good health, *boychick*."

The boy nodded. Clutching the bag he turned back towards Delancey Street, weaving and jostling through the crowd. As he passed the pushcart with the bric-a-brac, he glanced at the false teeth lying there. Who bought them? he asked himself. The woman at the corset pushcart was shouting out her wares in a loud voice, a shirt vendor's shout mixed with hers.

Outside, some of the stores displayed items for sale, some on wooden racks, or display bins, or hung from one inch by two-inch lengths of wood extending from their doorways. A suede jacket slowly billowing in the breeze caught the boy's eye, but he looked away. It was no use, he couldn't buy it. Not now. Maybe some day... Some day...

He reached Delancey Street and turned left towards the Williamsburgh Bridge. As he walked, the noise of Orchard Street began to diminish and fade. He went to Essex Street, where there on the corner, the large store open above counter level to the sidewalk, was Levy's. Fingering the nickel in his pocket he walked to the counter and said to the server behind it, "A hot dog and a root beer."

The young man behind the counter served him the hot dog flavored with a swipe of mustard and a layer of sauerkraut. The heavy glass stein of root beer appeared. The boy placed his nickel on the counter top, picked up the hot dog and bit into it. As he ate, he looked down the street, the wide middle of Delancey Street running into the Williamsburgh Bridge, the left and right side lanes of the street running down and merging beneath the rise of the structure.

The boy took a long sip of the sweet foamy root beer. Ah-h! He took another bite of the hot dog.

Well, anyway, he thought as he ate, still clutching the small bag with the tie, I didn't get a shirt, but I got something for the holidays. Not like last year when I got nothing at all.

MARRIAGE

They sat at the tan porcelain-topped table in the kitchen, her mother and father sitting next to each other and she, Claire, across from both of them. The overhead light fixture with its small electric bulb burned dimly. Across from her, past the heads of her parents, Claire could see the window in the kitchen, a wide window that was part of the wall that separated the kitchen from the unlit dining room, its bulky furniture dark shadows in the gloom of the other room. Another window, less wide, at the end of the kitchen looked out into the rear yard of the tenement building, the outside all blackened by night. Behind her, near the kitchen sink was the bathtub standing on its four clawed metal feet, the top of the tub covered with its large removable porcelain lid, black irregular chips showing here and there, especially at its edges. When David, Claire's younger brother, came home from school that was where he did his homework.

Her father was saying, "What are you talking about? Do you know what you're saying?" Turning to her mother, he said, "She's talking *narrishkeit*, foolishness, she don't know what she's saying. Go on, you talk to her." He threw up his hands in a gesture of resignation. "I can't talk to her." He turned to his daughter in a swift motion and asked, "What language am I speaking, hah? Do I speak a foreign language to you, do I?"

Her mother put her hand over her husband's tightened fist that now rested on the table. Glancing from her daughter to her husband, she said, "Listen, Morris, don't excite yourself. Don't get a heart attack. You come home from the shop, you worked enough. Don't get excited." And to her daughter just as her son, David opened the door of the flat and entered into the kitchen, "Your father works like a dog all day for them, the Margulies, in their shop. Don't let him get excited. You hear, Claire? Listen to him, he wants the best for you."

"*Ach!*" her father said angrily as he removed his hand from his wife's clutch. "What do they care, Claire, even David? Nothing. Not a thing. What am I to them?" Glancing angrily at David, he said, "You got a look on your face I don't like to see. You got something to say, I don't want to hear it."

Standing near the table, David had stopped to listen. Disregarding his father's remarks, he said, "What's going on?"

"What's going on?" His father said. "Don't you hear? Dear God, don't you have ears?"

Now his mother said to David, "Claire don't want to get married."

"Not to him!" Claire snapped. "I don't want him! Why can't you—?"

"You don't want him?" her father said incredulously. "He wants you, you don't know how lucky you are."

To Claire her father's voice went on and on, all the words familiar now, the slow drip of the kitchen faucet a soft punctuation to his words. She glanced across the room to where David's cot stood folded and erect against one of the walls, a flowered print material covering its bulk. She became lost in the flowers of the material as her father's voice droned on and on. It was the same thing over and over again, never ending, always hammering at her, beating at her, there was no escape. And always, however hard she tried to make her parents understand her feelings, there was total incomprehension, their words flung at her, Why was she acting like this? Didn't she understand the prize she would be getting? Other girls would do anything to get a catch like that. What was wrong with her?

David remained standing, a spectator, his eyes slowly moving over the three of them. Claire burst out, "He's forty-eight, he's an old man, I can't do it, I don't want to do it." She turned her head away from her parents, staring deeply into space, seeing nothing.

"So he's forty-eight, so what? He's still young. He's an accountant, he's got a good job. Who's working these days? We got a Depression, yeah? Who's making a living? Tell me. What do you want to do, marry somebody from your shop, someone who's always out of work? A *koptzint*, a pauper," her mother said.

"He'll make you a good husband," her father said leaning over the table, his face closer to Claire's. "He'll make a good living for you."

Her mother moved closer to Claire, her chair scraping across the scarred linoleum, and now her voice was pleading as she said to Claire, "You won't have to worry about what to eat, you'll have to eat, or about the rent, about buying clothes. You'll live in a nice apartment with steam heat, not like here," she said pointing to the black coal stove that was on the other side of the room. "Not like here, a tenement. A toilet in the hall for three flats. You like that, hah? You'll have a frigidaire, not the box that we got on the kitchen window outside, that metal thing nailed to the window outside we use in the winter, and that icebox there." She pointed to the aged wooden appliance in the room, painted green and peeling in scabrous blotches," and she said, "in the summer David has to *schlepp* up the ice on his back every two days and the basin underneath it is always running over with melted water. You like that? Or would you like to live like the rich people? He's a good man, he's rich, he makes," she accented the words, and said, "a hundred and fifty dollars a week, *ma-ma-nyu*, a millionaire."

"What kind of a life is this?" her father asked.

Claire said nothing. Breaking the silence David said, "Why don't you leave her alone? You're killing her with all your words. Leave her alone."

"Ah!" his father said furiously. "Now this one, here. With the big mouth. Fourteen years old and he knows everything. What do you know, you *pisher*, you baby?" His wife was tugging at his arm to stop his shouted flow of words but he was saying, "Do you know how to make a living? Do you know what it is to have no work and a family to support?" His words were racing now. "Do you know what it is to have the electric company shut your lights? Do you know what it is when the grocery store says they can't keep you on the books no more because you can't pay what you owe them? Do you know what it is," his father jumped up from his chair and glared fiercely at David as he said, "not to be able to pay the rent and they throw you out in the street, like the Goldsteins, hah?"

"Morris, Morris," his wife said as she jumped up from her chair and went to her husband. "Don't get excited. Sit down. Please." And to her son as she pulled on her husband's arm, "Don't be a fool, David. Keep quiet. Show respect for your father. You have no right, you hear me? No right! He slaves for you." Turning to Claire she said, "And for you too."

Claire was still sitting at the table, she looked up and said angrily, "I'm twenty-two. I work too. I bring in money."

"When you work," her father said, sitting down once more at the table. "Remember that. How many weeks did you work this year? Tell me. And tell me how many men you liked that the *shadchen*, the matchmaker, brought to you, hah? And you say, this one's too short, this one's too bald, this one's too old, that one limps." He was breathing heavily now and he roared out, "What do you want?" Glancing at all of them shouted, "What do you want from me?"

"Don't yell," David said. "The whole building will hear you."

"You shut up!" His father said. "Who asked you? Keep your mouth shut!"

"Is that the way to talk to your father?" his mother said angrily to David. "Go to the other room! Now!" David hesitated and his mother said, "Now, I said!"

David glanced at Claire, gave a great sigh. He turned and went into Claire's bedroom, a room off the kitchen. Inside, he pulled the chain of the electric fixture, the room became darkly visible in the anemic light. He sat down on the bed, its springs creaking. He was tired but he would have to wait until the family discussion, if it could be classified as such, was done.

His bed, the folding cot in the kitchen, could not be opened until the entire family had left the kitchen and gone to the two bedrooms. Now, from the other room, the kitchen, he heard the voices of his father and mother and Claire, and in the small silences between their hurled sentences, there was distant hum and sound from the other apartments in the tenement building, the creak of a floor when someone walked across it, the squeal of the small wheels of a folding cot being brought to the center of a kitchen, the flush of a toilet with its strangled liquid sound.

He lay back on the bed careful that his shoes did not touch the blanket beneath him. He stared into the dark ceiling, Claire's voice was saying, No, no, no, I don't want him! pleading now, her voice begging, almost crying.

"Goddammit!" he heard his father say. "I'm going to bed. To hell with all of this! I'm finished! You hear?"

There was the sound of his footsteps across the kitchen floor, the slam of the bedroom door. Outside, in the kitchen his mother was saying to Claire in a soft voice, "My child, listen carefully. Listen to me. Marry him. You won't have this kind of a life like this. Is this what you want? Better yourself." Claire mumbled something and her mother said, "What is love? Foolishness. Something from the movies. Go live on love, see if that will bring you something to eat. You can starve on love, your heart breaks for your children because they have nothing, nothing, because of love. A living, a man who makes a living for you, that is really love. So you can buy a dress, a pair of shoes, go to the country in the summer with the children. Don't live like a *schlepper*, a nothing. Listen to me." David heard the scrape of the chairs in the kitchen. His mother was saying to Claire, "Go to bed. Go. Think about what I said. Do you think your father and mother want bad for you? You are my child, I want the best for you."

"Yes, yes," Claire was mumbling. He heard the sound of the pull of the chain cutting off the electric light in the kitchen, he heard his mother go into her bedroom, he heard Claire moving slowly, the door of the bedroom opening as she entered the room.

David sat up in bed and as Claire wearily sat down beside him she muttered, "I can't, I can't."

"You don't have to," David said. "You shouldn't be forced to. This isn't the Old Country, this is a different time." There was the distance of years between the both of them, she an adult, and what was he? He didn't know, both of them living together yet living in different worlds, and he put his arms around her, his sister, her face now beside his. He could hear the sound of her breathing, loud and labored and he whispered to her, "Marry who you want, you listen to me. Don't marry that old man. Don't."

To his amazement he found that he was crying now, crying for his older sister who had suddenly, strangely, come back to him.

"Don't cry, David," she said to him in a strangled tone of voice. "Don't."

And David was saying, "I won't let you, you can't do it. You'll die. You deserve better."

And she, in a strange, haunted voice, lost, faraway, muttered more to herself than to him, "I must, I must do it."

THE CANARY
WHO PLAYED CARDS

The Canarrick they called him, the Canary, sitting at the table holding the cards of his poker hand close as he trilled a soft whistling tune through his teeth. His face a blank, he flittingly glanced at the other three players around the table, each of them studying his cards.

Bulldog, with his jutting lower jaw, his wide face and short flat nose, looked up from his cards towards the Canarrick, gave a humorless smile showing his uneven teeth as he asked, "You got a good hand, hah?"

"Maybe yes, maybe no," another player, Adler, said. "You sing that song and you say," and imitating the Canarrick's recent rhythmic words, "maybe yes, maybe no, hah, then I figure you got maybe two pair, at least. Yeah?"

"Maybe yes, maybe no," the Canarrick replied trilling his tune once more.

"At least a pair aces," Levin, the fourth player said. "The Canarrick he can afforda to throw this kind of money in. Me, I can't. I didn't have no work for a long time, it's a big slack season."

"What slack season?" Adler asked, shaking his head sadly. "Nobody's buying, nobody's selling, nobody's working."

Levin and Adler worked in the garment center but work was scarce, if at all. They spent their time in going to the shop and being told, no work today, maybe tomorrow, come back.

The Canarrick had become a professional gambler, he only worked at sitting in on poker games. Years before, he, Bulldog, Levin and Adler had all worked in the same shop in the garment center but it had all been too haphazard for the Canarrick, the long interminable stretches of no work and no pay, it was a crazy way to make a living. It had been too much for him and he had given it up and had, over time, found an aptitude for poker. That had become his livelihood.

Bulldog was a gambler too, having teamed up with the Canarrick, but now and then he would do some peripheral jobs for the local gangsters, nothing serious, picking up money perhaps, bringing it from one person to another, a sort of petty money messenger. Sometimes, just to pass the time away both he and the Canarrick would play this small meaningless game with their old friends.

Now the Canarrick was about to reply to Levin's remark but Bulldog said to Levin, "I know what the Canarrick's going to say, why only a pair aces? Why not two pair, a straight, maybe?" Bulldog discarded three cards from his hand, Adler two cards, Levin three cards. The Canarrick just sat there, staring at his cards, trilling a peeping tune. "Hey, Canarrick," Bulldog finally said. "How many cards?"

"I'll wait, I'll wait," the Canarrick replied.

"Wait? For what?" Levin asked.

"After we get our cards," Bulldog said. "I know him. He waits, he waits, just to see how things go." Bulldog gave a short laugh and said to Levin and Adler, "Makes you a little nervous, hah? What's he got there, the Canarrick, you ask? A straight, a royal flush, maybe? Maybe he's bluffing, maybe?"

"Maybe yes, maybe no," the Canarrick said in a singsong voice. "And why not? You think royal flushes are for everybody else and not me?"

Bulldog dealt the required number of cards to Adler and Levin, now he looked at the Canarrick and asked, "It's your turn. How many?"

The Canarrick shook his head. "I'm pat," he said in a flat almost distant tone of voice.

"Yeah, sure," Adler said without looking up, busy studying his cards. "He's got nothing. He's bluffing."

"Wait and see," the Canarrick said with a smile.

Levin, having studied his hand, stared hard at the Canarrick, shrugged and said, "Two cents," as he tossed the coins towards the center of the table.

Adler sighed and looked at the small pile of coins in front of him. "I'm out," he said in a disappointed tone of voice. "These cards are no good. Hey," he said to Bulldog, "what kind of a dealer are you, hah? Terrible cards, just terrible."

He sighed, threw his cards in as Bulldog said, "You must be lucky in love. *Ai, lieber!* Love, love! Adler, a regular movie star, hoo-hah!"

The Canarrick picked up a coin, nonchalantly tossed it into the pot where it landed with a clink on the other coins in the center of the table. "Five cents," he said.

"Hey!" Levin said somewhat angrily. "It's a penny and two. We're not millionaires around here. Come on, Canarrick, it's not right. We made an agreement, a penny and two."

"Look," the Canarrick said to him. "I'm your friend, yes? How am I going to tell you I got you beat? Sure, you put your money in already, but Bulldog, now it's his turn to get in or out. He's going to raise me." He turned to Bulldog and said, "Am I right? You'll raise me and I'll raise you and Levin, he'll put in his few more cents, he'll be caught. But he'll lose." He turned back to Levin and said, "You'll lose." And now to Bulldog, "And so will you. I got you all beat." He paused for a moment then said, "Look, I told you. Now it's up to you." Sitting there in that small silence he began his trill.

Bulldog laughed, a deep rolling sound. "*Ai,* Canarrick," he said. "An actor, that's what he is." And with a smile said in a confidential tone of voice to Levin and Adler, "Don't tell him but I'm telling you right now, I got him beat."

Levin dropped out of the game, stared moodily out the kitchen window of Bulldog's sister, Rifkeh's, flat. Rifkeh was working in a shop that miraculously had some work. Her eleven-year-old son was away at school and during the days when she worked and when he came home, one of the neighbors made lunch, sometimes supper for him. Her husband, Mottel, years before had come to America with her and their then small son but Mottel had found himself a complete stranger, an outsider in this alien land, and after a year of working in the shops had suddenly disappeared and gone back to Europe.

About six months later Rifkeh had received a letter from him, begging her forgiveness, telling her how impossible it had been for him, maybe America was for her, but it was not for him. After that letter there had been complete silence, Mottel, had become lost somewhere in that place beyond the ocean, buried by time and distance. A few years ago, she, still a pretty woman, had applied for and been granted a divorce by the court.

The Canarrick had attached himself to her, they were going steady, he had suggested moving in with her but she had refused. She wanted to get married and the Canarrick had told her he would marry her sometime in the future when he could support her so that she wouldn't have to work. Over and over she had pressed him, time was going by, why shouldn't they get married? Didn't he love her? She loved him. And he had replied, You know how I feel, Rifkeleh.

When Bulldog had moved out of Rifkeh's tenement flat to live with a single woman he had recently met, when he told his sister he was leaving, he said with a laugh, Rifkeh, I'll take *mein puhr zachen*, my few things, my fifty-three things, a deck of cards and my shirt and I'll go. He had roared after saying that but she had not been amused. She had stared angrily at him and had asked, And how will I be able to pay the rent, Bulldock? That was the way she pronounced his name. Well, Bulldog said, the Canarrick, he wants to live with you, yeah? Rifkeh attempted to control herself as she stared icily at her brother and Bulldog said, he'll help pay the rent.

Terrible, terrible, it had been awful for her and she had screamed at her brother, What am I, *a koorveh*, a prostitute? And Bulldog with a look of innocence had said to her, Who said anything like that? Did you hear me say that? When? You're a good woman, you will live with the Canarrick, he's a good man. He likes you, you like him. He tells me he will marry you just as soon he gets some more money together.

So Bulldog had moved out, his double bed in the second bed-room had come to be used by her son, Leo, and the Canarrick had moved in with her.

Now sitting at the kitchen table, Bulldog raised the ante, eased back in his chair and waited for the Canarrick's reaction.

"Your five and ten more," the Canarrick said tossing in the coins.

Through the swirl of cigarette smoke Adler, dismayed, looked at Levin and said to the Canarrick, "Hey! This is a penny and two game, a game with friends, yes? What do you want, blood?"

"Yeah, yeah," the Canarrick said glancing at Bulldog. "But this betting don't hurt you no more, yes or no, Adler? It's between me and Bulldog and he can afforda it."

Bulldog stared long at the Canarrick. Finally he said, more for Levin's and Adler's benefit, "I know you, Canarrick. I know when you're for real and when you're a bluffer. So you really got yourself a good hand this time, hah?" He threw his cards on the table.

The Canarrick grinned, dropped his cards face down on the table. As Bulldog began to reach for them the Canarrick said, "Hey! You didn't pay, you don't see." Staring at Bulldog the Canarrick scrambled all the cards, his hand became lost in the deck. "You know better, Bulldog. You and me, we been in too many games together. You didn't see me, right? So you don't see my hand."

"Agh-h," Bulldog said with a disgusted wave of his hand. "That's for real games, not this one, this penny game, we're friends here."

As the Canarrick raked in the small pile of coins, Levin said, "I'm finished here. Let's go to the cafeteria for a coffee. We can sit there and *schmooz*." Adler and Bulldog nodded.

The Canarrick had become tired of this game, there was no real tension, there was no real money involved, there was only cards dealt, a few pennies tossed into the pot, it all meant nothing, it was not a real game. Adler and Levin were his friends, but, well, this was not the game for them, they had no money. Maybe they thought it was money, but to the Canarrick it was nothing, just petty tokens. He yearned for a real game, one with the pot heaped with dollar bills, with suspicious eyes staring around the table looking at the backs of the cards held by other players, with the grunted remarks from some of them, with cigarette smoke clouding the air, where he felt alive, not like this boredom plastered on boredom.

"Bulldog," the Canarrick said. "We got to get us a real game." He glanced quickly at Adler and Levin and said, "Not that this ain't no game, but I mean, a real game. *Fahr gelt,* For money. You understand?"

Levin stared at the Canarrick. "What's the matter?" he said. "We're *koptzunim,* paupers, already?"

"No, no, no," the Canarrick replied. "It's a different kind of game. You know."

"Yeah, I know," Adler said." The *gelt,* the money. That's what makes it different, hah?"

Bulldog arose from his chair and said to them, "Adler, Levin, what *narishkeit,* foolishness, are you talking about? The Canarrick remembers his friends, you know that. It don't matter how much they make or how little. Come on," he said to the two of them, "we go to the cafeteria, we have a coffee, we *schmooz* a little, like friends do." Looking down at the table he saw the Canarrick still sitting there idly picking up a card at random and flipping it into the strewn pile near the center of the table. "Come on, Canarrick, let's go."

"Yeah, yeah," the Canarrick replied. Rising from the table he began to whistle while Bulldog began to rake in all the cards, formed them in a neat pack and stowed it into its box.

"Hey, let's clean up the place a little, yeah?" Bulldog said. "When Rifkeh comes home from work the place should be clean. She works late at the shop." He took the boxed pack of cards, stowed it in a drawer nearby, emptied the cigarette butts and ashes from the filled ashtray into the garbage can, opened the window

to air out the room. He was careful to replace everything as it had
been before they had started the game, he didn't want Rifkeh to
know they had idled their time away instead of looking for something productive to do.

Rifkeh knew they gambled like this sometimes during the day,
she knew that the Canarrick and Bulldog would not look for work
of some kind, for something honorable not like this gambling and
not like Bulldog's association with the gangsters, but she tried to
convince herself that both men were trying, were looking for work.
Bulldog wanted to keep it all that way, she with her fantasy, he
and the Canarrick with their gambling.

As they were leaving the flat Bulldog said to the Canarrick,
"Rifkeh told me you ain't staying out tonight, you'll have sopper
with her and the boy." The Canarrick nodded and Bulldog said,
"Me, I go to *mein maydel*, my girl, she's got a good sopper for
me."

"So that's what'll be," the Canarrick said. "There's no game
tonight, I looked. Anyway it ain't so bad eating with Rifkeh and
the boy. That Leo, he's a good boy."

"Good?" Bulldog said as he locked the door of the flat. "He is
the best. And such a smart boy, *ah zah yuhr ahv mir*, I should have
such a good year. He gets A's in school, you should see his report
card, AAAA, the teachers all talk about him, such an honest boy.
He'll maybe be a doctor or a dentist, a lawyer maybe, you'll see."

Adler, walking down slowly on the flight of stairs began to
laugh and said to Bulldog, "So when you're good and sick, you'll
go see him, the doctor, after all you're the uncle and you'll get a
free treatment. Not bad. I wish I had someone like that."

"*Mir zull nisht vissen fin duss*, We shouldn't know from that,
sickness, an accident. *Gutt zull oopheeten*, God forbid."

"A joke," Adler said to him. "What's the matter with you, you
forgot how to laugh?"

There was a real game, a heavy one, scheduled for the following week and the Canarrick wanted to prepare for it. First, the
money. He had enough. Then the cards. That was the delicate

part, getting the new decks marked, replaced in their wrappers, placed in their boxes and sealed. He always had five or six decks on hand, ready for use.

Having the packs placed in two or three candy stores around where the game would be played, that was the most difficult part. The candy store owner had to be approached by somebody he knew well, usually it was Bulldog, but not always, the decks had to be held somewhere in the candy store so that just before the game when the proper person entered the store and asked for a deck or two of cards, there could be no mistake in selling him the wrong cards.

The Canarrick knew how to play his own game. Usually he played in games outside of the neighborhood, there were games in the Bronx, in Brooklyn, in other parts of Manhattan. He didn't want to become involved in a game in his own neighborhood, sometimes, God forbid, something could go wrong, it never had, but better to keep it away from where he lived, from his street, from his part of the Lower East Side.

During the first game or two the Canarrick allowed the big shot, the sucker, to win a few dollars, maybe twelve, eighteen dollars, something like that. Then after that cause him to lose. Maybe twenty-five, thirty dollars. Depending. Then a small win, maybe six or seven dollars. Then get him good, a hundred dollars or more, if the sucker had that kind of money, and he usually did. The Canarrick played him real good, flung out his bait and made the sucker want to come back, made him want to up his bidding, made him so eager for the big kill, so he thought, that he was blinded to the fact that he had been hooked and was being taken.

But the Canarrick wanted to move up, he wanted bigger game. He yearned for winnings of five hundred dollars, maybe a thousand, and maybe, maybe, even more. It happened to other gamblers, why couldn't it happen to him?

Rifkeh had told him that her boss in the blouse factory, Kaplan, a married man, was constantly talking to her, stopping her as she was about to leave the shop after work, telling her, when there were just the two of them in that long loft that he would like to take her out, he really liked her, it was one of those things he couldn't help. He had been married for over twenty-five years, he just lived with his wife, that was all, they barely had anything to do with each other, they said hello, they said goodbye, they ate together in silence, everything was so polite and cold, the marriage was no marriage no more, it had become an endless terrible habit, something that was killing him.

There were no fights, they were beyond that, what was there to fight about? He gave her everything, she had a fur coat, dresses, jewelry, shoes, whatever she wanted. She got what she wanted, Kaplan had said, but what did he get? Nothing, nothing at all. He wanted someone, he needed someone.

"I know, I know," the Canarrick had said to her and laughing scornfully and rolling his eyes towards the ceiling, had said, "He wants to talk to you, yeah? Why not?" His tone had suddenly changed as he had said, "But that ain't all he wants." Rifkeh had averted her eyes from him. "But I tell you what," the Canarrick had said. "Invite him here, yeah, bring him. You tell him I'm your brother, I live here. The Bulldog, he's your brother, it's no lie and he's living with his *maydel*, and that's no lie. He comes around here to see you and the boy, yeah? You can tell Kaplan that too."

Rifkeh had remained silent, staring hard at the Canarrick as he was speaking. "No," she said.

"And why not? He's your boss, he wants to come, let him come. Invite this Kaplan for a glass tea, a little cake. Me, I'll come in later, maybe a half hour after he comes, me, the brother, we'll meet. I'll talk to this Kaplan and later on I'll talk to him about a game of poker, right here, in this place. He's got money, this Kaplan, yes?"

"Yeah," Rifkeh had replied, her eyes shut as she shook her head. "Canarrick, I can't. Don't make me do it. It's not nice. I don't want to do it."

"You want us to get married?" the Canarrick had asked, and Rifkeh, her eyes open, had nodded. "So we need some money to get married. I don't want you working in that shop no more, not my Rifkeleh. We got this Kaplan now, I take him for what I can get, a thousand? maybe two? who knows? I'll have enough to open up a shop with Bulldog, maybe a few other partners and then we'll get married, I promise you."

Rifkeh had pondered that for a while staring at the tabletop as her finger had made meaningless invisible patterns on it. As if the words had difficulty in being enunciated she had said, "But what about Leo? I don't want him mixed up in this *chazzarai*, this mess."

"The boy'll be all right. We know each other a long time, him and me. He calls me Uncle now, so to this Kaplan I'll be the boy's real uncle."

Rifkeh had remained silent for what seemed a long time. Shaking her head suddenly she had pushed herself up slowly from the kitchen table, heaved a great sigh and had said, "We'll get married? You mean it this time? You promise, Canarrick?"

"Yeah," he had replied looking up into her face. "I told you before. I promise."

Kaplan came to the house and sitting in the kitchen with Rifkeh, he was delighted. His eyes constantly followed her as she moved across the room. She served him tea and a slice of dark brown honey cake. He looked at her, a great smile on his face as she placed the glass of steaming liquid in front of him.

"*Ai*, Rifkeleh," he said to her between short sips of tea. "A *balabusteh*, a real good housekeeper. I expected that from you. See, I could tell from the shop. I could see it even there." She sat down at the table, dropped two cubes of sugar in her glass of hot tea and stirring the tea looked down into the swirling amber liquid. Kaplan said, "You got a nice place here, you keep it nice." Rifkeh took a sip of the hot tea and Kaplan said as he looked around the flat, "But you don't belong here, not in a place like this. You should have better than this. I mean it."

"Kaplan," she said to him as she held her glass motionless near her lips. When he had just entered the flat she had called him Mr. Kaplan as she always had but he had immediately insisted that she call him Kaplan. And now she said to him with a sad smile, "I can only afforda this. I got a boy to support, you know that. You should pardon me," and she began to laugh mirthlessly as she put her tea glass down on the table, "but right now I wish for a living, that's all. You know what I get paid."

Kaplan ate a small piece of cake. "Good honey cake," he said. Staring at her he swallowed, wiped his lips carefully, leaned forward over the table to be closer to her and said, "And so *schayn*, so pretty." He let the napkin drop to the table and said, "Listen to me, you don't belong in a shop, you don't belong here, in a place like this. Not you. Never. You're a-a-a-a princess," he said. And with a deliberate nod of his head, "I mean it. I don't lie, Rifkeleh."

She smiled a wan smile thinking how she hated all of this, this deception, this luring on of this old man whose senses had become blinded by the onset of his old age, his grasping for more out of life than a marriage gone wrong, that had become meaningless, of living in an empty house, with his three children gone, departed. Rifkeh had heard they lived in scattered sections of America, where? where? in some lost great beyond far away from New York.

And what about her? She was, what? A sort of *almooneh*, a widow. Yet, even worse. Like an *almooneh* she too lived without a husband, but Rifkeh's husband had not died, he lived lost and buried somewhere in that vast distance away that was the Old World, he was still alive. An *almooneh* received respect, the husband had died, been taken away, and that was final.

But with herself, Rifkeh, it was different. She was discussed in a terrible way, she knew what the gossip was. What was it that Mottel had found in her that had forced him to run away from her, to leave her and his son abandoned? What were her great hidden faults? Men thought about that when they were with her, she knew it. Those who had come somewhat close to her during those empty forlorn years when she had struggled alone, those men had kept a certain emotional distance from her. They had wanted only one thing, something shameful and defiling to her, something she could not do. She could not become their unpaid whore, their human mattress.

They promised nothing, yet wanted everything from her. She could not do it. Only the Canarrick had promised to marry her, only he had uttered those words she so desperately had wanted to hear. Only he had struck up some sort of a relationship with her son, those others they had disregarded Leo, her son, *her son*, and to them he had been merely a piece of furniture in the flat, if that.

Now looking at the man across the table from her, she thought, Kaplan, Kaplan, Kaplan. Go home. You're an old man, forget about such things like you're thinking. Go back to your wife, to what you have. You got more than me, more than most people. What do you want, the world? Go.

The Canarrick entered the flat then. Rifkeh introduced him as her brother to Kaplan, the two men shook hands. All three of them now seated at the table, Kaplan asked the Canarrick what he did, the Canarrick told him that he worked in the garment center, he was a finisher. Kaplan nodded.

Sipping his tea that Rifkeh had just served, the mist of steam rising up from the glass, the Canarrick asked Kaplan, "And you? What do you do?"

Kaplan formed a small smile, laughed softly, and said in a bantering tone of voice, "I work in a shop too. Blouses. For women." He gave a sly glance at Rifkeh, laughed once more, and said, "You could say Rifkeh and me, we work together, yeah, Rifkeh?"

"Yeah, sure," Rifkeh replied hating all of this. "We work together."

Leo entered the flat, Rifkeh introduced him to Kaplan. She could see Kaplan studying the boy. "You did your homework?" she said to the boy. He nodded as he stared at Kaplan. "You got more studying to do?" Again he nodded. She pointed to the second bedroom and said, "Go in the room and study." For a moment Leo remained in the kitchen, glancing towards the bedroom not knowing how to make an appropriate exit, grasping for something adequate yet completely elusive to say to the stranger, Kaplan. "Go," his mother said. "Mr. Kaplan knows you want to say goodnight to him." The boy mumbled something to Kaplan who smiled at him.

As Leo entered the bedroom Kaplan said to Rifkeh, "You got a nice boy there, I can see that right away. It comes from someplace, it shows what kind of a mother you are. *De appeleh fahlt nisht fahr fin de boim*, the apple doesn't fall too far from the tree."

Rifkeh smiled then, a true smile. "He is my life," she said.

"And why not?" the Canarrick said. "A good boy is precious like gold." Leo had shut the door of the bedroom. The Canarrick was talking to Kaplan, leading him slowly to a discourse of what he, Kaplan, did in his spare time. They talked on for a short while and finally the Canarrick asked, "Do you like cards? Me, I like to play. Poyker."

"Me too," Kaplan said.

"Sometime we'll play, yeah?" the Canarrick said casually.

"Here?" Kaplan asked looking at Rifkeh.

"Of course, here," the Canarrick said. "Why shouldn't it be here?"

So it had started. Once or twice a week, after work, Kaplan came to the flat where Rifkeh served him tea and cake. Kaplan met Bulldog and one of Bulldog's friends, someone who always joined the games that the Canarrick and Bulldog had set up.

Before Kaplan's second visit to Rifkeh's flat, Leo, finished with his homework went down to the street, stood on the stoop of the tenement when Kaplan appeared. Stopping near the boy Kaplan said, "Ah, Leo, yeah? That is your name?" The boy nodded slowly to the stranger. "Here," Kaplan said as he fished in his pocket for a coin. "Here's ten cents. For you. Go. Get something for yourself in the candy store. Enjoy."

Leo stared down at the hand holding the coin. He wanted that coin, oh, how wanted it! It was a magnet from which his eyes could not tear away. He wanted it but he could not take it, not from this Mr. Kaplan whom he did not know, whom he didn't really want to know, what was Mr. Kaplan doing there seeing his mother, why?

Leo, in the bedroom, had overheard the Canarrick in the kitchen telling his mother about the plans to ensnare this Mr. Kaplan and it had all seemed too wrong to Leo. How could the Canarrick do this, how could Leo's mother? Wrong was wrong.

Cautiously, as if it had a life of its own, his arm became extended, he watched as his hand took the coin from the man, and his eyes averted, he mumbled, "Thanks."

"Now that's what I like, a good boy who says thanks," Kaplan said with a smile.

In that first poker game Kaplan won approximately eighteen dollars. Bulldog and the Canarrick both lost a total of nineteen dollars, the other player won about a dollar.

After the game, when Bulldog and the other player had departed, Kaplan sat at the kitchen table, put his winnings away in his pocket, leaned back in the chair and said, "Rifkeh, you know, your brother don't look like you."

The Canarrick began to laugh and said, "Mr. Kaplan, you got *kinder*, children? Three, I hear. Tell me, they look like each other, hah?"

Kaplan shook his head. "No," he said. "Each one looks different. I don't know why it is but it is."

"That's the way things are," the Canarrick said stuffing the deck of cards into its box.

"What I'm saying is Rifkeh is so pretty."

"And I'm not," the Canarrick said with a shrug. "Lucky for her that she's the one who's *shayn*, pretty. A woman needs it. A man, he can get along without it. A woman should be pretty, beautiful, a man should be strong, that's the way the world should be."

Kaplan arose from the table, stared at Rifkeh as he slowly pushed his arm into the sleeve of his coat. "I'll see you on Thursday, yeah?" She glanced quickly at the Canarrick, looked back at Kaplan, and nodded. He reached for her hand, held it, warm in his hand, covered it with his other hand and said, "I enjoy being here, Rifkeh."

"It was a good game?" the Canarrick, still sitting at the table, asked.

"Yeah. Sure. I liked the game, why not? I always like to win. When do we play again?"

"Thursday?" the Canarrick said.

"Why not?" Kaplan replied. Still holding Rifkeh's hand he said to the Canarrick, "Thursday I'll win again. We'll start at seven and I'll stop by at half past six to see Rifkeh a little." He stared at Rifkeh and said, "Yeah?" She nodded slightly to him and he gave a short hearty laugh.

When Kaplan had gone, Rifkeh turned to the Canarrick and said with a wild shake of her head, "I don't want it, Canarrick. I can't do it and I won't do it, you hear me? I feel like a *koorveh*, you hear me? And what about Leo? What does he think? Men all around here. It was bad enough before, with you and me. But this Kaplan, what can Leo think of that? He's no fool, I tell you. He knows what goes on. He sees what's in front of his eyes—"

The Canarrick arose from his chair, went to Rifkeh. Lifting her face so that he could look into her eyes he said, "Rifkeleh, Rifkeleh, what's the matter, hah? Are you going to bed with him? Did you invite him to come here now? No, he invited himself, he asks to see you. Yes or no?" Now Rifkeh's head was resting on the Canarrick's shoulder and he felt her weak nod. "So, tell me, what's wrong?" She said nothing and he continued with, "And Leo? What can he think? A man comes, he plays cards with me and his uncle. So what? He sees me and the Bulldog play cards all the time with Adler and Levin. Yeah?" He looked down at her head and waited for her reply. There was none, and he asked in a somewhat higher tone of voice, "Yeah, Rifkeh?"

"Yeah," she finally said, the word muted against the Canarrick's shoulder. Still she felt that something was wrong. She lifted her head from his shoulder, looked up at him and asked, "We'll get married after this? You promise?" And in a more resolute tone of voice, "I mean it, this time."

"We'll get married, I promise," the Canarrick said. He kissed her, she held on to him for a moment and when they parted she glanced over her shoulder towards the bedroom where Leo slept as the Canarrick said, "You don't worry about nothing. I'll make enough to start a business, you'll see, to take care of you."

When Kaplan arrived for the following game, Leo said to his mother, "I'm going downstairs."

"Go to the movies on Cannon Street," she said. She looked for her purse but Kaplan had dug into his pocket and said to Leo, "Here, here's a quarter. For the movies and some candy too. Here, take it."

Leo hesitated. "Take it," the Canarrick said to him.

Kaplan's face took on a smile when Leo said faintly to him, "Thank you."

Leo slowly took the coin. "Ah-h," Kaplan said. "Like I said, a good boy."

Leo ran out of the flat, down the stairs of the tenement, two steps at a time, running from that Kaplan, that kitchen table, and that game that was to be. He would be glad with the darkness of the Cannon Street Movies, with the distraction of the two main features there. Of the unreal on the screen that somehow slowly evolved into a sort of reality, of the comedy short, of the newsreel, of the consumption of time.

He made up his mind that he wouldn't leave the movie house until after ten-thirty or maybe eleven, even if that meant seeing something over again. Mr. Kaplan had insisted to the Canarrick that the games end no later than eleven o'clock during weekdays.

Leo waited until a quarter to eleven before he left the movie house. Walking up the stairs, he met Mr. Kaplan as the man was descending. "You liked the movies?" Kaplan asked. Leo nodded. "Good!" Kaplan said. "You enjoyed the movies and I enjoyed being upstairs, in the house." With a laugh and more to himself than to Leo, Kaplan said, "I made twenty-four dollars." He shook his head in some sort of small admiration, said, "Not bad, not bad. But still, not a big game." And to Leo, "Go to bed, *boychick*, it's late."

"Yeah," Leo replied. He watched as the man descended the steps.

The Canarrick had it all planned. He had Bulldog plant nine or ten boxed and sealed decks of marked cards in the four candy stores in the immediate neighborhood. Should Kaplan demand a fresh deck from some outer source, someone, even Leo perhaps, would be sent down to the candy store, and its owner, primed by Bulldog in advance, would accept payment for and sell the marked deck. Bulldog had promised to pay the candy store owners a few dollars for this service and they had agreed, readily. Wasn't Bulldog hooked up with the gangsters and who wanted to start up with them? Who was crazy enough?

Leo had been in his bed hearing the Canarrick go over the plans for the upcoming game with Bulldog. Leo's head had rolled back and forth on his pillow as he stared up at the darkened ceiling of his room. He didn't want anything to do with the fake purchase of the cards, why were they involving him in this? He wanted desperately to separate himself from this—this thing, from all of it, from the card games, from Kaplan. Even the money that Kaplan gave him, Leo told himself, he wouldn't take any more money from the man, nothing, not even a penny. He didn't want it, it wasn't right.

And what dismayed him most of all was his mother. She had done nothing bad with Kaplan, he knew that. He had heard some of the bad things some women could do to men, how they led them on, and the men like some dumb animals became more and more entrapped. It was something Leo couldn't understand, what women did to men. And what disturbed him about the Canarrick were his promises to her that he would marry her. Sometime. Sometime. Leo had laughed caustically at that. Sometime never came. It was just a word, not even a promise, couldn't his mother see that?

He felt terrible about his mother. He loved her. He knew how lonely she had been before the Canarrick had come along, how she had cried alone, those long loud cries during the night when she thought Leo had been asleep, how her life had filled out after she had met the Canarrick. But to Leo it still was a life of uncertainty, of unfulfilled promises, of empty words, and now, this conniving, this involvement of his mother in this plan. That was wrong, that should not be.

And also that Kaplan, looking at his mother with those wanting eyes, touching her hand, Leo couldn't bear it. If only Leo could talk to his mother, warn her, tell her to stop. If only he could talk to the Canarrick. But why should he, Leo, be the one to do it when there was Bulldog who should watch over his sister? Where was Bulldog? What was he a brother for? Leo could talk to none of them.

It will work out, he said to himself attempting to console himself. It will. You'll see.

The next game Kaplan lost three hundred and eighty-two dollars. After he was gone, Leo heard the Canarrick say to his mother and to Bulldog, "I got him! I got him! He wants to raise the betting. Next time will be the big one." And to Rifkeh, "Be a little nicer to him next time, so far he gets from you is a little feel of the hands."

"You shut up!" Leo heard his mother shout out. "What do you think I am, hah? You got your *farrfoylteh* game, your rotten game, if that's what you do that's your business. And you, Bulldock, I don't want to hear from you either."

Leo heard the Canarrick's contrite reply, Bulldog's annoying laughter as if he hadn't heard his sister's words, that laughter angering Leo. When his laughter had subsided Bulldog said, "*Ai*, sister, sister. You still got the old fire."

When Bulldog left, Leo could hear his mother, in a pleading tone of voice, ask Canarrick, "When will we get married?"

"Right after I get Kaplan big this next game," the Canarrick replied.

A different Kaplan entered the flat for the next game. This was a serious Kaplan, his face contained no smile, his looks at the Canarrick and Bulldog had hints of hostility. Even as he looked longingly for an instant at Rifkeh, something steely had crept into those soft stares. He ignored Leo.

Leo went into the bedroom, and opened his schoolbooks to his English homework. He began writing into his notebook.

Rifkeh, as she usually did, served tea. Kaplan drank his in complete silence, staring emptily over the edge of the glass. Standing behind him, Rifkeh shrugged as she glanced at the Canarrick who sat slowly sipping his tea.

Before the other player arrived, Kaplan said in a clipped tone, "We got a new deck, hah?"

"Sure, sure," the Canarrick replied. "Leo," he called out. "*Boychick.* Come out for a minute." Inside the bedroom, Leo put down his pen, entered the kitchen. He approached the kitchen table, the Canarrick peeled a bill from a wad of money, said to him, "Go downstairs to the candy store and buy a *peckel*, a deck of cards. The good kind, not the cheap ones."

Leo stared at the Canarrick. He didn't want to look at Kaplan sitting there stiffly at the table. Leo stared at his mother. He didn't want to go. No, it wasn't fair, why should he be the one to go? Nobody asked him, they just told him, Do this, do that. He didn't want their schemes, he wanted no involvement with what they were doing.

"Go, Leo," Bulldog was saying. "Buy the cards."

Leo's mother, wordless, sat at the table, stared up at her son, her eyes moved to the Canarrick who said to Leo, "You'll have a treat, you'll go to the movies after. Go. Get the cards, *boychick.*" He held out a dollar bill.

Leo glanced once more at his mother who nodded. He took the money from the Canarrick, left the flat, and as he descended the stairs he was shaking his head, saying to himself, This is the last time. I mean it. I won't do it again. Never! He was down now, outside in the street and as he walked towards the candy store he thought, Why me? They want to do it, let them go for the cards. I won't.

He entered the candy store. The owner stood behind the counter. "A deck of cards," Leo heard himself say.

"Yeah. Sure," the man replied. His supply of playing cards was normally stacked in a slot in the wooden fixture against the wall which also contained packs of cigarettes. He reached down and removed a pack of cards from under the counter. Straightening up the owner asked, "Your uncle, he's upstairs?" Leo nodded, and gave the bill to the man.

After he received the change from the man for the purchase, after he left the store, Leo could almost feel the man's eyes following him. A wave of bitter resentment surged up in him. As he climbed the stairs of the tenement he banged his fist angrily over and over against the banister.

When he entered the flat, the tea glasses and the plates had been removed from the table, the other player was there. Without looking at Kaplan Leo placed the deck on the table, gave the change to the Canarrick.

The Canarrick, with a smile, gave Leo a quarter and said, "Go. Go to the movies. Buy yourself some candy."

Leo, the coin in his open palm, glanced at his mother, she nodded. Without a word, without looking at Kaplan, he left the flat.

One of the features at the Cannon Street Movies was a western with Jack Holt, the other starred Buck Jones. Somehow Leo became lost in the screen, lost in the intrigues of the plots.

It was a little after eleven o'clock when Leo returned to the flat. His mother, the Canarrick, Bulldog were there. Kaplan and the other player were gone. The room smelled heavily of cigarette smoke which still hung billowed and crawled across the kitchen ceiling. Bulldog was laughing, the Canarrick, trilling his song, was staring down unbelievingly at a stack of bills.

Leo's mother, her face impassive, looked at Leo as he entered and said, "Go to bed."

Leo went into his bedroom, shut the door. Outside, in the kitchen, he could hear the Canarrick say, each word stressed and elongated, "Over nine hundred dollars!"

"A fortune," Bulldog said. "Just like you said, Canarrick."

"Just like I said, yeah, Rifkeleh? Like I said, no?" the Canarrick said.

"Like you said," Leo's mother replied tonelessly. "You said other things too. Remember?"

"Remember? I remember," the Canarrick replied. "You don't let me forget."

"A-ha!" Bulldog said. "A fight already. Listen, Rifkeh, and you listen too, my friend, the Canarrick. Fights, I don't need. I got my money, Canarrick, you got yours. So I'm going. Good night. Fight in good health." And with that Leo heard the front door open and close. Leo undressed, turned off the overhead light, and was now in bed.

"What do you mean," he heard his mother say angrily, "I don't let you forget?"

"That you don't let me forget," the Canarrick replied. "All the time." And he mimicked Rifkeh's voice, "When do we get married? when do we get married?"

"Yeah. When?" Leo's mother said, her voice rising. "You're the one who tells me all the time we'll get married, don't you? So what are you saying now?"

There was a huge silence. Only the faint noises from the street below and from the few flats in the building in which people were still awake. Leo heard the soft pad of his mother, now in her stockinged feet treading slowly across the linoleum floor of the kitchen, the floor groaning slightly under her steps.

The Canarrick, his words slow and emphatic said, "I'm saying, like I just said, we'll get married. You hear that? What more do you want?"

"Nothing, nothing," Leo's mother snapped in return. Then suddenly, "Why do I have to say it, to remind you all the time? Why can't you say it, alone, without me asking you?"

"But I said it!" the Canarrick shouted. Lowering his voice somewhat he said, "Are you deaf? Didn't you hear me?"

There was another silence. Dimly Leo heard someone in the kitchen go to the sink, open the faucet, fill a glass with water. There was the mumble of words moving farther and farther away, lost in a vast distance, the distance curled and enveloped him and Leo fell asleep.

His mother didn't smile the next morning when Leo sat down at the kitchen table for breakfast. She had already eaten her meal, everything about her was grim. Leo, darting glances at her, began to eat his fried egg.

As she was about to leave to go to work, she turned and said to him, "You be good today." He nodded. "I'll be back when I finish work." Leo nodded once more as she said, "The Canarrick, he's still sleeping."

"I won't make noise, mama," Leo said.

"Make noise, make noise," she said to him. "Who cares?"

She said nothing more, then she was gone. Leo stared down at his food, his head nodding slightly. So the fight was still on. He sighed. Why did people fight? What did they want? Ah, if only they acted nice to each other, everything would be all right. If only.

When he returned from school, the Canarrick was gone. Leo washed the dishes that had been piled in the sink, swept the floor of the kitchen. The room still smelled of tobacco smoke, he opened the window, the fresh air rushed in, the vestiges of the smoke that clung to the walls and the ceiling began to disappear. He shut the window and left the flat.

Standing outside on the stoop of the tenement as the day was weakening and turning to gray, he searched the street for one of his friends. He saw nobody, it was too early, his friends, just as he, had come home from school and they were still in their flats. Leo leaned against the side of the entryway to the tenement. He felt tired, last night he had gone to bed at least an hour past his usual bedtime.

He was surprised when he saw Kaplan at his side. "Mr. Kaplan—" he stuttered out.

"Ah, Leo, Leo," Kaplan was saying, a fixed smile on his face. "Just the one I wanted to see."

"Me? What for?"

"You. Because I want to ask you something," Kaplan said staring into Leo's face. "You always looked like a good boy to me, an honest boy. Yes? I always said that, didn't I? Yes or no?" Still perplexed, Leo nodded slowly and Kaplan said, "I want to ask you for something, just one thing. And I want you to answer me *der emess*, the truth. Yes?" Kaplan waited for Leo's reply, there was none and

Kaplan said slowly, "Is the Canarrick your real uncle, hah?" Leo began to shake his head, not in reply to the question, but to rid himself of the words he had just heard. No, he didn't want to reply, he didn't want to be there. His heart was pounding, he looked away from Kaplan who said, "I can never see her alone, he's always there. Not Bulldog. Is Bulldog your uncle? *Der emess?*"

Leo didn't want to say anything, he wanted to run away but somehow he couldn't, his feet seemed cemented into the stoop. He shut his eyes, he heard his heavy breathing, and opening his eyes at last, he whispered, "Yeah."

"*Der emess?*" Kaplan asked. Leo nodded. "And the Canarrick?" Leo tensed. No, I won't answer that, no, I can't. Why does he ask me? what does he want from me? the words sped through his mind. Go away! he thought. Get away from me! Leave me alone! And Kaplan was saying, "The Canarrick, is he your uncle? Leo, you don't lie, you tell the truth, I know it."

It seemed forever, it was forever. He attempted, oh, how he tried! to say, Yes, he is. And that would be the end of it, the questions would be over, the tormenting would stop, Kaplan would go away, they would leave him alone at last, all of them. But the words did not come. Dimly, yet distinctly, he heard Kaplan's question once more.

"No," he heard his voice, something disconnected from himself say as he stared far into the distance.

"Ah!" Kaplan whispered and remained silent for a moment. Finally he said, "You're a good boy, Leo. One in a million."

Breathing heavily in and out, Leo felt that Kaplan at last was gone. He turned to look where Kaplan had been, the man had disappeared. Slowly, with great effort, he began to climb the stairs back to the flat. He shouldn't have told Kaplan. Who was Kaplan, what was he to Leo? But Kaplan had insisted on *der emess*, damn him! If Kaplan hadn't said those words, maybe he, Leo, would have been able to lie. Maybe.

When his mother came home later, she looked distraught. "What's the matter, mama?" he asked.

"Nothing, nothing," she mumbled with a wave of her hand. "Where's the Canarrick? Did you see him?" Leo shook his head, his mother said, "Go look for him. Go find him. Maybe he's with Bulldock. Go find him!" Leo was about to tell her that the Canarrick would come home, not to worry, but she said, "Go, Leo, go!"

She looked so beset with trouble that Leo felt he must obey her. He ran out of the house, ran all the way to where Bulldog lived. Running up the stairs of that tenement, two steps at a time, he arrived in front of the flat. Breathing heavily, he knocked on the door. Bulldog was at the door and when he opened it, Leo could see the Canarrick sitting at the kitchen table.

Leo said to the Canarrick, "Come quick! Mama wants you."

"What's the matter?" the Canarrick asked looking up from where he sat.

"She says for you to come. She says it's important. She's waiting. Come."

The Canarrick glanced at Bulldog, shrugged, lifted his eyes to the ceiling, pushed himself up from his seat and followed Leo out of the flat. Outside, in the street, Leo began to run, something was wrong, he knew it. He didn't want to think about what was wrong, maybe nothing was wrong, maybe his mother was still mad at the Canarrick, yes, that was it.

The Canarrick called out to Leo, "Wait! Don't run! Your mama will be there if you come two minutes later."

Leo stopped, turned back to the Canarrick and said," She don't look so good. Maybe she's sick. She said I should find you right away and you should come home. We could walk a little faster."

The Canarrick shook his head to himself, let his hands fall to his sides. "Go," he said to Leo. "Run. Fly. When you get home tell your mama I'm coming."

Leo began to run. Down the streets to the tenement where he lived. Up the stairs, to the flat. The door was closed but not locked. He burst into the flat, his mother was sitting at the kitchen table, her face held up by her right hand, her elbow on the table. A thin strand of hair had fallen on her cheek.

She looked up when Leo entered the room and he said breathlessly, "I found him. He's coming."

"You're a good boy, Leo. You're good to your mama," she said with a weak smile. Leo didn't know what to say. He stood, waiting for the Canarrick. Now he could hear ascending footsteps on the stairs. "He's coming?" Leo's mother asked and Leo nodded. "Go in the bedroom, Leo," she said. "I got to talk to the Canarrick."

The Canarrick came into the room as Leo entered the bedroom. When Leo shut the door he could hear the Canarrick say, "You wanted me? What is it?"

"I lost my job," Leo's mother said beginning to cry. "I got fired." She began to sob and Leo closed his eyes, prayed he could not hear anything else.

"You got fired?" the Canarrick said incredulously. "What for?"

"For nothing. I didn't do nothing. I came to the shop, I worked today like before. Kaplan, he looked at me once in the morning, then later in the afternoon I see him go out. Then he came back and he went to his office and soon the foreman, he came over to me, he said to pack my things, I was fired." Phrases and words were punctuated by sobs.

Lying in bed, Leo couldn't believe the words. Kaplan had gone out in the afternoon, that must have been—No, it couldn't be, no! And when he came back to the shop, soon the foreman told Leo's mother she was fired. No! no! It was impossible! How could it be?

Kaplan had told Leo to speak the truth, and he had. And now, for this to happen? Was that what happened when you told the truth? He tossed and turned on the bed, he banged the pillows with his fists. What had he done?

"Rifkeh, let me understand," the Canarrick was saying. "He went out, he came back, then you got fired."

"Yeah."

"He knows," the Canarrick said in a soft voice. Leo's mother said, No, it couldn't be, how could it? "He knows," the Canarrick said once more. Leo could hear the loud smash of the Canarrick's fist on the tabletop. "The bastard! Why did he do that? I thought he liked you, didn't he?"

"What do you want from me?" Leo's mother was sobbing. And now angrily, "What did I do, hah? Didn't I do everything you told me to do? Didn't I do everything even though I didn't want to?"

"He knows, the bastard knows," the Canarrick said quietly. "Okay, Rifkeh, all right, so he fired you, so it's not the end of the world, is it? There are other places you can work, you always tell me that. This place wants you, that place wants you. So you won't work for Kaplan, so what?"

"He knows, he knows," Leo heard his mother say. "I'm so ashamed, Canarrick, don't you understand?"

"What do you have to be ashamed for?" the Canarrick said. "You did nothing wrong."

Inside in the bedroom Leo couldn't bear listening to those words going endlessly on and on, emphasizing the terrible thing he had done. He pulled the pillow tightly up over his head and ears, held it there, damming those words that incriminated him, that had harmed his mother.

After school the next day, when Leo came home, he found his mother, Bulldog and the Canarrick there. But the Canarrick's face was a caricature of itself. The area around one eye was blue and purple, the eye was closed, his face and lips were swollen. He was holding a compress to his face.

"What happened?" Leo asked looking from one face to another.

"Nothing, nothing," his mother replied with a violent shake of her head.

"What do you mean, nothing?" Bulldog said to her, the cigarette in his mouth bobbing up and down as he spoke. "They beat up the Canarrick," he said to Leo. "The *shtarkers* , the strong-arm ones. From Kaplan, maybe." He nodded to Leo as he said, "No, not maybe. Who else? From Kaplan. He got that big shop, he's got a few *shtarkers* working for him there." He turned to his sister and asked, "Yeah, Rifkeh, am I right?"

She shut her eyes blurring her vision momentarily before cutting off the sight of that battered face. "Yeah," she said without emotion. "He got two, three, working for him."

The Canarrick said from swollen lips, "Yeah, it was Kaplan."

Leo wanted to run and hide. First, his mother being fired. Then, this. Why had he ever spoken to Kaplan? Why did he ever have to know Kaplan? Why should this have befallen him? Why had he opened his mouth to that stranger? What had been wrong with him? Crazy, senseless, he hadn't thought of anyone but himself and that damned *emess*. That *emess*, that was Kaplan's *emess*, not his. His real *emess* was that he had harmed his mother. And the Canarrick. And himself. That was the *emess*.

Bulldog was saying to the Canarrick, "Listen, if you want, I can get a few of the Cannon Street *boyiss* to see those *shtarkers*. And Kaplan too. Yeah?"

The Canarrick turned to stare one-eyed at Bulldog. His swollen lips began to form a small painful smile and he opened his mouth slowly to utter something when Rifkeh shouted out angrily to Bulldog, "*Messhugeneh*, Lunatic! *Idiot*! And now, this? You want to make a gangster from me too, now? It's not bad enough with the gambling? It's too much!" She turned to the Canarrick and said, "Enough! Enough with this *chazzerai*, this garbage, enough!" And to Bulldog, "Go already! Leave us alone! You heard me, go!"

Bulldog stared momentarily at his raging sister, then at the Canarrick who now sat slumped at the table watching the sporadic movement of his hands. Shrugging his shoulders in an emphatic helpless gesture Bulldog left the flat.

Rifkeh was glaring at the Canarrick. Leo couldn't bear to hear those angry hurled words, listen to his mother's grief. He thought, Kaplan, looking and acting so nice, what was he but an animal in beating up the Canarrick. What was wrong with everything?

He felt on the verge of tears, but he would not cry, that would be a complete, a total admission of guilt. And what was he guilty of? He had done nothing but spoken the truth. Was truth evil? He didn't know, he couldn't know. Maybe he would never know.

Outside his room, from the kitchen, he heard his mother's demanding voice, "Canarrick, when will we get married? You got the money now. So, when?"

"Soon. Later. What do you want, Rifkeh? Leave me alone for now, can't you see I don't feel so good? Later, you hear?"

"No," came Leo's mother rising voice. "Now. No more laters. Tell me now. I got to know. Your eye, your face will get better in maybe a week, two, but right now you have the money. When, Canarrick?" There was a heavy silence from the kitchen and suddenly Leo's mother began to shout, "I asked you, when? For three years you say to me, wait, wait. And me, where is my head? I waited. And I still wait. I will not wait no more, you hear me? No more. Soon I'll be old, soon men will not want me. I want to get married, you hear me? Now! I want you to talk about it. Answer me, Canarrick!" Leo could hear the slaps of his mother's hand on the porcelain top of the kitchen table, the stuttering echoes. There was no reply from the Canarrick. And finally Leo's mother, still shouting, cried out, "So that is your answer, hah? All right. So now I know your answer." And in a wounded yet angered tone of voice said, "Someplace in this world there is a man for me, who will marry me, who will be good to me and to my son. Somewhere. I will find him, he will find me—"

Leo couldn't bear to hear his mother speak this way. He had done this to her, he had caused all this trouble for her. He wanted to cry out, I am to blame, mama! Please, please, please, I'm so sorry.

The Canarrick finally said, "Why do you talk like this, Rifkeleh?"

"Don't Rifkeleh me. I talk like this because it is the *emess*. But what do you know about *emess*? What do you know about anything except your cards, your gambling? You don't have to get married, you're married already. To that pack of cards, to your gambling." Her words were speeding up, "You don't need another wife, you don't need me. Maybe somebody to trap a Kaplan, that's what you need me for. But I can't do it, I won't do it, not no more, not for you, not for nobody. And that's *der emess*." She gave a huge quivering loud sigh that came to Leo as something almost physical. "I don't need you, you understand?" Her voice was cracking as she said, the words rising, "I won't marry you, Canarrick, you hear that? I won't. Never. I want you to get out. Leave. Right now. Pack up your things and go. Get away from me, I don't want to see you, I don't want to hear you—"

The Canarrick was saying, in a shocked tone of voice, "Rifkeh, Rifkeh, what are you saying?"

"Get out!" Leo's mother said. "Now! That's what I'm saying. Go! I don't want you no more. Pack your things, I said!"

In the dark black cave, on that dark black bed on which he lay, Leo heard the scrape of a chair in the kitchen, the slow heavy tread of the Canarrick going into the other bedroom. Leo thought he could hear the heavy breathing of his mother, whether real or imaginary he heard something in his head and he wanted to shout out, I'm sorry, mama! I didn't mean it!

From the other bedroom, faintly, he heard the scrapes, the squealing opening of the closet, the opening of dresser drawers. He waited, breathing heavily in and out. He heard nothing from his mother. Finally there was the sound of the Canarrick's footsteps returning to the kitchen.

"Rifkeh—" he heard the Canarrick say.

"Go!" he heard his mother say. "Go now! I don't want you. I made of you what you wasn't. It was all a dream, a play, a movie. *Nisht der emess*, not the truth. I should know better. *Der emess iz der emess*, the truth is the truth. I don't want lies, no more lies."

In the bed, Leo suddenly understood her words. They came to him as salvation, the blackness around him began to disappear, was gone. I don't want lies, she said. Was that true? Yes, yes, and if it was so then that had governed his brief talk with Kaplan. He, Leo, had not lied, had not perpetuated what was false. In some unknown way he had known what to do, what his mother would have wanted him to do.

Maybe now, things would turn out all right for them. Now, there would be no deceit, no shame, no lies to spin. Maybe now his mother would find someone who would really take care of her, who would protect her. Maybe now there would be a real future for her.

He wanted desperately for it to be so. Make it so, he almost called out. This time it would all be better, mama, you'll see. I promise. Please, please, he fervently begged the darkened ceiling, let it be so, please, please.

THE RUN ON THE BANK

Frantic frantic frantic, she ran down the sunlit street clutching the sweat-dampened bankbook in her right hand, running as fast as she could down East Broadway on the Lower East Side, passing stores, houses, the Forward building on her left, running towards the cafeteria on the corner of Essex Street.

"Benny!" she gasped out as she ran. "Benny, *oy vay*, woe, woe, Benny. What shall we do?"

She came to the cafeteria and entered, going quickly down the aisle between the long counter and the sets of tables, her eyes eagerly searching for her husband. Benny Benny Benny, please be here. Benny, please.

It was eleven o'clock. Earlier in the morning she had sent one son off to school, later she had heard about the run on the bank from one of her neighbors.

The people were all taking their money out of the bank, it was a no-good bank, something was wrong with it, what could it be? Such a big bank, such a big building. How could a place like that be no-good?

Quickly she had rummaged in the old dresser drawer for their bankbook, their savings, all they had in the world. Two hundred and seventeen dollars. They had saved it all before the Crash, they had decided not to touch it, to let the little interest accumulate. After the Crash they had denied food from their mouths, they had denied themselves new clothing, shoes, everything. To ward off utter poverty, they had erected this barrier, this savings that they would not touch.

And after she had found the bankbook she had brought her other son, a boy of three, to be watched by the neighbor next door.

All the while saying to everyone she met, "How can it be? It must be wrong. It can't be true, can it?"

Another neighbor said to her, "Go! Go quick to the bank! Nothing is wrong, you are right, it can't be. But go. Find your Benny, go find him. Go to the bank. *Schnell*, Quick!

She found Benny in the cafeteria, seated at a long white marble-topped table drinking coffee with two of his friends from the shop. Lucky he was there, she thought, approaching him. Unlucky that there hadn't been work at the shop that day. When that happened, he would go to the cafeteria to drink some coffee and *schmooz*, talk a little with his friends.

"Benny!" she said urgently when she was near him. "Benny!"

He looked up at her, his eyes widened with apprehension. "What? What is it? The *kinder*, the children, nothing is wrong?"

"No, no, no," she said grasping him by his arm. "The bank. Something's wrong with it. All the people are taking their money out—" She stopped, unable to speak, tears began to stream down her face. "*Oy, Gutt!* Oh, God! It can't be true, it can't!"

People at other tables stared at her. Quickly, Benny quickly jumped to his feet. "What?" he said. "The bank?" He glanced at his friends, a baffled look on his face, he shook his head as he looked at his wife. He said to her, "No! It can't be! It's a national bank, the bank from the *rigeering*, the government. It's their bank, they will never allow anything to go wrong, President Roosevelt won't allow it, he will see that everything is all right."

Yet he joined her and now the both of them dashed out of the cafeteria, the babble of conversation of those inside cut off by its closing door.

Both of them now running running towards Delancey Street where the bank building was located, pushing people in their way, their breaths hot and cutting into their lungs, their eyes wild, glancing momentarily at each other as they ran.

"Who told you?" Benny gasped out as they raced on.

"Mrs. Levine. She heard it from a neighbor."

"Mrs. Levine," he said. "What does she know, hah?"

"She knows. She knows everything. All the time."

"She and her big mouth," Benny gasped. "She don't know nothing." He forced himself into more speed.

His wife was falling behind. He grasped her by her upper arm, pulled her along as they turned into Delancey Street. They ran towards Orchard Street, they could see a vast crowd of people milling in front of the bank building, police were there too, and from the crowd a moaning and crying of collective grief.

"*Oy vay*," Benny's wife said. "Look at that! *Mein Gutt!* My God! It's true!" She began to sob loud torrents of sorrow. Benny pulled her along with him as he ran. It took forever it seemed, his wife crying out to him, "I can't, I can't run no more, please, Benny!" But he dragged her along with him and now at last they were joining the crowd, both with fires in their chests, molten metal in their lungs.

They stood bent over, attempting to capture their normal breathing, hearing the shouts and the cries, the hurled curses from the crowd. Benny looked up, saw the white faces, the pleading eyes of those around him. At his side his wife was holding her chest as she heaved breaths in and out.

They tried to force themselves forward into the crowd but it was impossible. They joined the solid mass of humans packed together, wedged together, unable to move. Standing there, those who could, stared at the shut bank doors, others looked at the police as they motioned the crowd into a more solid mass.

"My money!" Benny shouted out. "Where is my money? Two hundred and seventeen dollars! Where is it?" Others were shouting too, their clamor a scrambled din rising up into the air.

Up ahead, at the head of the mob, people were pressed against the doors of the closed bank, banging on the doors with clenched fists, shouting, yelling, screaming, demanding their money.

"*Ganovim! Ganovim!* Thieves! Thieves!" Benny's wife shouted out from beside him. "Give us our *gelt*, our money back!"

Other frantic people had formed behind Benny and his wife and from somewhere in back of them a woman cried out, "What shall I do? It's all I have, everything!"

The policemen pressed, shoved the crowd back "*Cossackin! Cossackin!* Cossacks! Cossacks!" people roared out. "Why are you doing this? What have we done? It's our money, give us back our money!"

The police pushed against the shouting people, the cries of the crowd unheard, unheeded, lost in the wind.

"Go home!" someone up front shouted. From where Benny and his wife stood it seemed like a voice emanated from the visored blue cap of a policeman standing somewhere at the fringe of the crowd. "Go home," it said with authority. "The bank is closed."

"How can we go home?" someone shouted out furiously. "When they won't give us our money? What will happen to us?"

"Go home!" the authority voice said.

Benny looked around him. Not too far away stood a man, a stone man unmoving, ashen, mute, only the trickle of a large tear running slowly down each side of his face.

Someone in front of Benny said, "They say we will hear from the bank."

Benny, his face white and gaunt, looked at his wife. Tears streamed down her face, she stared at him, shaking her head in complete bewilderment. Her mouth opened to say something, no words came out.

"Two hundred and seventeen dollars," Benny said in a whisper. "*Alles*, All. And now, nothing."

He tried to control himself, he felt as if he would burst out into tears but he must not allow himself to do it, not even like that stone man he had just seen. He, Benny, was the man of the house, the man didn't cry, it was not allowed, never. Yet he felt he was crying, deep down inside he was crying.

At last he said to his wife, "The *rigeering*, the bank was from the *rigeering*."

"No, no," a man near him said in an English almost without accent. "It was just a bank. Private."

"No, no," Benny said shaking his head vehemently. He felt beaten, lost, alone. "It can't be. It's a national bank, the building is so big, it's like a palace. It's the *rigeering* I tell you. Why would they have a name like that if it wasn't?" he said to nobody and to everybody, to anybody who would listen and help him. He found himself suddenly crying, and he shook his head like a wounded animal, the tears flooding down.

THE ORDEAL OF
MR. COOLIDGE

Early spring, those spring fever days, were crazy days. Your body wakes up from the cold bitter winter. It wants to move, to jump, to kick out. Your mind becomes unfrozen, you want to sing, strange ideas race through you like roaring locomotives, speeding here, there, everywhere.

Nothing seems the same, not even at the all-boys junior high school on the Lower East Side that I attended, not even what went on in its playground, its classrooms. Even the Depression takes on a somewhat different tinge, maybe now, soon, something good would happen and the bad days would be gone. Just a bad dream.

That sunny spring day, for some strange reason, all of us, the students, had congregated early in the outdoor playground. We had begun our handball games, a few-minor fights, mostly pushing and shoving matches, had broken out among some of the rougher boys, while many of the other boys, influenced by the new-born bright sun just stood silently, waiting for something unknown, something good to happen.

I was playing handball with Goldie and Max and Joey DeSimone. The four of us were good students, good friends. We studied together for the mid-term and final exams and especially for the most important New York State Regents exams.

Since almost everybody had a nickname, I was called Lion because my first name was Leo and there was a Leo the Lion that roared out when they showed the Metro-Goldwyn-Mayer movies. That was my nickname.

The students of our school were almost all Jewish, the few non-Jewish boys were those whose families lived on the fringes of the Lower East Side.

For some time, almost from the beginning when I had first met him, I had called him Joey, Yussel, or Yussie, its Jewish-Hebrew equivalent. He didn't care, he seemed at home with us and when he visited my house when we studied together my mother didn't even know he was Catholic-Italian.

"Yusseleh," my mother would say to him on those occasions, "it's good to see you. You feeling all right?" Yussie, smiling, would nod. "And your mama and papa, they're all right?" Again Yussie's nod. "Your father's working?"

"Sometimes," Yussie would reply. "You know how it is."

My mother knew that Yussie's father was a bricklayer. It wasn't a usual Jewish trade, she thought, but after all, work was work, you did what you had to. Anything to make a living, anything to feed your family, anything to exist.

"You make good marks in school?" she would ask him.

And he, embarrassed, would squirm somewhat in his seat and say nothing and I would reply, "He's an A student, mama."

That was always the catechism when he visited us. After that my mother would serve us a glass of milk and some cookies or a piece of cake, and all of us, Yussie, myself, Goldie, Danny, Max, Izzy, whoever was present, would move all the chairs close to the porcelain top of the bathtub set against the wall in the kitchen and we would begin our studying, asking each other questions. Someone, any one of us, would correct the answers if they were wrong.

My mother, as she worked on the other side of the kitchen, would occasionally stop to stare at us, a huge smile on her face. "Good boys!" she would whisper to herself. "Such good boys!"

For some reason, Yussie preferred to come to my house to study although sometimes we did go to other houses. When I asked him about it he said, "Lion, I feel comfortable in your house, there's something there that's okay, you know?"

Even his speech, his cadences, had become like ours. To my mother, to all of us, he was a Jewish boy whose name was Yussie. Only in school when he was called up by the teacher, "Joseph DeSimone," his last name pronounced by the teacher,"Dess-Si-mohnee," were we reminded that he was Italian. But even that, over time, had ceased to penetrate our minds. Yussie was Yussie, he belonged with us, he was part of our group.

Once my mother had asked him, "*Fahrshtayst Yeeddish*, Do you understand Yiddish?" a phrase she had used with all of my other friends.

And Yussie had replied, "*Ah bissel*, A little."

My mother had smiled broadly at that. Ah! Here was a Jewish boy who was learning Yiddish, less and less of the young ones were, here was a good Jewish boy, a good boy for Leo to be friends with.

Yussie ate the Jewish food, the kugels, the pickled herring, the chopped liver, he ate it like all of us, there was nothing that was served to him that he didn't eat. My mother liked that tremendously, a good eater!

And when he went home, to his own neighborhood, his speech patterns changed, the Italian rhythms and words returned to him, even in his English. Yussie was a language chameleon.

He was my partner that morning on the handball court. We lost. As we left the court, I said to him, without malice, "You're a lousy handball player. You don't have that swing."

"I know, I know," he replied. "But I sure as hell can run, can't I?" He had won a number of track events during our school's Field Days in the nearby park where athletic competitions were held. "You can't have everything," he said with a smile.

"Try," I said. "Practice that swing. You swing like a rusty gate. If you got a real good swing you could be good in handball too."

Goldie was leading the way to the school building, we were following him. Max, Goldie's partner in the game said, "We sure as hell beat you, didn't we? We skunked you."

"Come on," Yussie said. "All you need to win is Goldie. Put him on the court without a partner and he'll beat any two of us. You know that."

"What's he saying?" Max turned to me as he pointed his head in Yussie's direction. "That I can't play? Is that it?"

"Maxie," I replied. "What he's saying is that Goldie don't need any of us to win, that's all. You're not bad, Maxie, you play a good game, but Goldie don't need you."

Max said to me with a trace of anger, "I can beat you. Anytime." And to Yussie, "And you too."

"You're on," I said. "Lunch time I'll play you."

"Me too," Yussie said to him.

We went to our classes that morning. None of that closed bitter winter feeling remained, it was all gone, even the good students began acting up, laughing loudly at whispered jokes. In the hallway we engaged in the game we called Baseball, when someone with his clawed fingers ripped at an unsuspecting student's fly. If two buttons were whisked away from their fly eyelets, it was a two-bagger, if the fly was opened totally, it was a home run. There was always a roar of laughter from the onlookers, especially if there was a home run. If there was time before classes, victims became perpetrators, the game went on until it was time to enter the classroom.

In the classrooms, the rough boys, the older boys, began their thumb tack maneuvers. When a student who was not of their clique would go to the blackboard to write something, or went to the front of the class to read or recite, a few members of the older clique surreptitiously would place five or six thumb tacks, points up, on his seat.

The entire class, aware of what was going on, would watch and wait while the intended victim returned to his seat, sit down, shout out a surprised, "Ouch!" and jump up from his seat as he ran his hands gingerly across his bottom to remove the tacks.

We would all laugh at this spectacle, it was impossible not to. We held our laughter bottled inside of us, staring goggle-eyed at the teacher, our hands on our desks while the teacher said sharply, "What is it? What?"

"Nothing, nothing," the victim mumbled, sitting cautiously down in his seat after he had made certain no more tacks remained to harm him.

Everybody, every student, before sitting down, would run his hand across the seat of his desk, flicking the thumb tacks away to the floor, if there were any. It didn't take too long for a student, when called to leave his desk, would swing his seat up, so that at right angles to the floor, it was impossible for the tacks to be planted.

Impossible, until one of the older boys brought some chewing gum, chewed it slowly and imperceptibly so that the teacher wouldn't notice, the gum turning soft in his mouth. When someone not from his clique was called upon to go to the front of the room to recite, the gum chewer would secretly remove the wad from his mouth, tear it into small pieces, and would implant the thumb tacks, points up, into the soft wad. He would place each small pointed piece onto the seat and slowly raise the seat to its upright position.

The class waited. The victim would return to his desk, pull his seat down, sit down and immediately spring up yelling a pained, "Ouch! Ouch!"

We could not contain ourselves, the uproar became tremendous, the teacher banged on the desk shouting, "Will you be quiet! Will you be quiet!"

That day, the assistant principal, Mr. Burger was passing by in the hall, heard the noise of a tack attack and immediately entered the room. "You! You! You!" he pointed to three laughing students. "Go to my office! Immediately!" The room suddenly became quiet, we sat erect in our seats, unsmiling. Nobody moved. We knew what would go on in his office, the sharp stinging slaps of the heavy wooden ruler on the palms of both hands, sometimes one, two or three times depending on how Mr. Burger felt. He asked the teacher, "What happened?"

She told him all she knew was that there had been several outcries of ouches! a tremendous burst of laughter in the room, but the last time had been the worst. Mr. Burger glared ominously at us, his face turned on his body as on a swivel, his steely eyes on each of our faces, he made us feel guilty. Finally he left the room.

The last two victims of the thumb tack war remained in the classroom. Two innocents and one perpetrator were in Mr. Burger's office receiving their punishment. That was the way Mr. Burger operated. Over the school term he managed to get everybody in the class to his office, the innocent as well as the guilty.

Once, some time before, during the early winter, a substitute teacher, a young woman, perhaps twenty-four, had taken over the English class for the day. The regular teacher had taken sick. The class, at least the one I was in, was unmanageable from the start. Whistles, laughter, conversations shouted across the room while the powerless young woman had banged frantically on the top of her desk, asking for quiet.

I had felt sorry for her, she was young, she seemed nice. The students, not all of them, mainly the rougher and older ones made her life miserable. She had blinked several times behind her glasses, on the verge of tears.

Someone, I thought it was Gimpy, the tough one who been born with a limp, had made a paper airplane, dipped its tip into the inkwell on his desk, and had thrown it in her direction. The paper plane had flown in the air, gone between the substitute teacher's glasses and her cheek, its tip had hit the side of her nose and had streaked ink on it as it had slid down her face. She had looked up for a moment in shocked anguish, had run her hand down her face, stared at her fingers stained with ink and had begun to cry, almost uncontrollably.

Someone, one of the students had laughed, almost a bray. For some reason, out of nervousness perhaps, we all began to laugh, the sound welled up to a roar while that poor woman stood crying. Suddenly the door of the classroom had opened, Mr. Burger stood there, and his finger pointing had said, "You! You! You!" I was one of them. "Go to my office! Right now!" I had tried to protest but he hadn't listened and he said to me, "To my office, I said!"

Three of us had sat in his office, we waited for him as we looked at the long wide ruler that lay across the green blotter on his desk. About ten minutes later he had finally appeared in his office, red-faced, angry.

I had begun to say to him, "Mr. Burger, I didn't do anything. Honest. I really didn't."

"You just shut up," he had said to me. "It's a shame what you did to that woman, a terrible thing! Come here!" He had said loudly to me as he went to his desk and picked up the ruler.

I hadn't moved. "But I didn't do anything," I had said.

"Come here!" he had shouted. "When I tell you to do something, you do it! You're going to learn, all of you." He had glanced at the other two sitting in the chairs beside me, "that you can't do these things. You're going to behave like human beings, even if I have to beat it into you." And to me he had said, "Get over here!" Against my will I had moved cautiously, slowly, in his direction. "Put your hand out!" he ordered.

I had begun to shake my head, begun to recite my phrase of innocence when he had grabbed my hand, whacked it once, twice, hard, with the ruler, snatched the other hand, whacked that one too.

It had hurt, a pain of fire. He had wanted to hurt me. He had meant to make me cry. But I had made up my mind, in that instant, that I wouldn't, that at least in that, I would thwart him. I hadn't done anything! Hadn't I felt sorry for that poor teacher? What did he want from me?

Our next class was Miss Mason's music class. It shouldn't have been held that crazy spring day, not with that spring fever going around. For the protection of everybody, students and teachers, the school should have been closed down. Now the old rumors cropped up again, Miss Mason, an attractive brunette lady in her early thirties, it was whispered, was doing it with Mr. Coolidge in the students' clothes closet in her room when there was no class scheduled at the time.

The students who recited the story had practically sworn they had seen both of them go into the clothes closet, slide the doors shut and had emerged smiling about ten minutes later. Sure, what do you know, they did it, they did it in the clothes closet, sure, sure I'm telling you, I seen them go in. Those sliding doors closing up and later they shook, I can tell you what a banging went on!

Gimpy raised his hand and said in a sugary voice to Miss Mason, "Miss Mason, I got to go to your clothes closet. I got to pick up," and here his words had become slower and slower, "a double breasted—" now the class erupted in a howl of laughter drowning out Gimpy's other words.

Miss Mason looked uncomprehendingly at him. "Sit down," she said to him but Gimpy disregarded her, his words going on and on, lost under the roar of prolonged laughter. "Sit down!" she shouted at him but her words could not be heard. She stared wide-eyed at the class and shouted, "Will you be quiet!"

Uproar. Her words had melted into the tumult. Gimpy, in a shout that was a blast that everyone could hear said, "I slid it into your closet earlier, Miss Mason." The class again exploded in laughter.

Her face averted from the class, Miss Mason now began to cry. She was vulnerable and we knew it. There were two classes she couldn't control, ours and one other, that one also contained some older, rougher boys. With her other classes she managed to exercise control, the students were younger, more fearful of authority.

In this class the older boys exercised authority. There was bedlam when they wanted it, there were leering suggestive words and phrases as they, acting innocent, spoke them to her. There was temporary peace when they became bored with it all and allowed her to run her class. To them she was a small step above a substitute teacher whom they devoured, ate alive.

I stopped laughing. Maybe at first it had been funny, I couldn't help it if I had laughed, but it wasn't funny anymore. But I said nothing, nobody said anything to stop what was going on. The laughter subsided slowly, came to a slow silence. Miss Mason was drying her tears with her handkerchief, here eyes were red. Gimpy was leaning to one side of his seat whispering something to his neighbor.

Someone else said in a loud voice, "Mr. Coolidge likes to put his things in the closet all the time." The class began to roar once more. Someone hooted wildly. Miss Mason sat stunned, her mouth open, her tears running down her cheeks.

No music was taught in that class that day. Fortunately, Mr. Burger was nowhere in the vicinity of that part of the building.

I looked at Goldie seated near me. He shrugged, what could he do? I looked at Yussie, he shook his head and shrugged. I leaned over to my neighbor and said, "It's enough. Enough. She's crying."

The period finally ended, we left the classroom, Miss Mason was sitting at her desk, her eyes closed, her head rocking slightly from side to side, her crumpled handkerchief balled in one hand.

Now we would be going to Mr. Coolidge's algebra class and that would be an entirely different thing. Early spring, spring fever, whatever it was that caused this craziness, all that would have to be set aside in Coolidge's class. There would be no fooling around, no shouted out words. There would be order, strict order. As we entered his classroom, one of the students from the preceding class told us that it looked like the stock market was down, way down, Coolidge was on the war path.

That was our barometer with Mr. Coolidge, the stock market. Someone, sometime ago, had spread the rumor which had become wildfire, that when Mr. Coolidge was mad it was because the stock market was down. And when he was glad, stocks were up. Rumor or not, true or false, it had become a hard fact with us, we believed in it although we didn't really know what stocks were, or the stock market, what did you do there? All we knew was that you bought or sold something, but what did you buy? What did you sell? And if you bought, who did you buy from? And who did you sell to? All we knew was that Wall Street had crashed in 1929, and what did that mean?

"Stocks are sure down," I heard Gimpy whisper to another older student as they entered the classroom. "He gave the other class hell and it's going to be hell for us today. We better watch out."

Mr. Coolidge was at his desk looking down at some books spread on the green blotter. A younger student, someone whom I recognized as belonging to Miss Mason's class that followed ours, approached Mr. Coolidge and handed him a folded note. Mr. Coolidge read it, glared up at us several times, finished reading the note, nodded to the messenger who left the room.

Standing erect now, his body tense, his face rigid and red, we could feel his anger as he stared stonily at us, pointed with a steel finger to five of us, I wasn't one of them, ordered them to the blackboard, told each one of the selected students, Gimpy among them, "Do the homework problems," and gave each one of them a specific lesson number. Gimpy's was the second problem. "Move!" he said to them in a murderous voice. "Fast!" All of them scurried to the blackboard, books in hand. Gimpy quickly waddled to the blackboard, stepping only on the ball of his left foot, his heel set rigidly and permanently high above a normal position. Looking out at the rest of us, his anger boiling in his words, Mr. Coolidge said, "You'll all stay right here, very quiet, all of you, while I go out for a few minutes. Not-a-peep-out-of-any-of-you!" he shouted slowly, hesitating before each word to give it emphasis. "If I hear anything, anything! You'll wish you'd never been born! You'll be quiet now, you'll be quiet while I'm gone, you'll be quiet when I come back." He turned abruptly and left the room slamming the door shut.

There was silence in the room. We glanced at each other but didn't say a word. Now and then, at the blackboard, chalk squeaked across the slate. Gimpy was busy at the blackboard writing the answer to his problem. All of us knew that he had copied the homework from somebody else, someone he had intimidated earlier that morning before school started.

He passed exams by cheating, having small written notes passed secretly on to him by allies during the tests. Gimpy was totally unaware of algebra, it was a foreign language to him, everything, the words, the concepts, had never entered his head.

When he was finished with his work at the blackboard, he glanced around furtively, saw nobody at the door and he whispered out, "Is it okay? Is it right?"

Yeah, yeah, yeah, were the soft hissed replies. Shut up, someone whispered fiercely, Coolidge could come back any second now, you want to get us in trouble?

I stared down at my lesson book, reading a problem and its solution. Mr. Coolidge entered the room, everybody stiffened. Glaring murderously at us, he shut the door with a slam and walked slowly to his desk. The students at the blackboard turned away from facing us and were looking at their work. There was a heavy silence.

"Who do you think you are?" Mr. Coolidge said in an angry whisper. "Just who? You think," now his voice rose until it was a shout, "you can do anything to anybody? To a teacher? You think so, huh?" In a quick movement he picked up a book from his desk and hurled it at us, all of us ducked down in our seats as far as we could. The book flew over our heads, hit the wall in back of us and fell to the floor as Mr. Coolidge was shouting, "I'll teach you to be human beings if I've got to break every bone in your bodies!" He turned to Gimpy, pointed his finger at him and said, "You! You got something to say?" Gimpy, looked at us for a moment, his look begging for help. He shook his head. "I hear you've got a lot to say," Mr. Coolidge was shouting, his voice hoarse, spit shooting out in small mists from his mouth. "A lot! Plenty! Too much!" Sneering at Gimpy who shrunk away until he was stopped by the blackboard, Mr. Coolidge slowly approached him and said, "You got no words? It's a shame, isn't it?" He glanced at Gimpy's work on the board and said, "Explain that problem to me." His voice was still furious, though now somewhat contained. "Talk!" he commanded. "Now! You know how, I hear!"

Gimpy began to read what he had chalked on the blackboard. When he was finished he glanced momentarily at Mr. Coolidge who said, "Oh, that's fine. Great. Now tell me how you arrived at the concept. What's the rule?"

Gimpy looked dumbfounded, he said in a voice a little above a whisper, "Rule? What rule?"

Now Mr. Coolidge shouted out, "A rule! Yes, a rule! Do you know what it means?" But now all restraints were off, he picked up a piece of chalk, and full of anger, threw it at Gimpy, hit him in the leg. Gimpy said ouch! and began to rub his leg, Mr. Coolidge scooped up more chalk, hurled it at us, he ran to his desk and heaved his other books at us. He picked up his heavy square glass inkwell, hurled it, the ink spilled out dark trails in the air. All of the students ducked, the inkwell hit Yussie in the upper arm, he yelled out, clutched his arm as the inkwell fell to the floor.

Yussie looked at his arm in amazement, it had begun to bleed, I could see the blood slowly seeping between his fingers, his shirt had been cut by the glass missile and I yelled out, "He's bleeding! He's bleeding!" Everything stopped, sound, movement, everything. Mr. Coolidge saw the blood oozing between Yussie's fingers, stared uncomprehendingly at his wounded student while I ran to Yussie's side and said, "Come on, I'll take you to the toilet to wash it off there." Mr. Coolidge nodded dumbly. Goldie came up behind me and had pried Yussie's hand from the wound. The shirt at the wound was ripped, now bloody from the gash in Yussie's arm. Goldie looked at the dumbfounded Mr. Coolidge and said to the teacher, "His shirt's ripped too."

"Go," Mr. Coolidge whispered.

We went to the toilet, the three of us, where we washed the wound, swabbed it with pads made of folded toilet paper. It was hurting, Yussie's face was grimacing in pain as he said, "What'll I tell my mother? My shirt's ripped."

"Forget it, Yussie," I said to him as I placed a wad of dry toilet paper on the wound. "Just hold it. Like that. Yeah," I said. I looked at Goldie, shook my head and said, "I got to get him someplace, a drugstore. Doc Stern, that's the drugstore near where I live, I'll take him there. Doc'll fix him up."

"Go on," Goldie said. "You go. I'll tell Coolidge what you're doing."

"No," Yussie said as he pressed the paper wad to his arm. "I'll go back with you." He had been crying but he had surreptitiously wiped away his tears so that we wouldn't see him like that. Now his face was dry.

We returned to the classroom. Mr. Coolidge sat at his desk, staring down blankly at the green blotter. The flung books had been picked up and now lay on one side on the top of his desk, the inkwell, empty, was in its usual place. The class was silent, hunched over desks, working at a problem of some sort.

I said to Mr. Coolidge, "It's still bleeding. I better take him to my drugstore, it's not far from here, just a couple of blocks." Coolidge, silent, nodded, and I said, "Then I think he ought to go home." Coolidge shut his eyes and nodded.

We left the school building using the staircase that was near an exit door. We were out in the street, walking swiftly. Goldie asked Yussie, "How's it coming along?"

"It hurts," Yussie said. "It hurts! I didn't do anything!"

"Yeah," Goldie said. "It should've been Gimpy and some of those others." He shrugged. "It should've been them."

"But it was me," Yussie said bitterly.

The drugstore was on the corner of the street. I could see one of its display windows with its two large urn-like glass vases of a design peculiar to drugstores. Inside the glass vases, was a colored liquid, each vase a different color. A large cardboard sign advertising Ex-Lax was in the window with small dummy cardboard boxes of the product stacked neatly throughout.

We entered the drugstore, it was empty of customers. Doc was working behind the prescription counter, he looked up across its wide wooden partition, saw us, and he came out to meet us. "Doc," I said to him, "I got a friend who hurt himself."

"So I see," Doc said. He picked up a chair at the side of the store and said to Yussie, "Sit down, let me take a look at it. A-ha!" he said as Yussie removed his hand from the wad of paper.

Doc acted as neighborhood doctor. Except for prescriptions, which he was forbidden to write, he could only fill them, he advised us about our ills, telling us what patent medicine to use for our colds, our stomach aches, our cramps, for the thousand and one things we came down with. He talked to the women in soft, discrete, secretive tones, he listened attentively to them. He was also excellent in removing cinders from eyes, something quite usual. He did everything but write prescriptions, fill and pull teeth, set broken bones and operate on people. Because there was no money, everybody I knew only used doctors and dentists in the most dire circumstances.

Yussie had removed his shirt, Doc ran behind the counter, returned with bandage, tape, a bottle of antiseptic. He knelt down beside Yussie asked, "How'd you get it, hah?"

As Doc swabbed gently, removed the blood, cleaned the wound, Yussie, wincing, was saying, "I ran into something."

"Yeah. Sure," Doc said, nodding slightly. "That's what they all say." He swabbed antiseptic into the wound, Yussie stiffened with the pain and Doc said, "Yeah. It hurts. I can't help it, but that's what I got to do." He applied a bandage to the wound and he said to me, "Leo, how is your family?"

"They're okay," I said. Doc nodded, finished his bandaging. He arose groaning against the tightness in his knees and said to Yussie, "You don't have to go to the dispensary or see a doctor. It'll heal okay. I don't think it'll need stitches." As Yussie was painfully putting on his shirt, Doc said, "Keep it clean. Leave the bandage on, don't take it off until it's healed." Yussie, fully dressed now, nodded.

"Thanks, Doc," I said. "Thanks for everything."

"Eh," Doc said. "What else am I here for? Give my regards to your family." To Yussie he said, "No more fights, you hear? You don't think you fooled me with that monkey business you ran into something."

Yussie stood undecided for a moment then finally said in a tentative voice, "What do I owe you?"

Doc stared at him for a moment, waved his hand in front of his face, said, "What should I charge you, a hundred dollars? Come on, *boychik*, don't talk *narishkeit*, foolishness."

"No, I owe it," Yussie said. "How much?"

Doc snorted. "*Oy vay?*" he said to himself. "A sport."

Yussie was reaching into his pocket for a coin and I said to him, "Forget it. He does it for all of us."

Yussie stared at Doc and said, "Thanks."

"Now, that's it," Doc said. "A polite boy, that's what I like."

We left the drugstore. Outside, I told Goldie I would take Yussie home, there was no sense in all of us tramping to Yussie's house. Goldie agreed, he said he would return to school. "I'll tell Coolidge everything looks like it's okay. I shouldn't, he doesn't deserve it, but I will. Anyway, I want the guys to know that Yussie's okay."

He left. Yussie and I walked through the streets, I looked at him, he was holding his arm attempting somehow to minimize the pain. He was really a nice guy, a good friend, I liked him. Sometime ago he had told me that he wanted to be a lawyer and I looked at him in amazement. I hadn't determined what I wanted to be. To me, commitment seemed ages away. For me, it was enough that my family and I just got through each day.

A lawyer? I had said. Yes, he had replied, I don't want to have to live like we all do now, there's got to be something better, I look around and see what we have and then I think about what we don't have. Don't you? I don't want to be a bricklayer, a cement worker like my father. Not that there's anything wrong with it. But I don't want to have to beg for work. Do you know what it's like to get that kind of work today? You got to know somebody, you got to kiss behinds, that's what you have to do. And then when someone does you that big favor and lets you work, you got to do him a favor, someday. I don't want to have to go to people and beg, I want people to come to me. They do that when you're a lawyer.

And I had said, they come to you because you're a good lawyer, a great one, yes? And he had said, Yes. And I had asked, But what about the ambulance chasers, didn't some of them want to be great lawyers too? Yussie had smiled sadly and said, At least I'll try, I got to try. If you don't try, you die, you're kissing behinds all your life.

We walked through the neighborhood, Yussie winced with pain every now and then, his hand clutched his arm. Now we were out of my immediate neighborhood, into another area of the Lower East Side. It was still Jewish, but I rarely went there, I remained mostly in the few blocks around my house. I ventured out only to visit a friend on the other side of Delancey Street, on the other side of the bridge, or when I went down the teeming business section of Delancey Street with its shops, its restaurants, its movie houses. Or those few times when I went to visit relatives in the Bronx or Brooklyn.

But when I went to study at Yussie's house in the part of Little Italy that was at the edge of the Lower East Side, it was really a different world, it was a completely foreign world to me. The tenements looked the same, but the stores were different. The pork stores, we didn't eat pork, it was forbidden, we had no pork stores on the Lower East Side. The cheese stores with their sharp pungent smells reaching strongly to me, I could not become used to it. The restaurants, different from ours, each with a small painted statue of a cook with a chef's hat in the window, his one hand holding a tray of pizzeria, the other holding up almost at the figure's eye level, a string of ropey cheese rising up from the tray to the fingers of that upheld hand. The words on the stores were different, the speech there was different, native Italian or English spoken with Italian rhythms. The gestures of the people there were different too, we had our distinctive ones and they had theirs.

Every time I had gone to Yussie's house to study, his mother would offer me a dish of spaghetti. I liked the spaghetti but the sauce was too tart and spicy for me. Whenever I could I didn't take any cheese with the spaghetti, it was too strong for me. "You like the spaghetti?" she had asked me.

"Yeah," I had said sipping up the strands, their ends flopping at my mouth.

"You mama, she make the spaghetti?"

"Well," I had said wiping my lips. "We don't eat spaghetti too often. Just sometimes. We eat something like it, noodles, we call it *luckshin*. We eat wide noodles like when you eat spaghetti. We eat fine noodles when we put it in soup."

Yussie's mother had been nodding her head. "And the sauce when you eat the noodle, you mama, she make it like me?"

"Well," I said. "When she makes it with sauce, she buys it in the grocery store."

"In the grocery store?" she had said perplexed. "What can you buy in the grocery store?" Her shoulders had gone up in a huge shrug.

"Del Monte tomato sauce," I had replied. "In the little cans. My mother uses that."

"She use the can, what she buy in the store?" Yussie's mother said in wonderment. "I make my sauce, that what make the spaghetti, the sauce." She had become silent for a moment then she had asked, "This Del Monte, they are Italian?"

"I don't know," I had replied. "They put all kinds of things in cans, fruits, vegetables, fish, tomato herring, things like that."

Yussie's mother's head had gone back and forth in a puzzled motion and she had said, "We no buy things like that. Maybe *tonno*. You like *tonno*?"

"Tuna?" I had asked and she had nodded. "No, we don't eat that. We buy salmon in cans. Bumble Bee."

His mother had shrugged once more, picked up the plate I had just finished and gone to the sink. Yussie had been watching me, an amused grin on his face. I had smiled at him and he had whispered to me, "I was lucky. Your mother didn't put me through that. Lucky she thought I was Jewish. Maybe what you ought to do is become Italian."

We had both laughed at that. Yussie's mother had turned to stare at us then returned to her work at the sink. "You want the fruit?" she had asked the both of us over her shoulder.

"No, thanks," I had replied. As it was I had been embarrassed to eat in a stranger's house. And strange food at that.

We had gone back to studying, Yussie and I. Now and then his mother had stopped to listen and look at us. Once she had said, "You smart, you two. Be smart. You be something good, you understand?"

Once, only once, his father had come home when I had been there. Seated in the kitchen, Yussie's father had turned to both us, listened to our studyings, our replies. He had said something in Italian to his wife and she had replied in a quick rush of unintelligible sound.

Although I had tried to learn Italian, I hadn't understood it at all, not a word. I had envied Yussie and his quick grasp of foreign languages, I had yearned to be able to do what he did.

"You no understand?" Yussie's father had said to me.

"Italian? No," I had replied.

"Why not? You smart, no? Why you no understand?"

"I never learned," I had said to him.

"What you learn now, what I hear you say, that make you smart?" he had asked. I had not replied, I sensed it was a rhetorical question. "No," he had said. "What make you smart is what you do with what you learn. But don't get so smart, you forget you family. I see it happen. That's no good, no good. Family, that's what count. You understand? You, Joey's friend," he had said to me, "you get so smart you forget you family?"

I hadn't known what to say. "I don't know what to tell you," I finally had said. "I've never really thought about it."

"You think about it," Yussie's father had said. "Think about it good. You no hurt you family. Study, learn, be somebody, that's good, but no leave the family, that's no good. Understand?"

Later I had asked Yussie what his father and mother had said in Italian. Yussie had laughed. "He asked if you were the smart one, the one with the brains. And my mother had told him, yes, then she told him not speak in Italian, you didn't understand, it wasn't nice."

That had been some time ago and now I was walking into Yussie's world, still an alien world to me, the pork stores, the bakeries, the grocery stores with their windows stacked with cans of imported olive oil, the dairy stores with their sharp-smelling cheeses, the fish stores with their strange wares. The language, foreign, and still foreign to me, a rush of words I couldn't understand.

Yussie had dropped his hand from his wounded arm. A young man stopped and asked him as he looked at me, "What you doing home so early? Ain't you supposed to be in school?"

Yussie became Joey, replied in his Little Italy English, "We got off, the two of us. We're doing some special thing together." The young man went off and Joey said to me, "He's one of my cousins."

We passed older men seated and standing clustered in front of a restaurant. One of them called out to Joey, Joey waved at the group, said something in Italian. Some young men in good suits also stood outside the restaurant, watching us. One of them called out, How ya doing, Joey? Joey replied with a smile and a wave of his hand.

Women, tending their baby carriages, sat in the street, at the same time watching the doings of their older, pre-school children who were yelling and running and milling around. Some of them called out to Joey. All eyes followed us as we walked down the street, comments were made in Italian. Joey and I just walked on.

We entered the gloomy tenement and Joey's hand went back to his wound. We climbed the stairs, the smell of cooking surrounded us. To me the odors were different, entirely different from those where I lived. Here were sharp smells, ones I was not accustomed to, and the smell of olive oil, fish in olive oil, everything in olive oil.

Joey went slowly up the stairs. He said to me, "You can't walk down the street here without everybody watching you. They know what you're doing, who your friends are. They gossip and gossip. I think," he said with a laugh, still holding his arm, "I'll tell them your name's Leonardo, they'll like that."

I laughed. "Hell," I said. "Yours is Yussie, back there. Mine could be Leonardo, back here. Why not?"

Just before we reached the fourth floor where Joey's family lived, Joey stopped. I, too, stopped on the staircase and he said to me, "My mother's going to go haywire when she hears what happened. I can't tell her. How can I?" He looked at the door to his family's flat. "I wish everybody would forget it. It's over."

I had been looking at that flat's door. "Listen, Joey," I said. "You don't have to. I'll tell her."

"You kidding? You think you can do it?" he asked eagerly. "You mean it?" I nodded. He put his hand down from his arm, took a deep breath, smiled weakly at me and said, "Okay, let's go. Let's get it over with."

I knocked at the door. Inside Joey's mother called out something in Italian. Joey replied. There was the sound of a quick shuffle of feet to the door, Joey's mother opened it quickly. She stood staring at Joey, her eyes darting from him to me, she said something to him in Italian, she stared at me and asked, "What's-a-matter? What happen? You don't have no accident, no?"

"No accident," I said to her in a soothing tone of voice. Her eyes were scanning Joey, looking for something, a wound, a scrape, something, anything. At the same time she backed away from the door. I entered, Joey followed me in and I said to her as Joey went to a chair at the kitchen table, sat down, and looked away from his mother, "No accident, honest."

"Why you here? Why you no in school? You do something wrong, eh?" she asked her son.

"There's nothing wrong, Joey did nothing wrong, " I said to her. She turned towards me and I went on with, "We got some time off."

"No, no, no," she said shaking her head. "I know something is wrong. What? Tell me, what?" When I told her, her eyes went back to her son. As I told her about the hurled inkwell and Joey's wound she slapped her hands to her cheeks, her eyes widened and stared up at the ceiling and she called out, "*Mama-mia*! They hurt my Joey? Where? Where?" She bent towards her son who began to remove his shirt.

When she saw Joey's bandaged arm, she began to cry out, "They hurt my Joey! They hurt my Joey!"

And for an instant I could hear my mother. If I had come home with Joey's wound, I could hear her in a different voice and a different language, in a different English, crying out similar words.

"He's not hurt," I said to Joey's mother trying to calm her. "I took him to the drugstore, Doc took care of him, he fixed him up, said it was okay."

"*Mama-mia!*" she screamed. "Look at that!" she shouted hoarsely pointing to the bandage around Joey's arm. "That murderer do that to you?" she asked her son.

"Coolidge did it," Joey replied. Looking up at her said, "He didn't mean it, it was an accident."

"Acc-ci-dent?" she said almost uncontrollably. "You call that accident?"

"I'm okay, mama," Joey said. "Honest. See. It's all bandaged up good, it'll heal in a couple of days. It's okay, mama."

"I kill that murderer!" she shouted out, tears streaming down her face. "He do this to my son, I kill him!"

I could almost see my mother there, I could almost hear her, echoing those words. They were twins, the two mothers, born at different times, in different countries, from different families, speaking different languages, but somehow, they were the same.

"Mama," Joey said rising from the chair. He put his arms around her and held her close. "I'm okay. Everything's okay."

She was sobbing, "Why he do this to you? Why? You do something wrong?"

"Joey didn't do anything wrong," I said to her. "Honest."

I left them after that and trudged back to my Lower East Side. It was too early to go home, I didn't want to have to go through explanations with my mother. She wouldn't wait for explanations, if I came home when I should have been in school it had to mean I had done something wrong. So, instead, I went to the library and in the quietness there, picked up a book from one of the shelves, sat down at a large table and began to read.

The next morning I met Goldie outside the school building. Yussie hadn't yet arrived. Was he coming? would he be in school today? Sure, I told myself, he'll come, he would never want Coolidge to feel that he, Yussie, had no guts. Yussie would be in school today.

Yussie showed up a few minutes later. "How's the arm?" I asked.

"Okay, okay," he replied. Then he gave a huge sigh and said, "My cousins, Nick and Rosario, are coming. They'll be here during lunch hour." He glanced around. "Promise you won't tell anybody about it. I swore to them I wouldn't say a word. Promise."

Both Goldie and I made our promises. "They're coming for Coolidge?" I asked knowing that they were. Yussie nodded. I said, "Are they the two cousins who—? you know—"

Could I say the word, gangsters, to Yussie? I couldn't. But I had heard from Yussie and others about Nick and Rosario. They were petty gangsters, strong-arm men, who went from store to store taking protection money from storekeepers.

And once I had been foolish to ask Yussie, "Protection from what?"

"From themselves," Yussie had explained. "You pay protection, nothing happens to your business, or to you. Your arm don't get broken, or your leg, something like that. You don't get hurt. If you don't pay . . ." his voice trailed off then he had said, "Rosario's a wild man. But Nick, he's quiet, he talks nice and low, but he's even worse than Rosario. People pay, they sure as hell pay them the protection money."

"They're going to kill Coolidge?" Goldie asked in an amazed tone.

"Naw," Yussie replied. "They'll scare him." He paused, sighed, and said, "I didn't want them to come, I begged them to forget it. But my father when he came home last night and found out what happened, he hit the roof. He got Nick and Rosario to come to the house, he made me tell them what happened. I didn't want to, I told them I didn't want to, but Nick said to me that you always pay back. Always. If you don't, they'll do it to you again. The way they're going to do it, a guy like Coolidge will learn."

"What're they really going to do to him?" I asked.

Yussie shrugged. "I don't know. Like I said, they'll scare him but I don't know exactly how, what they're going to do. I just hope Rosario doesn't lose his temper."

There was a silence. We looked at each other and finally Goldie, with a laugh, said, "Stocks sure as hell will be down today." I began to laugh and a tentative smile appeared momentarily on Yussie's face.

We couldn't wait for our classes to end that morning.

I kept watching Yussie. At times he sat fidgeting in his seat, looking at his hands, staring into space. Several times I glanced at Goldie who nodded imperceptibly to me. Luckily Yussie wasn't called on by any of the teachers, he wasn't concentrating on class work at all. I know I couldn't concentrate if I were in his shoes.

When the bell rang for the lunch hour, Yussie was ready. His books in hand he raced down the stairs. He was gone before Goldie and I had a chance to leave our seats. Gathering our things together we ran down the staircase and there, almost at street level, coming up quickly as we were descending was Yussie followed by a tall man and a squat man, both in business suits. The tall man was carrying a brown paper bag containing something. We passed each other without saying a word, Yussie's eyes went to mine in a fleeting moment. Then the three of them went up those stairs to the third floor. Exchanging glances, Goldie and I descended to the exit.

Outside in the street, the students were spreading out into rivulets running in all directions. Some of the students went to the playground, where they ate their lunches taken from brown paper bags they had brought from home. Those who had begun to play handball would eat their lunches after their games. Other students had gone to a corner grocery store a few blocks away where they were buying a five-cent tomato herring sandwich on rye bread. A few had gone home to eat. The school building had emptied out, Goldie and I stood out on the sidewalk near its exit door and looked up at the closed windows of Mr. Coolidge's room.

"Let's go back up," Goldie said to me. "Let's see what's going on."

"Good idea," I replied. We entered the building once more, ran up the three flights of stairs, arrived panting on the third floor. As we moved quietly and furtively down the corridor I was whispering to Goldie, "Sh! Sh! Let's not make any noise."

We stopped at the closed door of Mr. Coolidge's room. The upper half of the wooden door was composed of small windowpanes set into strips of wood. Standing near the door, at one of its sides, I glanced into the room. Mr. Coolidge was saying something to the two cousins who faced him, the tall one in front of the squat one. I couldn't see Yussie, he was somewhere out of my sight.

"What's going on?" Goldie whispered to me. I told him what I had seen. "Let me look," he said.

I was still looking into the room. The squat cousin said something to Mr. Coolidge, had suddenly reached under his jacket and held out a gun. Mr. Coolidge's eyes widened, his face fell apart, he was staring uncomprehendingly from one cousin to another.

"He's got a gun!" I whispered wildly to Goldie.

"What? Come on, let me look," he said. I moved as he pushed me aside. I was behind Goldie now as he stared into the room. I glanced down the hallway, it was empty. Goldie said, "The tall one, he's waving to the small one to put his gun away. Now the big one's saying something to Coolidge, it looks like Coolidge doesn't know what he's saying, and the big one's opening the paper bag in front of Coolidge, he's taking out something from the bag. It's Yussie's shirt with the blood on it. He's waving it in front of Coolidge's face, Coolidge's looking away—"

I thought I heard something in the hallway and I looked around. Nothing. But from somewhere I heard a murmur of voices growing nearer, it came from the staircase.

I hissed to Goldie, "Come on, let's go! Someone's coming!"

We ran to the boys' toilet on the floor. Standing inside, we caught our breaths and listened. Outside in the hallway we could hear voices, a pleasant conversation between two teachers, it grew somewhat louder, then slowly disappeared. They had passed Coolidge's room and had walked on.

Goldie was staring at me as he said, "Coolidge, he gave the tall one some money, I saw it."

"Yeah," I said suddenly realizing what had happened. "He got the money for a new shirt for Yussie."

"Gee, I wonder what's happening," Goldie said. "They sure looked mean, those two cousins."

"Yeah," I said. "I think the tall one's Nick. The other one's Rosario, he looked wild waving that gun. A gun, did you see that gun?"

"Yeah. Big," Goldie said. "I'd hate to have that waving in front of me."

"Let's go down," I said to Goldie. "We can't stay here anymore. More and more teachers'll be in the hallway."

"Good idea," Goldie said. "But I sure would like to see what's going on."

We sneaked down the hallway. As we passed Mr. Coolidge's door, I glanced quickly through its panes into the room. Yussie was standing in front of his two cousins, I couldn't see Mr. Coolidge. I went by the room, we entered the stairwell, ran down the stairs and were out in the street.

Breathing with relief, I said to Goldie, "Did you ever see anything like that?"

"Never," Goldie replied.

We looked up at the window of Mr. Coolidge's room. The bottom half had been raised halfway, we could see nothing else. A few minutes later both cousins emerged into the street, Yussie following them carrying the brown paper bag. The two men went off, turned the corner and were gone.

Yussie stopped at our side and I said to him, "What happened?"

"Come on, let's get out of here," he said. We walked down the street as Goldie asked him what had happened. Shaking his head Yussie said, "They came up, Nick and Rosario, you saw them. We went into Coolidge's room. Rosario, he shut the door. Coolidge, he sees me, he sees my two cousins, he says, What are you doing here? Get out! Nick, he says in his low voice, you know, he never sounds angry, he says, We came to talk to you about what you did to our cousin, Joey. Get out! Coolidge says, beginning to look wild. I was standing in the back, and I saw Rosario take out his gun, point it at Coolidge who all of a sudden looks like he's going to faint.

"Nick told Rosario to put the gun away. Rosario didn't want to, but he did. Coolidge, he was real quiet now and Nick says, First thing, you ripped the kid's shirt, that's two dollars. We want it now. Coolidge almost said something, but he didn't. He reached in his pocket, got two dollars and gave it to Nick who didn't turn around but handed it backwards and I came to get it. Then they got down to brass tacks and Nick said, You hurt my cousin, we don't like it when you do things like that, and when he said it Coolidge was shaking his head mumbling, No, no, no.

"Rosario got wild and began to say something and Nick told him to be quiet and Rosario shut up and Nick said to Coolidge, You like to fly? Coolidge looked like Nick was crazy or something and Nick said to Rosario, Open the window. Rosario opens the window, Coolidge looks like he's going to die, and maybe he is dying, he begins to say something, his tongue is licking his lips, his eyes are real wide and Nick says again, You like to fly? And Coolidge says, No, please don't, please, no, and Nick is smiling now only he ain't really smiling. He calls me over and tells me to stand in front of Coolidge. I walk over to Coolidge, he can't control himself, he keeps saying, I didn't mean it, I didn't mean it, and he keeps looking at Nick who says to him, Get on your knees. I thought Coolidge was going to faint, he thought Nick was going to shoot him while he was on his knees and he begs Nick with his eyes and Nick says, I told you to get on your knees, and Coolidge gets down on his knees, he's looking at Nick, begging him with his eyes, and Nick says, Apologize to Joey. Coolidge looks from him to me to Rosario and Nick says, I'll say it just one more time, apologize to Joey. If you don't, you fly. Understand? Coolidge wipes

his lips with his tongue, he looks at me and whispers, I'm sorry.
And Rosario says, Louder! I can't hear you, Joey can't hear you.
And Coolidge says it louder this time. Then Nick says to me,
Where's that thing he hit you with? Go get it. I ran to Coolidge's
desk, got the inkwell, it's filled with ink and I say to Nick, It's got
ink in it. He says, Spill it out, I want the thing. So I spilled the ink
in Coolidge's wastebasket and gave Nick the glass inkwell.

"He holds it in front of Coolidge's nose and says, I ought to
make you eat it, but I'll do you a favor, I'm taking it away. He
wraps the inkwell in my old shirt and puts all of it in the paper
bag. Then he says to Coolidge, You ain't to touch the kid again,
you understand? Coolidge nods his head. Not never, Nick says.
You touch him, just touch him and we come up here and you fly,
oh, you will fly all right. Another thing, Nick says, Joey's a good
student. Right, Joey? he says to me over his shoulder, What kind
of marks you been getting? A, I say. And Nick with that smile of
his says to Coolidge, The kid still gets an A, right? Right? Coolidge
mumbles a yes and Nick says, I don't want you to take advantage
of him just because you're the teacher and he's the student, that
wouldn't be fair, right? Coolidge nods and Rosario says to him, I
didn't hear you say, right. Say it! And Coolidge says in a kind of
whisper, Right. And then we left, was I glad to get out of there,"
Yussie said.

"Just like in the movies," I said.

"Yeah," Yussie said slowly. "Only it wasn't a movie, it was for
real."

SHOOTING DICE ON CANNON STREET

Down beneath the corner street lamp, on the corner of Cannon and Stanton Streets, in the late afternoon pale sunshine, they stood in a wide circle in their form-fitting topcoats and their fedora hats as they looked down at the cement sidewalk. It was late fall and with the slow approach of evening just beginning to tinge the sky, a chill had come into the air.

When they spoke the men in the circle spouted misty plumes from their mouths. They were shooting dice, one man was bending down to pick up the cubes from the sidewalk, another threw a fluttering bill to the ground as he said, "One says he won't make it."

Someone else threw a bill down. "You're covered," he said.

Another man laughed, said to the man next to him, "He's on a roll, I wouldn't bet against him."

"Yeah?" said the first man to him. "Put your money where your mouth is. I say he won't make it."

The few passersby avoided the group. They crossed the street to the other sidewalk, never coming close to the circle. A few young people, boys in their teens, stood on the other side of the corner, and watched the gamblers with an intense curiosity.

The gamblers themselves disregarded everyone and everything around them. The game and the other players was all to them. They laughed and joked with each other, all the time staring intently at the cubes hopping and skipping across the rough cement. Someone there bet two dollars.

Nearby, standing on the stoop of his house, Marty looked at the scene. There, there, in the circle there, near the dice thrower he thought he saw his cousin Kalman, whom he hadn't seen at all for over three years. Kalman visited nobody from the family. Kalman, whose mother was Marty's Aunt Tessie, she had cried when she had said bitterly that he, Kalman, only wanted to be called Cal, this was America here, wasn't it? Not the Old Country, Kalman didn't want those Old Country names, how did it sound to be called Kalman? He lived someplace else, not in the Lower East Side anymore, Kalman was ashamed of his name, of the place where he had lived.

Marty had almost started to go to his older cousin, but reconsidering, he had stopped. He had been warned by his father and mother never to see Kalman, never to talk to him, and if he saw him, to walk away. Kalman was a gangster, he hung out with the other Jewish gangsters, those that had become a part of Murder Incorporated, those who killed for a price, twenty-five dollars it had been rumored, to rub out somebody and drop the body somewhere in the barren wet forsaken lands in New Jersey, across the river from New York.

Marty had seen Kalman on some other occasions when the group had congregated to shoot dice under the street lamp. But he had never approached his cousin, had never spoken to him, had never told his parents that he had seen him.

Now, soon, soon, when the real cold weather came, when winter froze the city, the group would disappear from the street, probably move somewhere else where it was warm. Occasionally during the winter, Marty would see some of them inside the warmth of the corner candy store, all similarly dressed with their wide-brimmed hats, their form-fitting overcoats, their polished shoes.

Where did they get their money? he had asked himself time and time again, the details of which he couldn't imagine. They threw away dollar bills just in gambling. One, two, sometimes five dollar bills. It was a fortune.

Once during a conversation with his mother when she had cautioned Marty not to acknowledge Kalman if he saw him, Marty had asked, "They got money all the time. When, how, did they get it?"

"From holdups," she had replied after dry-spitting quickly three times to exorcise the evil. "From robbing people, from going into stores at night when it's closed, from killing people, from all of that. From being gangsters, what else? *A bruch ov zay*, A curse on them."

He couldn't imagine it, holding up stores, businesses. All those other things. It was movie stuff, things that he had seen James Cagney do, Edward G. Robinson, Paul Muni, George Raft. But that was the movies, make-believe. It seemed real while you were sitting in the dark movie house, but it wasn't real. Someone wrote a story, a script, the actors were chosen, given their parts to read, the camera recorded the acting, that's what they did.

But it was never real. Although, almost. Everything in the movies was although, almost. Those beautiful women, the cars, the apartments, the things that people owned that were real in the movies, but when you thought of it, a movie was just a screen with pictures, and pictures weren't real.

Sure, gangsters in the movies had money, but how did real gangsters get their money? Who gave it to them? How was it gotten in the first place? He didn't know, he couldn't know, he couldn't find out, nobody would really tell him. It was like a big secret in a secret society sworn to secrecy and only those inside knew.

Marty glanced at the circle of players on the corner. Kalman placed a bet on the sidewalk and was joking with the man beside him. Coming down the street, he saw the slow plodding approach of the policeman. Strung from his wrist was his club, which he swung and flipped expertly, to be caught up by his hand then repeated in his walk ritual.

Seeing the gamblers, the cop stopped, immediately turned around and walked the other way. Marty had heard that the police were paid off. Someone, one of the gangsters, met somewhere with a cop, a lieutenant or a captain, and paid him off for the entire precinct, so that none of the gangsters would be touched. So that way the police would act as if the gangsters never existed.

A small shout went up from the gamblers, someone had made his point. There were shouts of triumph from those who had bet on him, words of disappointment from the losers. Marty saw Kalman bend down to pick up the money he had won.

Marty, now twelve, remembered Kalman from years before when Marty had been six or seven. Kalman had been his big cousin. One day Kalman had fought someone who had bullied another older cousin almost Kalman's age, a small frail sickly white-faced boy. Kalman had been unbelievably good, yes, Kalman had taken a beating but he had fought on, never stopping until the bully had begun to cry and had run away. Kalman had been the protector, the big powerful cousin with the iron fists, the brave one, Marty had looked up at him. But that was then, before Kalman had become a gangster. Before.

Marty was waiting for his mother. He had promised that he would go shopping for food with her. She was going to the push-carts on Rivington Street to buy a few fruits and vegetables, mainly potatoes. The bundle would be too heavy for her to carry, potatoes weighed a lot, so he would carry the purchases in the large black oilcloth shopping bag she usually carried.

He turned and looked into the gloom of the tenement hall-way. There, barely visible, he saw the bulk of his mother growing more distinct as she approached the door of the building. "We go," she said to him when she was at his side. "Fast. It's getting late." Her breath puffed out a scant white trail.

He didn't know what to tell her about Kalman, it would make her angry he knew. As they left the stoop he began to tell her, in hurried fashion, of what had happened at school that day. Standing beside her, hoping he was acting as a barrier so that she wouldn't see the circle of men at the corner, he tried to keep her on the other side of the street from the group.

To divert her, he said, "I got an A in French on my test."

"Good, good," she replied almost abstractedly. Normally she would have been delighted. She expected and demanded A's from him, but she had barely been listening. She had seen the gamblers on the corner, she slowed her walk and was staring intently, searching the ring of gamblers. "Kalman," she said quietly to Marty. "Is he there?"

"I don't know," Marty replied not looking at her.

"You got eyes," she replied. "See, look, is he there?"

They stopped walking. Marty attempted to block her view as he said, "They're all dressed the same. You know, the same kind of hats, the same coats. It's hard to tell."

"Move a little so I can see. And you look again. Look good," she said squinting her eyes, attempting to see better. "Kalman, is he there?"

Marty couldn't lie to her, not anymore. "Yeah," he finally said. "He's there."

She nodded violently. Suddenly her face set into a fierce rigidity. "*A bruch ov im*, A curse on him," she said vehemently. "A gangster. *Feh!* Disgusting" she said roughly grabbing Marty by the arm. "We go across the street."

"Mama," Marty began to plead. "What for? We got to go shopping, yeah? It's getting late, right? Why should we go see Kalman? What for?"

"Because I want to," she replied pulling him along as they began to cross the street.

He stopped his resistance, began to walk alongside of her. Staring at the gamblers now, he saw Kalman in conversation with the man beside him. Someone there was just beginning to shake the dice in his hand and was blowing into his loose fist saying, "Come on, baby, come on! Give me a six!"

His mother's grip still tight on his arm, Marty walked along with her to the rim of the gamblers circle. Some of them were fluttering bills down to the sidewalk. Letting go of Marty, she approached Kalman. One of the gamblers on the other side of the group noticed her and said, "Hey! What're you doing here? Beat it!"

Everything stopped. All of the men turned to stare at her. Kalman, seeing his aunt, began to shake his head in annoyance. "Go on home," he said to her as he glanced quickly at the men around him. "You don't belong here. Go. Go."

"Why should I go?" she said loudly. "Because you say so? You go, all of you." Her voice was rising and she shouted out, "Go away from here! *Merderers!* Murderers! Go, Kalman! You go! I belong here, not you!"

Marty tugged desperately at his mother's arm. "Mama! Mama! Come! Let's go! Come on!"

She didn't hear him. One of the men in the crowd glanced at Kalman, angrily said to her, "Go, missus. Go home. Go on. Get a move on."

Marty turned to him and shouted, "You don't talk to my mother that way, you hear?" He found himself shaking with fear and with anger.

The man stared at Marty. Hard. His eyes, steel agates in his face. "Listen, kid," he finally said. "You'd better learn to keep your mouth shut. Understand?" Marty's trembling increased, he didn't want to show it, there was an earthquake inside of him.

Marty's mother had begun to shout to the man, "You'll do something to my son, hah? You think so? You don't touch my son, you hear me?"

The man, his face still emotionless, his voice flat, said coldly, "Go, missus. Go home." When she hadn't moved and hadn't replied, he said quietly to Kalman, "Talk to her. Get her going."

Kalman was shaking his head angrily. He turned to his aunt and moved slightly away from the other men in the circle. Now, close to his aunt and Marty, he said to her, "You came to talk to me. All right. So come. Let's go up the street, so you'll talk to me."

Marty's mother disregarded him. Marty could see the heavy heave of her chest and now she yelled out, "*Momzerin!* Bastards! It's a *shandeh farr dee Yeedin a shandeh farr alleh menschen!* A shame for the Jews, a shame for all the people! *Zulst nuhr alleh gehargit verren!* You should all get killed! Gangsters, *alleh!* All of you gangsters!" She turned her head and spit heavily on the sidewalk.

The man who had been speaking to her stared coldly at her. His face had turned nasty and he said, his lips barely moving,

"Get out of here, lady, I'm telling you. Aunt or no aunt, you're asking for trouble, a lot of trouble, you understand?"

"Come on, come on," Kalman urged his aunt, pulling her by the arm. She attempted to wrestle out of his hold and he, still grasping her arm turned to Marty and said, "Tell her to walk with me. Come on, will you?"

Marty tugged at his mother's other arm. "Mama, mama," he said. "Let's go. Please. Please."

His mother stared defiantly at the men and said to them with contempt, "So you'll go and kill me, hah?" She turned away from them, pulled her arm roughly out of Kalman's grip and began to move away from the group saying, "A *schvartz yoor ov zay*, A black year to them."

Kalman was walking at her side. Marty, on the other side of his mother, glanced at him, then in silence, looked at his mother, the oilcloth handles of the shopping bag around one of her wrists. They walked past two or three houses up the street when she stopped and suddenly said to Kalman, "You are killing your mother. Day and night she cries. Night and day." Kalman's face took on a look of anger. "You don't like it, hah, when I talk like this? How should I talk to you? Should I be afraid, hah? You'll maybe kill me too? You kill your mother, you kill your *tanteh*, aunt, yeah? You live with that *koorveh*, that prostitute—"

"Stop!" Kalman shouted. "Will you shut up!" His face had become red with anger. With great effort, he had begun to control himself and he said as he reached into his pants pocket, "You need some money? Here!" He took out a small roll of bills, pulled out a ten-dollar bill from the wad and held the bill out to her. "Here. Here's some money. Go. Buy something."

She stared at him with contempt. "Your money, hah? With blood on it, I should take it? Never."

Kalman shook his head in disbelief. He turned to Marty and offered the bill to him. "Here. You take it. A present from me."

"Don't touch it!" Marty's mother commanded. Marty stared at the bill then at his mother who said, "It's murder money, don't take it!" Kalman was about to say something but she went on, her voice became softer, "Kalman, Kalman, you have my father's name, your *zaydeh's* name, your grandfather's name. He was an *ehrlicheh mann*, a moral man. It's a sin to do this to his name, you hear me? Why do you do this? Why? Why do you have to come to Cannon Street with them?"

Kalman became silent, everything had become silent. He shrugged, stared at the ten-dollar bill in his hand, looked at his aunt, at Marty. He shrugged once more, returned the money back into his pocket. As he turned to leave, he said, "I'll tell you, *Tanteh*—" he began.

"I'm not your *Tanteh*. No more."

He shrugged again and said, "I'll come over with the boys anytime they want to come. You don't like it, don't look. Don't come to talk to me. If you don't come to us there'll be no trouble."

"A-ha!" she said, her eyes flashing. "Orders now. Let me tell you what I will do. I'll sit *shiva*, I'll do the mourning for the dead for you. You're dead for me." She turned to Marty, said to him, "You got no cousin Kalman, he's dead, you hear?"

Marty said nothing. He glanced from one face to the other, both stony now, both set with a cold fury. Kalman finally said, "Do what you want. But stay away."

He began to walk away taking swift steps. Marty's eyes followed him. Marty's mother too was looking after her disowned nephew. Now she turned, reached out for Marty's arm as she said to him, "Come. Let's go. Away from this *drek*, filth."

The two of them walked on slowly, passing another two tenements. She stopped, her arms went out, half raised, the thumbs of both of her hands touched the tips of the three adjoining fingers. Her hands rose up and down in small beseeching arcs as she stared up at the huge sky and said, "*Tateh! Tateh!* Father! Father! You have no one that has your name now. *Ai, Tateh!*" She looked up at the wide deep sky for another moment, turned to Marty and said in a more subdued tone of voice, "When you have a son, Marteleh, you'll name him after your *zaydeh*, yes? You hear? Promise me."

Looking into his mother's face, Marty nodded. His mother sighed deeply and said, "Come. We go to Rivington Street, away from this *drek*."

Walking slowly alongside his mother, he glanced backward briefly towards the ring of men under the street lamp on the corner as he thought, just for a fleeting moment, What was it like having all that money? Being rich like that?

GOING TO SEE
CAB CALLOWAY

Now past Sixth Street they were walking down Avenue B, the three of them, Eddie and his two classmates, Aaron and Heshy, were on their way to Fourteenth Street to the theater where Cab Calloway and his band was the stage attraction.

Aaron was saying, "I hope Cab Calloway will play 'Minnie the Moocher'."

"What're you crazy, or what?" Heshy said. "Sure, he'll play it, that's what he's famous for. His band will play it and he'll sing it."

Aaron began to sing the song louder and louder as they walked on. They were out of the Lower East Side, they had passed its fringes, having gone down Clinton Street past Houston Street into the beginning of Avenue B where the ragged edges of the Lower East Side were located.

Now they were in another country where there were no kosher butcher signs with Hebrew lettering on their windows, where the grocery store windows displayed types and brands of food some of which were unknown to Eddie. The signs on the stores, while in English, had funny sounding names to Eddie, names that came from foreign languages that he didn't understand, perhaps Polish or Russian, or some other Slavic language. Maybe it was Danish or Swedish. Who knew? Or German or Italian? No, it wasn't Italian, one thing Eddie knew, Italian words ended in an o or an i, there were none of those on the windows of the stores, no it wasn't Italian. Or even German, sometimes German words sounded like Yiddish. Only the candy stores seemed the same, with their windows open for the summer, selling cigars and cigarettes, soda and candy to people out on the sidewalk.

They had passed St. Mark's Place which normally would have been Eighth Street, and outside in the street some women sat on old folding chairs tending baby carriages, small groups of boys and men stood here and there, some young girls were skipping rope.

"Hi-dee-hi-dee-hidee-hoh!" Heshy roared out. "Hee-dee-hee-dee-heedee-hah!" Eddie and Aaron, in unison, shouted out to the rooftops.

Now in front of them, staring at them, were two boys, older than any of the three of them, a taller one with blonde hair, the other with dark hair. The blonde one said to the singers, "Who in hell do you think you are, making all this noise here?"

Eddie and his friends suddenly stopped singing and Heshy said in a polite voice, "We're just going along minding our own business, that's all."

"We ain't harming anybody," Aaron said in a quiet voice.

"You're making too goddam much noise here, in these streets. You don't belong here. These are my streets, not yours," the blonde one said taking a step forward.

Eddie glanced quickly at his friends, began to move sideways to walk around the two strangers. He knew, his friends knew, not to stop and argue with someone like these two. Hadn't Eddie's mother told him so many times, Don't look for trouble, Eddehleh, someone wants to make trouble for you, go away, you hear? *Zull ehr nuhr schluggen zein kupp in vant*, Let him bang his own head into the wall. Go away, you hear?

Eddie had always replied, Yeah, I hear. I'll go away.

The blonde boy made two quick side steps and stood in front of Eddie, the dark-haired boy blocked Heshy and Aaron. The blonde said to the three of them, "This ain't your neighborhood. Get the hell out of here! And don't come back!"

"This is the street, the city owns it," Aaron said reasonably. "Everybody can walk in the street, can't they?"

"This is our street, this is our part of town," the darkhaired one said. "You got your own streets where you live with those crazy words in that crazy Jew language that nobody understands. Jewboys, go back to your Jew neighborhood. We don't want you here."

Silence. Cold silence. As the blonde and the dark-haired companion stared with contempt at Eddie and his two friends, Eddie's heart had begun to beat violently, bang! bang! It sounded like a bass drum in his head. He glanced at his friends, Heshy was staring at him. Aaron's face had turned pale. Eddie's mouth had turned dry, the fear in it tasted sour, almost like dry vomit.

Again he remembered his mother's words, You don't fight. When there's trouble you turn around and you go away. You run away. You hear me? If you fight, you get hurt. You like to get hurt, hah?

No, he said silently to himself as if answering his mother. I don't want to get hurt. No, mama, I won't fight.

He glanced at the blonde standing in front of him, at the face with the contemptuous smile and Eddie felt suddenly weak, his knees felt weak, his hands were powerless, useless.

The blonde was saying, "You Jewboys better not come here. Me, I don't like Jewboys, they think they're so smart. You like to talk, don't you? With your hands, right? But you can't use your hands to fight, can you?" His contemptuous smile grew broader and he approached closer and said, "Come on! Let's see you fight, you bastards!"

Why was he doing this? Why was he saying this? Eddie asked himself, the questions racing through his mind. He had friends in school, the Adams boy, he was called Harry by all of them, his real first name was Harrison. Harry wasn't a Jew but he and Eddie were friends. There was the Smith boy, his father was a janitor in one of the tenements on the Lower East Side, there were the few Italian boys, another one who was Polish, they were all friends of Eddie's, some closer than others, they never acted like this.

But why, this, now?

The dark-haired boy was grinning at them, he said to Heshy who was the tallest of the three friends, "We'll play a little game, Jewboy. You don't know the game so I'll teach you, right?"

"You Jewboys can always learn something new, can't you?" the blonde said with a laugh. "I hear you got your long noses in books all the time. Right?" he asked his companion.

"Right," the dark-haired one said. "And sometimes they make a mistake," he began to laugh, "and they close the damn books fast, their noses are stuck in the books and bam! the noses get longer." His laughter grew louder and he jabbed a finger into Heshy's chest and said, "Now, about the game."

Eddie wished desperately to avoid what was about to happen, wished fervently, Please, no fights. Please, please. He edged slightly to one side hoping to get around the blonde one. "Where the hell do you think you're going?" the blonde asked.

Eddie's mouth was a desert of dryness, his legs trembled as he stopped his movement. He cleared his throat and said in a hoarse whisper, "Look, we're not doing anything to you. We don't want any trouble, we just want to walk down the street."

"That's what he says," the dark-haired one replied. "But that's not what we say, right?"

"Right," the blonde said. "Now, like my friend said, we're going to teach you something." The dark-haired one had picked up a small thin stick and gave it to the blonde who approached Heshy and balanced the stick on Heshy's shoulder as he said, "I put this on your shoulder, like this, and I say," and he began to chant, "three six nine, a bottle of wine, I can fight you any old time." His chant finished he said to Heshy, "And I knock it off, then you're supposed to fight me. Otherwise you're a no-good Jewboy coward."

The dark-haired one laughed. "Yeah. And we got to teach a Jewboy not to be a coward, right?"

In spite of himself Eddie blurted out, "What did we do to you? Let us go by."

"Hey, small Jewboy," the blonde said. "Keep your damned

mouth shut! When I want your advice, I'll ask you." He took a step towards Eddie.

"Let him go," Heshy said in a strained strange voice. "He's not doing anything to you."

The blonde disregarded Heshy and said to Eddie, "This little bastard's too goddam snotty." He lowered his face to Eddie's level as he said, "You hear that? A snotty Jewboy from a snotty Jew family—"

"You keep my family out of this!" Eddie said, feeling terribly fearful, feeling himself tremble inside.

"Your Jew family, they're all no good. You got a sister? She's a whore." He grinned then, those white teeth near Eddie's nose.

The words blasted out from Eddie, "You can't talk that way about my sister, you hear!"

The blonde moved even closer to Eddie. Deep inside Eddie once again he heard his mother's words. He felt a tremendous fear yet mixed with that was a roiling of anger, Who in hell was this bastard to say these things? To stand there and stop them from walking on?

The blonde was saying to Eddie, "Your mother goes up on the roof with men for a quarter. She—"

A tumultuous anger suddenly erupted inside of Eddie. "You bastard!" he roared out. "You shut your mouth!" He was still fearful, but this huge fury was exploding out of him, moving him. He lunged at the blonde in front of him, his fists were hammering out, the blonde's face took on a startled look as he fell back, then regained his balance and he moved in towards Eddie. Somewhere to the side of him Eddie glimpsed his two friends beginning to battle the dark-haired one.

In the haze of the furious battle now, Eddie could only see flickers of the blonde's face and body, could see the fists aimed at him, he could dimly hear the commotion around him, he could hear the drum of his heart in his head. Movement, fists, grunts, roars, that was all Eddie saw and heard.

His nose suddenly dripped blood, he had run his hand across

his lips and with surprise noticed the red streaks on his fingers and hand. He rushed at the blonde, kicked ferociously at his shins, heard the blonde gasp with pain and surprise, saw him retreat, crouch once more in fighting position. Eddie bored in, felt the smash to his eye, heard as if from far away his cry of pain, but still he crowded in and in, was able to put his arm around the blonde's throat. Eddie rode up his back, Eddie's arms were now coupled together, he heard the strangling sounds from the blonde's throat.

Eddie began to shout, "I'll kill you!"

He felt hands around him prying him away from the blonde's back. He held on even more tightly and shouted at the blonde, taunting him, but the strangers who were pulling him away now had separated him from the blonde, and one of them, a man, asked, "What the hell's going on here?"

"Let me at him!" Eddie shouted straining against the hands that held him back. "I'll kill him!"

"You and who else?" the blonde was saying breathing heavily, blood seeping from his lips to his jaw.

Some men had intervened between Eddie's two friends and the dark-haired one, all fighting had ceased. A man was saying to all of them, "Stop this fighting! Right now! Now, go home, all of you!"

While Eddie, was saying to the blonde, "Me! That's who! I'll kill you! I'm saying it.."

"I'll fight you any old time," the blonde said as he touched his lips gingerly. "Who's scared of you?"

"You are, you bastard!" Eddie said, his anger suddenly gone. Yet acting defiantly he said, "I'm not afraid of you." Held there by the men the two of them glared at each other. Eddie pulled himself away from the men who were holding him, he turned to Heshy and Aaron and said, "Come on, let's go." They walked past the other two boys, past the small group of men.

From behind them the blonde's voice shouted out, "You Jew bastards, stay out of here!"

Eddie stopped, turned, glared at the blonde and said, "We'll go wherever we want to go!"

He turned his back on the blonde and began to walk away. Eddie felt the pain now, the aches in his body, the growing stiffness at his knees, his nose was an aching blob. As he limped forward he dabbed away at the area under his nose with his handkerchief. He glanced at his two friends, Heshy had a welt on his cheek, Aaron was sucking on his bloodied knuckles. Eddie looked down, there was dirt on the knees of his pants. Luckily, the pants weren't torn, his shirt either.

"What'll we do now?" Aaron asked. "Should we go home?"

"Nah," Eddie said limping along. "We said we were going to see Cab Calloway and we're going to see him."

Heshy said to Eddie, "After you wipe all the blood from your face, we'll go to the toilet of the cafeteria near the theater and we'll get all washed up. Then we'll go see Cab Calloway."

"We ain't letting any of those bastards stop us from doing what we want to do," Eddie said, dabbing away at his face.

Aaron said with a loud laugh, "We sure did give those two bastards hell, didn't we?" He shook his head in admiration and said, "Did you see how Eddie went after that blonde sonofabitch, did you see that? Did you see him after Eddie got through with him? We let those bastards know we were there, didn't we?"

"Yeah. We sure did," Heshy said. "Eddie really gave it to him." And to Eddie, said, "Gee, I didn't know you could fight like that."

"Yeah," Eddie said almost to himself.

He walked along thinking of some of the other times when something similar had happened, everything in him had turned to pure panic. His heart drumming, his lungs scalded by tortured gasps, he had run away from the tormentors, feeling great pain but there had been a greater shame, he had shown fear, he had run away. The tormentors had laughed at his flight, how they had laughed! And a long way away from the danger he had stopped, bent over to catch his breath and that unending snake of a thought had uncoiled itself from somewhere deep inside his brain and had hissed out, Coward! Coward! He had berated himself for his failure to fight, he shouldn't've run away, he should've killed them! A huge catalogue of what he should have done but hadn't came to him in his mind. He had felt debased.

Yeah, sure, he had had a few fights in school, a few skirmishes, a few minor battles, but he had known that those fights were not because he was a Jew. Those times he had also been afraid but that fear had been different, there hadn't been that something additional, something similar to what had just occurred, something of terrible helplessness.

This time he had shown them, hadn't he? He sighed and walked on, congratulating himself. Glancing at his friends at his side, a small smile appeared on his lips. Disregarding his aches and pains, he said, "We sure were in a fight, weren't we?" His friends began to laugh softly. But now, Eddie, thinking of his mother's words, of his promise to her, said, "You know something? If my mother finds out about it, she'll kill me, she sure as hell will kill me."

GOLDIE'S
ONCE ONLY COUSINS

That year, somehow, his father had scraped up enough money to buy new clothing for the family. Danny didn't know how his father had done it, maybe he had gone to his Old Country society here in New York where they loaned out money, maybe there had magically materialized a little more work at his shop than before. Anyway, that day after his father finished his work, the three of them, his mother, his father and Danny would be going out to the stores to buy him a suit for the holidays.

Danny couldn't wait. Not for three years had he had a new suit, last year he had gotten a hand-me-down, something one of his cousins had worn until it had become too small for him. Danny's mother had altered it, she had done a good job but even with her expert sewing, the thread hiding the frays here and there, nothing could hide the worn condition of the cloth itself, the shine at the seat of the pants and at the elbows of the jacket.

Even before he had gotten it, it had been an old suit. It had been a hand-me-down even then when his cousin had been given it, it had been altered even then, stitched and sewn a number of times and when it had come to him, he, Danny, had hated it from the start. Any time that he had worn it he had considered it his bosom enemy.

It had been decided that while he and his parents would go out shopping for the suit, his younger brother and sister would stay at home. Their time for shopping would come another day soon, Danny's suit would be the most expensive item of all the children's clothing, therefore the first to be bought.

As he was walking home from school with some of the guys, Danny told them, "I'm going to get a suit today."

"Yeah?" Max said. "A suit, a real suit? For real? You mean it? What kind?"

"What kind do you think?" Izzy said. "A suit. A jacket, pants and a vest. A suit."

"Come to where I work," Goldie said. He was going to his house where he would have something to eat before he would go to his after-school job. "I'll get you a good price."

Goldie had found work with one of the small men's suit and coat stores that, beginning at Clinton Street lined Stanton Street down past Suffolk and Norfolk Streets. Fifteen now, big for his age, with those huge hands, he had gone to one store asking for work, the owner of the suit store had glanced at Goldie's powerful hands, at the size of him.

He told Goldie to remain in the middle of the store, while the owner had gone to his partner in the rear somewhere, where they had held a muted conversation, their heads nodding as they spoke, both of them occasionally casting quick glances at Goldie who stood there, motionless, waiting.

The first owner of the store had returned to Goldie, offered him a job standing outside the store. He had said, "You got to pull them in, you understand? Somebody stops in front of the store, somebody looks at the suits in the window, you go over, you say, Mister, they got good suits here, good bargains." The owner had paused for a moment, then added "You hear that? What's your name?" Goldie had answered. The man had looked squarely at Goldie and said, "You take them by the arm, so," he had put his hand around Goldie's upper arm and had begun to lead him deeper into the store, "and you bring him in. You don't hurt him, God forbid, you hear that? Just, a polite boy, that's what you are. Polite. I can see that you are, and then you tell them about the cheap prices like a good friend, you bring them in here to us. That's the job." While he had been talking, now and then, the owner had been staring at Goldie's large hands. "You want the job? You got it."

Before entering the store to ask for work Goldie had noticed the man outside, waiting, the man whose job obviously was the one being offered. Goldie had momentarily wavered in his decision but then had accepted the job. Goldie had said to the owner, "That's the job? I thought there might be something else, like running errands, delivering things maybe. A job like that."

"That's the job," the owner had said. "Like I said, a puller-inner." He had come closer to Goldie and asked, "What're you waiting for? It's a good job, no?"

Afterwards, the other outside man had disappeared. Goldie had been working there for about a month, had become practiced at it, his huge hands had learned how to hold a prospective customer's arm gently enough, yet firmly enough to lead the man into the store where one of the owners stood waiting for him.

And now, as they walked from school, Danny said to Goldie, "They got nice suits there? Not too much money?"

"Plenty of suits. You'll get a good price, I'll see to that," Goldie said. "Come there, I'll be there. I'll tell the boss you're my cousin, to give you a good price. But," he said as he stopped on the sidewalk and all of them stopped along with him, "don't take the blue suit with the purple color in it. It's a dog." Danny gave his friend Goldie a serious look as Goldie said, "They got it real cheap, they thought they could get rid of it fast. But nobody wants to buy it. I think it's your size, maybe a little bigger but they'll cut it down for you. They'll try to make you buy it. Don't. But if you do," he shrugged, "don't give them more than maybe eight dollars. They'll ask for eighteen, twenty."

Danny nodded. "And the other suits?" he asked.

"They'll ask eighteen, twenty, they don't care what they ask. That's where they start. Tell your father to bargain hard, they'll sell at fourteen." Danny began to smile as Goldie said, "But don't forget that we're cousins. Right?"

"Right. We'll be there. Thanks," Danny said.

They parted. There in his house, Danny did his homework while he waited for his father, knowing that his father wouldn't be home this early. Finished with his homework, he told his mother he was going downstairs. When he was outside, in the street, he stood on the stoop of the tenement, waiting for his father.

To do something he walked around the neighborhood. None of the guys were around, he stopped at the candy store and bought a frozen twist for a penny, the candy stiff, hard with cold. He bit off a chunk with effort, it felt good as the chocolate slowly melted in his mouth. He passed the fruit and vegetable store where the red-headed girl he silently liked to watch worked after school along-side her mother and father. She wasn't there. He shook his head sadly to himself in disappointment, returned to the stoop of his house. And waited. Some of the other tenants of the house pushed past him to enter the building, they said something to him, he said something polite to them, he waited.

He went up to his flat. There he sat at the kitchen table while his mother was busy cooking food, the good food odors encircled him and made him hungry. Busy with her preparations, without looking at him, his mother said, "Poppa will come, he'll come, don't worry."

"Who's worrying?" Danny said.

His brother and sister were there, he could hear their voices in the bedroom, they were playing a game. He looked at the Ingersoll alarm clock ticking loudly away on the kitchen shelf. He arose, went to the kitchen window, his hands jammed into his pants pockets while he looked out into the yard below. It was darker outside now. He didn't want to look at the clock, time seemed not to move, however his head, as if belonging to somebody else, turned slowly and looked at its dial.

His father finally arrived. "Eat sopper, fast," he said to all of them. "We got to go out, get Danny a new suit. Tomorrow," he said to the younger children, "we will buy things for you."

Their meal finished, the dishes piled in the sink, as the three of them were leaving the other two children, Danny's mother said to them, "Don't do nothing wrong, we'll be back soon. Don't open the door to nobody. Do your homework. You hear? Be good."

Danny's mother, his father and he left. They were in the street, walking quickly towards Stanton Street.

Danny had told his parents about the place where Goldie worked, that Goldie was negotiating a good deal with his boss for them.

"We're cousins, hah? Goldie, he's a good boy," his father said nodding his approval as they walked down Stanton Street. "What we'll do is first go to a couple other stores." He put up his hands as Danny began to protest. "Just to see what they ask this year. But we'll buy at Goldie's place."

"Listen to your poppa," his mother said. "You'll get a suit, but poppa's got to know what everybody else is asking. Just to be sure. He don't want to pay too much."

"But Goldie said he would speak to his boss," Danny said.

They went on, passed Clinton Street. They stopped at one clothing store, entered without being pulled in by the man who was leaning on the wall near the doorway. They spent over twenty minutes with Danny being jacketed, the owner talking without stopping as his hands patted the wrinkled places in the jacket into smoothness.

They left, the owner called after them, "Mister, missus, it's a fine suit. Listen to me. Come back—" But they were on their way to another store where they wasted more time.

Now, away from the second store at last, Danny's father said, "So now we go to Goldie's store."

They passed three other clothing stores, the outside men calling to them, their phrases attempting to lure them. As they approached the store where Goldie worked Danny could see him standing outside, surveying the sidewalk, looking for a prospective customer. The three of them stopped in front of the store as Danny's father glanced at the display in the window.

Goldie had seen them. "Come on in," he said softly. His hand crept out and circled Danny's father's arm. Danny touched Goldie's arm and when Goldie looked at him, Danny shook his head as he pointed to Goldie's hand on his father's arm. "Oh! I forgot!" Goldie

said as his hand dropped away from the older man's arm. "Listen,"
he said, "I talked to the boss. He'll give you a low price."

"What's low?" Danny's father asked.

"It depends," Goldie said. "You know, you could buy a good
suit, you could buy a better suit, or you could buy the best suit."

"A suit that's good and *billig,* cheap," Danny's father said.

"Go on in," Goldie said, "I'll go in with you."

They entered the store, both sides lined with recessed racks of
clothing, a long mirror on each wall.

Goldie introduced them to his boss, a short, bald-headed man
who said as he appraised them, "So, this is the cousins." Goldie
nodded. Danny looked away pretending to gaze at one of the suits
in the rack and the man was saying, "We'll treat them good, Goldie,
don't you worry. They came to the right place." He turned to
Danny's father and asked, "A suit for you?"

"No. It's for the boy."

"Aha!" the man said in reply. He glanced at Goldie, shooed
him away with a quick head motion. Goldie left them to return to
his station outside. The owner led them to the middle of the store
as he was saying, "The best suits." He studied Danny and said,
"Let's try on a suit."

His hand reached out, lifted a jacket from a wooden hanger in
the rack and in the yellow light of the store Danny saw it was the
blue suit with its strong purple hue that Goldie had mentioned.

"No, no," Danny said. "I don't want that suit."

"It's just for size," the owner said. "To see how it fits." Danny
began to protest once more and he looked up at his father who
nodded silently. The owner helped Danny into the garment, pulled
down sharply on its lower back, the wrinkles at the shoulders disappeared. "Ah! A nice suit," he said as he looked into Danny's
father's face, then his gaze went to Danny's mother. "Like it was
made for him."

"I don't want it," Danny said.

"He don't want it," the owner said to nobody shrugging his
shoulders. And to Danny's father, he said, "And you, mister, what

do you think?" Danny's father stepped away, stopped, as he studied the jacket. The owner was saying, "A fine suit, yes? You, mama, it's a nice suit? Something special, fits the boy like a tailor took his measure, you can believe me."

Danny looked up at his father, his eyes pleading, as he said, "Let's try another suit."

"You're missing a bargain," the owner said. "Sixteen dollars. And only because you're Goldie's cousin."

"Let's see another suit," Danny's father said. "They're all bargains, ain't they?"

"Sure," the man said as he reached into the rack for a gray jacket. "They're all bargains, that's all I sell, but there are suits and there are suits. This one cost a little more. Twenty dollars." He waited for a reply from Danny's father, there was none. With a silent shrug, the owner removed the first jacket, worked Danny into the gray one. "See," he said. "A diamond." He was watching Danny's father's face carefully, and sidled up to him he said in a confidential tone of voice, "Believe me, they're both good. But that blue suit is a real bargain. You won't get that suit no place else for less than twenty-three dollars, believe me."

Danny had listened in to the conversation and as much as he wanted a new suit, as much as he needed one, he said, "I don't want that suit. I won't wear it. No."

The owner said to Danny's father, "You got yourself a boy with a mind of his own." And turning to Danny, he said, "But poppa pays for the suit, you understand that?"

Danny's father said, "Let's try on another suit. A brown one."

The man removed the gray jacket from Danny then reached into the rack. When Danny was fitted with the brown jacket the store owner said with a smile to all of them, "A beautiful suit, wonderful. Twenty dollars, worth fifty, sixty, maybe more. But that blue suit fits the boy, a marvelous fit and it's *billig vee borscht,* cheap."

Again Danny protested and looked into his father's face. His father said to the owner, "We want to talk together for a minute."

"Sure, sure," the man said. He walked away, into the depths of the store where his partner was servicing a customer Goldie had recently escorted in. The first owner motioned to his partner who excused himself, approached his partner. There was a short huddled conversation between the two of them.

Now, Danny, his mother and father stood together near the rack. "That blue suit—" his father began.

"I don't want it," Danny said.

"I like the gray," his mother said.

"It's maybe two, three dollars more," his father said to her.

"But he don't like it," his mother said in an exasperated tone. "What's the use buying it if he don't wear it?"

"He'll wear it, he'll wear it," his father said. "For that extra three dollars I can buy a pair of shoes for the little girl."

"I'll work for the three dollars," Danny said clutching his father's arm. "I'll pay you back, you'll see, I will, honest. I don't want the blue."

"You got money already for shoes for the *kinder*, children, yes?" his mother asked his father who nodded. She said, "Danny says he'll work for it, maybe he'll find a job like Goldie, it don't have to be in a suit store, maybe someplace else. Buy the suit, the gray one." She turned to Danny and asked, "You like the gray one best?" Danny nodded. "See?" she said to her husband.

His father put his hands out in a helpless gesture and said, "*Ai*. You think I don't want Danny to have the suit he likes? What am I, a stone? That I don't know that he wants the gray one? But there's the other *kinderlach*, children, too, we have to get them new things too. And there's us, yes?"

"Ah," his mother said softly. "It will work out, you'll see." A pause, then, "The gray one, yes?"

"Let it be the gray one," his father finally said with a great sigh of surrender. He looked down the depths of the store, motioned the owner to return.

Now both owners approached, the first one saying to Danny's father, "You'll take the blue one, it's a wonderful suit." He turned to his partner as he plucked the blue jacket out once more from the rack, said, "Morris, a wonderful piece goods, no?"

Danny was saying, "No, no!"

Danny's father said, "The gray one."

"The gray one," the first partner said in a flat tone of voice. He glanced at his partner who shrugged his shoulders and returned to his customer at the rear of the store.

"How much? The cheapest price," Danny's father said. "Twenty's too much."

Danny felt a great happiness. Almost from the beginning he had felt that finally, he would have to capitulate to all of them, to agree to the blue suit. But his parents, his father, his mother, they had understood. The blue suit was hideous, it was something he could not bear to wear, but if his parents had bought it, he would have had no choice but to wear it. Detesting it, he would yet have to wear it.

He smiled at his parents who were listening carefully to the owner who said, "Twenty is too much? Tell me, mister, what do you want to pay?"

"Nothing," Danny's father replied. "I would like to have it, if I could, for free."

The owner gave a false high laugh. "Don't talk *narishkeit*, foolishness, excuse the word. You got to live? I got to live too. I got expenses with the store, I got to pay your cousin, Goldie, out there. How much do you want to pay?"

Danny's father glanced at his wife, finally said. "Twelve dollars," he said.

The man lifted his eyes to the ceiling. "Twelve dollars?" he said in mock astonishment. "Mister, I run a store I got expenses, I got to live, I can't give the suit away and lose money."

"Let's go," Danny's father said.

They began to move towards the door of the store. "Wait!" the owner called out. "What's your hurry? Listen, because you're Goldie's cousin, I'll make it special for you, eighteen dollars."

"Twelve dollars," Danny's father said. They stood, motionless, and finally he said to his family, "Let's go."

They went out into the street, Danny was certain that they had lost the suit, that he would have nothing, that perhaps it would all end up with his having to accept the blue suit, but he didn't want it. Now Goldie sidled up to Danny, asked what had happened. Danny managed only to shake his head and mumble an unintelligible sound.

The owner was at the door, he called out, "Come back for a minute. What's your hurry? Come back." Danny stopped momentarily, his father urged him to walk on and the owner called out to Goldie, "Bring your cousins back! What's their hurry?"

Goldie said to all of them, "Why don't you go back? He wants to talk. What's the harm in talking to him?"

"All right," Danny's father said. "So I'll talk." They returned to the store, the owner put on a wide sales smile. Goldie had stopped at the doorway and was leaning against one of the side windows. Danny's father said to the owner, "So talk."

"Sixteen dollars," the man said with a serious expression on his face. "Not a penny less."

"Let's go," Danny's father said.

The three of them were outside now, the man appeared at the door and he said, "Fifteen." Danny's father shook his head and the man said, "Mister, I can't sell it for twelve, I can't lose money. Make it fourteen."

"Thirteen," Danny's father said.

The man sighed. He clapped his hands to his sides in a futile gesture. "My partner will kill me," he said almost in a whisper. Then, "All right. Thirteen. So it's thirteen."

Danny had been watching all of this, certain this his suit was gone, vanished, that it wouldn't be bought, that it couldn't be bought, that in the end he would have to settle for that other terrible colored suit. But now, suddenly, the good suit was his. Somehow it didn't feel real.

His mind returned to the store once more, the owner called out to his partner, "Morris, come over, take the measurements for the boy's suit, "Danny knew, at last, the gray suit was his. "Ai, yai,

yai," the owner was now muttering to himself as he hung the jackets of the unwanted suits on hangers. "*Mein mazel,* My luck, that Goldie should have such cousins."

THE EYE IN THE MIRROR

He was staring into the mirror once more. How many times had he told himself not to do it, to hell with the damned mirror, he didn't want to look into it, never, not again, to see himself, always staring at the eyes, one of them crossed, cockeyed, that was the terrible word, damn it all! Cockeyed!

He couldn't bear to look at that eye, yet he did, forced by some compulsion to take that rectangular mirror in its peeling green-painted wooden frame, to pick it up from the shelf over the kitchen sink in that tenement flat and to look into those mismatched eyes again, once more, again.

Why? Why him? What had he ever done to deserve this? What awful crime? What terrible thoughts had he had that deserved this kind of punishment? What had he done? If only someone could tell him. Tell me, tell me.

Nothing. Nothing. It wasn't his fault, how could it have been? He had been born with it, he had always had it ever since he could remember, it wasn't his fault. His parents were to blame, they had done something wrong to cause this. He wore that crossed eye as a stigma that would go on forever and there were times when studying that eye he felt that he could pick up a small razor-sharp knife from the table drawer and with one decisive stroke cut something there at the side of his eye, or maybe in back of his eye, the eye would become straightened, that curse, that heavy burden would be lifted from him once and for all.

Cockeye, they called him. He had a real name, damn them! His name was Harry. Harry Blau. If only they would call him that, or Heshy, that would have been wonderful, but no, they called him that damned word, that cockeye, something he could not bare to hear.

Sometimes when he passed girls on the street, girls gathered together on a stoop of a tenement, girls he didn't know, they would whisper to one another, they would suddenly begin to laugh. He knew, oh, how he knew! He told himself bitterly those many, many times, they were laughing at him, all laughing at that crossed eye, while he was secretly crying.

On innumerable occasions he had fought with boys at school or on the streets when they called him that damned name. And fighting, he had lashed out at those tormentors, those sneering lips, at that laugher. And lashing out as well at that eye that mocked him. He would show them, he would show them all. Wait and see! Just wait!

Once, a few years before, he had taken those automatic pictures in the special booth with its black heavy curtain in the Five-And-Ten. He hadn't moved at all during the process, he had just sat there posing full-faced forcing his eyes to remain open during the first three blinding flashes of light, but he had not been able to maintain it and had shut his tear-brimmed eyes on the fourth flash.

When it was all over he had waited for the strip to be processed and disgorged from the slot in the machine. For a minute or two he had stared at those pictures, those first three, the fourth was a failure showing him grimacing, his eyes shut.

When he had gone home and was alone he had meticulously cut out a small pattern of an eye on white blank paper, inked in a pupil in its center matching as much as possible its twin, the other good eye, and had pasted the manufactured eye on the photograph over the bad one.

There! That was how he looked, how he would look, should look. That person there was someone else yet still Harry Blau, someone who looked like every other human being, not like some freak in a sideshow in Coney Island. Someday, damn it all! Someday. . .

He had done the same thing with the other two good photographs and had discarded the fourth one, thrown it into the garbage after he had cut it into small pieces. He had kept one of the photographs in his worn wallet, and occasionally, when he was alone, took it out of wallet to stare at it.

The other two he had hidden in one of his books and had used one when the first photograph had become frayed and tattered with handling. Now, years later, he carried the third and last good photograph in his wallet. When that became worn he would make himself a new set.

His mother was out when he came home from junior high school that day. He imagined she was out shopping for food but he didn't care, to hell with her, his father too, they were the ones who had caused this to him. When they were gone, when he was alone in the tenement flat, that was when he felt the best that he could, considering.

He wanted nothing to do with them, they were the worst of his enemies. The others, those in his class at school, except for the too few who didn't call him Cockeye, he hated them too. All, all, with a terrible hatred, a long hatred, one that had grown over time.

And this, the mirror. If only he could rid himself of this cursed compulsion. Every time he passed it, it was a huge magnet drawing his eyes to it. Damn! Again with the eyes!

Outside on the street when people weren't watching he always found himself looking into the plate glass windows of the stores staring at his pale phantom image there marching along with him, always studying his eyes, his eyes looking back at him and always that damned eye.

Why had his parents done this to him?

There was a knock on the door of the apartment. "Yeah?" he called out as he hastily replaced the mirror on its shelf. "Who is it?"

"It's me, Abe," came from behind the door. Harry went to the door, opened it there stood his friend, Abe, one of the very few who called him Harry. Abe entered the flat, asked as Harry shut the door, "What you been doing? The exercises?"

"Yeah," Harry replied. "My mother wasn't home so I did them."

Some time before, a half year at least, Harry had picked up somewhere a copy of a magazine, was it Amazing Stories or Astounding Stories? Maybe it was G-8 And His Battle Aces, a magazine with short stories about the Allied and German airforces during the World War. Having finished reading the stories Harry had noticed the full-page strip ad of Charles Atlas, about the 98 pound weakling on a beach somewhere who had had sand deliberately kicked into his face by a burly stranger and because of fear had done nothing about it. But later, after having bought Charles Atlas' home body-building program, had come back to the beach and scared off his oppressor.

The ad had shown Atlas, with his powerful physique, his broad chest, his arms tight and flexed showing his bulging steely muscles, he had won a title of some sort. And Harry, thin and rangy, had over months hoarded his money until he had been able to buy the Atlas course.

Despite Abe's initial skepticism, Harry had begun to fill out, his chest had broadened, his arms began to show more muscle.

Abe said to him, "You know something, Harry? You're beginning to look good, almost like in the ad."

"I do it every day," Harry said, "without fail. I'm going to have a body like Charles Atlas." He couldn't stop the flow of words, "And I'll kill them all who call me that—that name and who laugh at me. And I'll get my eye straightened out too. You wait and see."

"But the doctor told you it was around two hundred dollars for the operation, didn't he?" Abe said.

"Yeah. Maybe two hundred dollars," he said, "I'll get it some way." Now stressing the words, "I won't let it stop me."

Harry and Abe had become friends after school when they had discovered they each liked to make model airplanes. Harry had made one of the Red Baron's, The World War German ace, Baron von Richthofen, whose plane had triple wings, while Abe had carefully put together a Spad. They both read G-8 And His Battle Aces whenever they could afford to buy a copy or to borrow one or swap one. Except for Harry's rampages about his bad eye, which Abe had always tried to ignore whenever possible, Abe had found Harry to be a good friend.

At least a year before Harry had asked Abe to go along with him to the clinic. "What for?" Abe had asked. "You ain't sick."

No, no, Harry had replied. He would be going there for his eye. And Abe, confused, had said, What for? Harry had said he would make his eye red, real red, and go in the clinic for treatment, see if they could help him, maybe they would operate on the bad eye and straighten it, they could help him, weren't they there to help people? Harry had to do it, he had to have his eye fixed and the way things were now they wouldn't do anything at the clinic to fix it, they didn't do things like that. Abe had said, Maybe they'll help you. They sure as hell will, Harry had said.

Abe had seen Harry take a few pinches of sand into his hand from a paper bag and begin to rub it into his eye. Abe, startled and alarmed, had said, What're you doing? you crazy, or what? The sand was in Harry's eye, he was groaning in pain he was still rubbing away.

When Harry had finally finished, he was holding his hand to his eye and they had walked on towards the clinic. You'll come with me? Harry had asked. Yeah, yeah, Abe had replied, I'm going with you. And Harry, his hand still at his eye like a fleshy eyepatch let Abe guide him along the way.

Entering the clinic, Abe had been struck by its medicinal smell, the sharp odors that always reminded him of the times he had gone there when he had been sick. Harry had gone up to the desk, had groaned with pain as he cried for help, His eye! His eye! Help! Help! When finally a nurse had led Harry into a nearby room Abe had been able to hear the conversation between the doctor and Harry.

How did you get it? What happened? The wind blew something in my eye and I tried to get it out and I rubbed it and it hurts, it hurts! Harry had replied. The doctor and nurse had worked on Harry who had cried out in pain and when they were almost finished Harry had asked the doctor were they going to operate on his eye, could they straighten it out? And the doctor in a sort of surprised tone had replied that he was there only to take care of emergency cases and that Harry's irritated eye was being attended to. He gave Harry instructions what to do to speed its recovery.

Harry had begged, cried out, The operation! The operation! The doctor had replied that that was another matter, nothing the clinic could handle, it would have to be handled by a private doctor, a specialist, while Harry had repeated over and over again, Fix the eye, please! It has to be fixed! The doctor had replied, go to a specialist, but it'll cost money. Money? How much? Harry had asked, the doctor hadn't wanted to say but Harry had persisted and finally the doctor had said it would probably be around two hundred dollars, maybe a little less or a little more.

Abe sitting there in the waiting room, having heard this, had thought, It's a fortune, all the money in the world!

Now back in the kitchen of the flat, there was a rapid knocking on the door. "Open the door," Harry's mother called from behind it. "I got a lot here, it's heavy. Open!"

Harry shook his head. "Okay, okay," he said angrily. "I'm coming."

He opened the door for his mother. She entered wearily carrying an oilcloth shopping bag filled with potatoes. Outside in the hallway propped up against the frame of the door she had deposited another smaller shopping bag containing onions and two large cabbages. She was breathing heavily, sagging into herself as she deposited the bag of potatoes on the kitchen table.

"Harry, go get the other bag," she said to her son. Harry didn't move. He stared stonily at his mother, said nothing and finally Abe went to the door, picked up the bag and brought it to the table. Harry's mother glanced contemptuously at her son, looked at Abe and said, "Abeleh, you're a good boy. Thanks." Glaring at her son, "And you? What's the matter with you? You can't move, hah?"

"What for?" Harry replied furiously. "What do you do for me?" He pointed to his bad eye and said, "You won't pay for the operation, why should I do anything for you? Or for him?"

"Him? He's your father, who works for you, who goes out looking for work so you can have something to eat and a bed to sleep in. What is he, an animal, you should call him like that, hah? What am I, an animal too, *schlepping*, dragging all this to make *essen*, food for you?"

"Only for me?" Harry said mockingly. "Don't you eat too? Don't he?"

"I don't want to hear he, him, you hear that! He's your father, I'm your mother! I don't want to hear words like that in this house." Glaring at Harry she removed her coat and sat down heavily in one of the kitchen chairs. She turned and looked up at Abe and said plaintively, "You hear that? Is that the way a son talks to his mother, I ask you?"

Abe wanted desperately to leave. He glanced at Harry and slowly began to walk to the door. "Don't go. Wait," Harry said to him. And to his mother, "I asked you a thousand times. I asked both of you. It's two hundred dollars for the operation. I want that operation, I got to have it. You don't care, he don't. But I care!" he began to shout.

"*Mein Gutt!* My God!" His mother said frantically looking at Abe. "Two hundred dollars! Who has it? What are we, millionaires? We don't have two extra dollars. What should I do, steal, maybe rob a bank, hah?"

"I don't care," Harry said not looking at her. "Go rob a bank. Go. Do anything! I want that operation!"

"He's crazy, a *meshugganeh*," Harry's mother whispered to herself. "He don't know what he's saying." Rousing herself, she turned toward her son, looked up at his icy stare, and said, "You go get the two hundred dollars, you think you're so smart. You think it's so easy, hah?"

Harry bent over, his face near his mother's. "I will!" he said between tight teeth. "I'll get it and when I do you won't see a penny from it, not one, you hear me? And you won't ever see me again!" He straightened up, turned to Abe and said, "Let's go. I'm getting out of here."

Harry's mother stared after him in a huge still silence, her arm rested heavily on the kitchen table. Abe didn't know what to do. He managed to say to her, "Goodbye, Mrs. Blau."

She made no reply, sitting at the table with her eyes closed, statue-like, her body scarcely moving with each breath. Harry pulled Abe by the arm, closed the door of the apartment after them with a ferocious bang that filled the hallway with heavy echoes.

Downstairs in the street, Harry said, "I got to get out of that house."

Abe said to him, "You shouldn't do and say those things to her, she's your mother."

"She gave me that eye!" Harry began to shout. "She and him, they did it, I didn't do nothing, did I? Why shouldn't I be mad at them? Why shouldn't they help me?"

"You know they don't have the money," Abe said. "There's no work, there's no money, you know that."

"I don't care!" Harry shouted. "If they cared, they'd get the money!"

Harry had fought with his parents. There had been the repeated times when he had cursed his father, begged him too, asked him to have the operation done. His father, in exasperation, had asked where he was to get the money, he worked when he could, when there was work, there was barely enough to pay the rent and to eat. What do you want from me? his father had cried out. Why are you tormenting me, torturing me? Harry had answered, You gave me that eye. You and she. I didn't ask to be born, did I? It's your fault! There were times Harry's mother had come between them to prevent a fist fight.

Harry and Abe had been walking slowly down the street. Abe said to him, "It's your parents' problem but it's also your problem too."

Harry suddenly began to hurry, he pushed his way between a couple who were approaching. Abe trotted to catch up, and he could hear Harry say, "They don't care how I feel. Sometimes I feel they never wanted me. I don't need them either."

Abe shrugged. There was no use in being with Harry when he was raging like this. So enveloped was he by his eye obsession he didn't listen, he was deaf too. He said to Harry, "I got to go."

"Go. Go on," Harry mumbled with a wave of his hand.

Abe walked away. Harry continued walking on with fast angry

strides. As he passed a group of stores he slowed down staring into the plate glass windows to see his image, his eyes, that eye.

He told himself, I'll get the money, the two hundred dollars, I will! I'll steal, I'll rob a bank, I'll do something, anything! But I'll get it!

Damn you! he said to his crossed eye as it appeared fleetingly in the store windows. You're the whole goddammed trouble! Without realizing it, he was crying, the tears coming down from both eyes, the good and the bad one.

You—, you—, you! he said to the bad eye, You're doing this to me. Tell me, what did I ever do to you?

The next day before classes, outside the school building, Abe saw Harry approach. Dumbfounded, Abe stared at the black patch over Harry's eye, its elasticized string circling Harry's head. "What—what's going on?" Abe asked.

"Listen," Harry replied. "Yesterday I thought about it. I can't get that money for the operation, not right now. I was so mad yesterday I could've killed my mother and father and when I passed the drugstore I thought of the time I really had something in my eye and how I went in there and Doc, he took it out, you know how he does it, he lifts up that eyelid and just puts that thing in your eye so light you don't even feel it and he gets out the dirt. And remember how if your eye is real red he puts a piece of bandage over the eye? Then I remembered that he sells these things, he calls them eye patches. And I remembered that story in G-8 And His Battle Aces, remember?"

"What story?" Abe asked.

A group of three or four classmates had formed around Harry and were all pointing at the eye patch asking, What's that for? What's with the eye? Harry disregarded them and said to Abe, "You know, the story about the American pilot. How he gets shot down by the German pilot, that German ace like Richthofen, who's killing off the American's buddies. And when the American pilot crashes—"

"Yeah, yeah," Abe said snapping his fingers in remembrance. "He crashes but he's in Allied territory and he gets rescued but he loses an eye and he's in a hospital not far away from the Allied airfield and they tell him when he gets better that because of that eye he ain't got, he can't fly a plane no more—"

Harry, caught up in the story interrupted with, "So this American pilot, he's wearing an eyepatch like I got on now, he mopes around, at first he feels useless because he can't fly no more but one day he sneaks away from the hospital, comes to the airfield and when nobody's looking he hops into a plane that's warming up and up he goes praying to meet that German and sure enough, a little later, he sees him in his airplane with the three wings and wham! he goes after the German, they go round and round in a dogfight, the American dips and loops, goes from side to side, some of the German's bullets slam into the American's plane but there's no real damage and he's coming out of an Immelman roll and straight ahead he sees the German's plane in his sights and he gives a burst, just one burst, tat-tat-tat-tat-tat and the German plane begins to smoke, it begins to fall and spins and crashes."

"Yeah. You remember good," Abe said.

Harry said, "And I figured if an American fighter pilot, someone who shot down a German ace, if he could wear one of those patches and still do what he did, I could wear one of these things too." He tapped the outside of his eyepatch. "I'll wear it till I can get the money for the operation. It ain't so bad. Better than being called Cockeye."

THE OLD WOMAN

Outside, in the dimly-lit hallway, she sighed. A heavy sigh, quivering her body, mixing unevenly with her anger. She stood facing the door of her tenement flat. Die! she said silently, willing her thought through the door. Get killed!

From inside the old three-room flat she heard her daughter's hurled words, "Bastard! You're the one! It's your fault!"

The old woman sighed once more. Shook her head in disbelief, lifted her arms slightly and let them fall heavily to her sides.

To come to this, she thought. God! God! What do you want from me?

She turned away from the door, went to the landing where the anemic light of an electric bulb poked helplessly at the gloom. She grasped the banister tightly and slowly, one heavy step at a time, began the descent from the third floor.

It was cold in the unheated hallway. Bitter. Despite the closed door at the entrance of the tenement, the winter wind howled and swept up the stairway, spilled into the halls.

Down the old woman went, plodding, her body taking an angled metronomic quality as she took each step. The tenement gargled, sighed, strained, squeaked. Water running through the pipes burbled. Here and there a child cried, a voice was raised.

Ah-h! the old woman thought. Mrs. Epstein fighting with her son.

"You can't make me do it! I won't!" she heard the Epstein son shout out, the words smashed through the door of the flat the old woman had just passed, the sound blotting out the other noises of the building.

As she heard Mrs. Epstein's muted reply the old woman thought, *Ach!* You can't make me do it! mimicking in her head the Epstein boy's phrase.

And the things we learn to do, we have to do... she said to herself. Her thoughts went back to her daughter, up there, in the flat above. Whore! she thought. Filth!

The old woman sighed, tears sprang to her eyes as she thought of herself, widowed, alone except for her daughter, Selma. "Nachum," she whispered into the freezing cold as she approached the heavy door leading out from the tenement. "Why did you leave me? Why?" For a moment she was silent as if expecting an answer, then she said, "God's will. But what is God's will? Who will tell me, what rabbi, what holy man?"

And now she thought, Who will help me, a widow for almost fifteen years? Nachum, Nachum, why did you leave me?

He had died of influenza during the epidemic of 1918 when she had been forty-eight. Now it was 1933, and she was sixty-three.

Sixty-three. Time to die, to leave this pestilential world.

She pushed the heavy door open. The wind wailed, whipped her coat and dress, billowed her shawl. She muttered to herself, To have to live and have that one... She raised her eyes to the third floor of the tenement and stared at the window of her flat.

She was on the stoop of the tenement. Although the sun shone, it was colder outside than it had been in the hallway of the tenement. Somehow with the sun came a creeping, sliding sort of courage, courage to look Mrs. Rappaport in the eye as Mrs. Rappaport, on the stoop, said to her, "A good day, Mrs. Goldfarb. And how are you? And your daughter?" Not waiting for a reply Mrs. Rappaport clicked her tongue and shook her head. "Did you hear the *geshrei*, the yelling, at Mrs. Epstein's just before? *Ai*, it's not good! it's only trouble. Terrible!" Mrs. Rappaport shut her eyes, her head became a rocking pendulum. The eyes opened. "And how is your daughter, Selma?" she asked once more.

"Fine. Just fine."

The old woman looked Mrs. Rappaport in the eye. You should be our *kappurreh*, our stand-in for all the evils that are destined to befall us, for my Selma and me, you old evil-tongued witch!

She went past Mrs. Rappaport and into the street.

It was late morning, shadows crossed the sidewalk and gutter. Here and there an automobile went by, sounding of warmth and money.

She shook her head. No! She couldn't do it! Not this time, not again, not ever! What did they want from her, all of them? Was she made of stone, of iron, of steel?

She turned a corner and trudged past pushcarts lining each side of the street. Here and there fires crackled and leapt out of large open metal drums. The heavily-clothed puchcart peddlers yelled out their wares. Occasionally one would approach a drum topped by writhing leaves of flame to warm his hands which were clutched with cold.

A sweater-layered woman standing on a wooden box behind her pushcart of stockings, socks, gloves and handkerchiefs called out to her.

The old woman plodded on, a mounting dread coming over her as she neared the end of the four or five blocks that she considered her neighborhood. After that she would be in streets that felt strange to her, the people wouldn't know her, and she could begin.

Faces and shapes passed her. She put her frozen hands into the pockets of her shapeless coat. With each step now, inside her tightened right fist she nervously began to crush the little paper memo book in one of her pockets; the book that the grocer used to note the amounts of her purchases and what she owed him.

Now she was there. Long ago she had set up the boundary of her neighborhood as being this street. She was five blocks away, in another world. She turned at the corner, away from the people and the pushcarts and the noise.

She almost stopped, fervently wishing to go back, yet she forced herself on. Searching the street, looking. Halfway up the street she saw a man, a stranger, approach, he looked a little over thirty, about Selma's age. She lowered her eyes, tightened her hold upon her herself, clenched her fists in her pockets and walked forward. She dare not look up, she could not, she sensed in some fashion how close to her the stranger now was.

When she was about three feet from him, she looked up suddenly and said to him, "Pardon me, are you Jewish?"

The man stopped. "Yes," he said.

She swallowed hard and said, "*Ai*—" somehow the words were blocked in her mouth. Forcing herself she began once more, now blurting out the words, her eyes wide with a horror in them, "There is a girl, a nice Jewish girl, there on Rivington Street, 192, 192 Rivington Street, apartment 3-D. Why don't you go up and see her, you will—"

"What!" the man shouted. "What are you—?"

"A girl, a nice girl—"

"You must be crazy," he said hoarsely as he walked swiftly away. "My God!"

Inside her coat pocket the grocery memo book was a crushed wad in her tight quivering fist. *Mishuggeh*, it's crazy, she thought as she lowered her head, me too, a mishuggeneh, a lunatic...

She shut her eyes tightly, tears formed behind her lids, and she said to herself, Why? What do they want from me, all of them?

She opened her eyes and began trudging once more. The wind blew, tears ran from her eyes, spilled down her lined parchment face. She moved on, searching. And up ahead, another stranger, younger. Perhaps twenty-five, smoking a cigarette as he stared into the small glass display case in front of a shoe store.

"Mister, mister," she said to him as she approached, her voice hoarse, almost breathless, her face partially hidden by the depths of her shawl. "Are you Jewish?"

"Yes," he replied looking up.

"There's a girl, mister, a nice Jewish girl. Why don't you go up and visit her and—" the words spilled on, the same phrases used so many times before.

The man's face changed from politeness to bewilderment. He shrugged at her, stared hard at her, all the while listening to her with his head cocked. And he said, "But I have no money, I have no job."

"No money, no money," she replied. "Go quick. On Rivington Street, number 192, flat 3-D. Go." The man was undecided and she said in a louder voice, "Go! I swear it, no money! A nice girl, as God is my witness!" She stopped, the words were vomit in her throat, but she had to go on while the man stood still, staring at her. She said, forcing out the words, "You know the address?"

He nodded slowly. "192 Rivington Street. Flat 3-D," Finally he shrugged and said, "Okay."

She stood there leaden, lost, sagging inside, the iron gone from her, only water there, all water, so that she felt she couldn't move, not ever, that she would remain there and die and not have to return to that flat on the third floor. Not today, not tomorrow, not ever.

God! she called out silently. Who will help a poor widow? Who will give me peace? And looking up at the clouded sky, at the sun's rays splintering gold from the rims of the clouds, she asked, What do you want from me?

She began to walk slowly, placing one leaden foot before the other. She would go to the grocery store to shop while... while ...

But she would have to be sure. She could see the man turning the corner, she followed, going as quickly as she could yet aware that she didn't want to be noticed. Sometimes pretending to be interested in the goods at the pushcarts, stopping once for some brief moments to warm her frost-clawed hands. But watching the man as he moved in the direction of her apartment.

She saw him stop in front of the tenement and peer up at the number of the house. Go! she willed to him. Go inside! What more do you want? She saw him shrug to himself, enter the building. Yes, she thought bitterly. Yes, now it has come to this.

She went to the grocery store. Inside the store she would listen to the neighborhood gossip as the grocer cut an eighth of a pound of sweet butter from the tub, as he placed three white eggs in a bag, as he scooped up sugar by the pound. She waited in the store, dawdling over this, pretending to be interested in that, allowing other customers who had come in after her to be waited on. Almost a half-hour later, through the plate glass windows of the store, she saw the man walking by on the street.

Now she was free. She finished with her shopping, gave the grocer her crumpled memo book in which he made his notation.

And she was out, the paper bag clutched tightly to her. Now, into the tenement. Up the stairs, each step an agony to her lungs, to her heavy feet and clattering heart.

To have to come back to this, she thought. To have children, a daughter, and to live on and on in this filth. To have only one daughter, and that a cripple, unable to walk who periodically became a howling devil, who made the house a hell, who possessed the fires of the living that had to be quenched.

The old woman was on the third floor, at her door. She knocked. "Selma," she called out softly. "Selmaleh, is everything all right?"

"Yes," she heard the voice reply. "Come in, mama."

THE ENTREPRENEUR OF CROTONA PARK

I don't know about your relatives, but there was only one Uncle Max in our family. One of a kind. And in the Thirties when the Depression killed the spirit, when everybody I knew was praying for a job, any job, a little something to be earned, something to buy the cheap food we ate, Uncle Max, he was different.

Somehow he was able to purchase (ah! That was the word, it denoted having enough money to spend for things other than the barest necessities of life), to purchase many things most of us could not afford. He was able to buy dresses for his wife, pants and suits and shoes for his two sons. While my family's clothing hung sadly and lonely in our closets—one suit, perhaps a hand-me-down, one good dress years old for my older sister, and that mended one for my mother. My father had his one suit from those earlier times, the good times of the Twenties.

Uncle Max always dressed well. I remember when he wore spats, carried a wooden cane with a metal lion's head handle, that was during the Twenties. Summers he wore a flat-topped straw hat, that was the fashion then. Later he gave up the cane because people thought that he had gone lame. Natty was the word for him then.

He lived in an apartment in the Bronx while the rest of the family, including us, lived in the tenements of the Lower East Side. He had a car, a Ford, he had bought it used, but it was the only car owned by anybody in the family.

How he did it, we didn't know. But we knew, we really knew. He was a boss, not a worker. He had been a boss ever since those lost and missed days of the Twenties when he had quit his job as a cutter in the garment center and gone into the *schmateh* business with his two partners. Well, not the dress business, it was aprons that he made, also housecoats for women.

"Listen," he said in his accented English, accented, yes, but he had accumulated a large English vocabulary, from where I don't know. "The women, they will always need aprons. Sure, they like dresses, they want dresses. But aprons, housecoats, they got to have. When they clean, when they cook. And they wear out fast, faster than dresses. Why should they dirty their dresses when they clean, hah?"

"But aprons, they cost less than dresses so you charge less for them so you make less on them," my mother, Max's sister said.

"Sure. Sure," he replied nodding. Now he spoke as teacher, "I know. But everybody's in the dress business. A hundred, a thousand, more even. Who knows how many? Each one competing (he said the word slowly, enunciating clearly), each one cutting the price to get the business. You think S. Klein's, Macy's, the department stores, you think the dress stores, they buy just like that," he snapped his fingers, "because you just come in and ask for a certain price?" He shook his head. "That's not the way it is, believe me."

"So why don't they do it when you come to sell your aprons?" my father, a presser in a now defunct garment factory said.

"But there's less com-petition than in the dress business," Uncle Max said with a broad smile. "So department stores, the other stores, they play their game and you play your game. You know how much each piece costs you. You know how far down you can go. So you play."

But that was before he found out that Belsky, one of his partners, had stolen him blind, had ruined the business. We didn't see Uncle Max for over eight months, not even at the family get-togethers. Every time someone in the family spoke about him they would ask, What was he doing? Where was he? He seemed to have disappeared. Not a word from him, not even from his wife, my Aunt Mollie. They had become lost in the Bronx while we lived in the tenements of the Lower East Side shadowed by the Williamsburgh Bridge. Even his two sons had been lost with him.

"I worry about him," my mother said to my father. Max was her youngest brother. "What happened to him?"

My father shrugged. "I don't know." But with a knowing nod, "Max is Max. We will see him someday. He'll show up."

My mother rocked her head sadly. "Like the earth swallowed him up." Leaning towards my father, said, "Why don't he come to see us?"

What was there to say?

Then one day he did show up, a broad smile on his face. Natty as ever. My mother, startled, said almost in a whisper, "Max, Max, you're here."

My father, my sister and myself, we stared at him, a ghost reappeared. My father whispered, "*A gahst in shtetl*, A guest in town."

Uncle Max didn't hear my father's whisper, he turned towards my mother as he said to her, "I'm here. And why not? This is the family, yes?"

"Yes, yes," she replied. "Come. Sit down. I'll make you a glass tea." She placed the kettle on the stove, cut a slice of lemon while my sister set the table. My mother searched the shelves for the jar of strawberry jam. There was none. "I don't have the jelly," she said to Uncle Max. "I know you like tea with some jelly."

"So does the world come to an end, you don't have the jelly?" Uncle Max, now seated at the table, said, "Come, sit down."

"After the tea," she replied. "And how is Mollie, the family?"

"Fine, fine."

While we were having our tea my father asked, "And what are you doing, Max?"

"I'm in the soap business," he said sitting back in his chair.

"What?" my mother said, startled.

Uncle Max, grinning, nodded. "Soap. To wash, to clean. Soap for the wash."

My mother, holding the fingertips of both of her hands to her mouth in wonderment, whispered, "The money. Where did he get the money?" while my father said to Uncle Max, "What do you know about the soap business? You know the *schmateh* business, the apron business. But, soap—?"

"I know how to sell, that's what I know. You're in the dress business, you sell dresses, you're in the apron business, you sell aprons. If you can sell one thing, you can always sell another. You sell what you got to sell. It's not such a big thing, I can tell you."

"You work for somebody?" My mother asked.

"Me? I should work for somebody? What are you talking about? You think I want somebody telling me what to do? Never."

"You make soap?" my mother said slowly in wonder. "Make it? *Takeh*, really?"

"Yeah," Uncle Max said. "Businesses make things. I make soap."

"Like Lux soap?" My mother asked. She loved Lux soap, its smell and its lather. She bought it whenever she had a few cents extra to spare.

"No. Not yet," Uncle Max said. "Soap for the laundry, soap flakes, soap powder, things to clean."

"You mean it?" my father said bewildered.

"Here," Uncle Max said as he removed a card from his vest pocket and handed it to my father. "It says the Brite White Company, right? Right?"

My father reached for the card, stared hard at it, his glance darted to Uncle Max as he said, "I don't understand."

Uncle Max took a sip of tea, put the glass down on the table and said, "After that Belsky, that *goniff*, that thief, he should only get killed, the *momzer*, the bastard, he stole from me the apron business, I sat down and thought it all out."

One sure thing, he told us, no more partners, that was rule number one. Partners steal. What did he, Uncle Max, want? A business where the investment was not as great as the dress, the *schmateh* business. So he began to look around, there were plenty of businesses for sale, wasn't this the Depression? Too many businesses, not enough customers. And he found it, the soap business, it was going bankrupt this little place in the Bronx—

"In the Bronx, a factory?" my father said.

The only time I had been in the Bronx were those few times when my mother and father and my sister had attended those parties Uncle Max had had in his apartment opposite Crotona Park. We went to the Bronx as little as possible, the trip was too long. We had to walk to the 2nd Avenue El, take it to the interchange uptown with the 3rd Avenue El, take that train and get off somewhere in the 170's in the Bronx. Then, later, we had to make that long trip back. It was all just too much.

"What do you think?" Uncle Max said to my father. "They don't have factories in the Bronx? There's factories. Plenty." My mother shrugged her I-don't-know shrug as Uncle Max went on with, "We sell to laundries, big laundries, other places that use a lot of soap. You would be surprised, there are lots of places like that and I'm getting in some of them. I picked up some good business."

"You make Fels Naptha soap?" my mother asked. It was the bar of soap she used for her laundry.

"Yeah. Well, that too. I got a soap like that that's better, believe me." He took a slow sip of tea and said, "When I got the business I made up my mind I would be the outside man, I would do the selling. But I would still run the business, you understand?"

"What's not to understand?" my father said. "But who makes the soap?"

"Somebody inside," Uncle Max said with a satisfied grin.

"You got people working for you?" my mother asked with surprise.

"When you make things you have workers working for you. That's the way it is. I got three working for me and the girl in the office. And sometimes when it gets too busy, I get two or three more. And sometimes my two boys come in to help out too. One man I keep all the time, he's the one knows how to make the soap. He's," Uncle Max said with a laugh, "a chef of the soap. He worked before for the people I bought the business from and he was *takeh*, really, glad to have the job from me."

We looked at each other, awed by what Uncle Max was saying. How was it possible that this had happened when businesses failed every day, when people had no jobs, when a multitude of people were on New York City's Home Relief? How had Uncle Max done it?

"So why not a job for the family, Max? You got a good business, yeah?" my mother said. "You didn't think of that?"

My father tensed at her words. He searched for work every day and occasionally he would find something for a short time, I knew that he had no desire to work for Uncle Max. Staring at Uncle Max my father muttered more to himself a caustic, yeah, yeah, oh sure.

"Because," Uncle Max said placing his half-filled tea glass deliberately on the table, "nobody in the family knows how to make soap, how to be a good soap chef, yeah? How to make soap flakes, how to boil the things that go into my White-O, it's a liq-uid," he said the last word with a deliberateness as if he had just learned it. He turned to my father and said, "Can you do that?" My father said nothing and looked away from him. "Hah?" Uncle Max persisted. "Can anybody from this family do that? So what do I do? I get somebody who can."

Silence. Slowly Uncle Max looked into our faces. Then, slowly, he picked up his unfinished glass and sipped more tea. My mother said, "What about the other ones who work for you?"

"A truck driver? He owns his own truck. You got a truck? He gets—I wouldn't tell him this but I'll tell you. A little secret. He gets *bupkiss*, almost nothing, but he's glad he's got a job, he's satisfied. If he's satisfied, so I'm satisfied. The same with the others. You know what they do? They mix, they pack, they *schlepp*, haul. Would you be able to do that?" he said to my father. My father said nothing.

Uncle Max sat there like a king. This was Uncle Max, whenever we saw him, he somehow established himself as the center of things. Even when earlier in his career, when he was still in the apron business. Especially in the earlier days whenever he needed the money, which was on a regular basis, he made the rounds of family members and friends, those who had small grocery or candy stores. Or those like my father who made a decent living before the Depression, Uncle Max gave them what he called 'head checks' dated ahead three or four days for which he received immediate cash.

He squeezed out fifty dollars here, one hundred dollars there, that way he had cash for those days before his checks cleared. He may have had others who exchanged cash for lesser or more amounts but we were not aware of them.

But even then, while writing his check, he was still the success, the boss, the someone. Even then. But that was in the early days of the apron business. His check exchange business stopped a few years later.

"So from this you're making a living?" my mother asked him.

"Yeah. Sure," he replied. "You make a living from selling anything, even shoelaces, if you sell enough of them. Come," he said as he suddenly arose from the table. "Come downstairs. Come look at my new car."

"A new car?" my father said in disbelief. "You got a new car?"

"Sure. Why not?" Uncle Max replied. "A Pontiac. Come see it."

"A Pontiac?" I said in awe, thinking at the same time, What's happened to the Ford?

We trooped down the dimly-lit stairs of the tenement following Uncle Max. And there outside, parked at the curb, was the new automobile shining and glimmering in the late afternoon sunlight. A bunch of kids had gathered around it and were peering into its windows, studying its interior.

"Hah!" Uncle Max said as he stopped to point at the vehicle, "There it is. What do you think?"

What could we think? Wonderment, disbelief even in belief. Awe. Who bought a new car at that time? Who could afford it?

But that was Uncle Max again. A show man, a boss, a success. Maybe not a Rockefeller, but still he was a success. And later, after he had gone we still questioned why he had come. He had asked for nothing, no 'head checks,' no favors. As if we had any favors to bestow upon him. Why had he come?

About a month later he was back again. This time he carried a half-filled shopping bag. He said to my mother, "We'll have the tea later. Come see what I got to show you."

All of us circled the kitchen table. "What's all this about?" my father asked.

Uncle Max said, "I want you to tell me what you think." I stared at him as he removed a box of laundry soap and placed it on the table.

"What is this, you show us Rinso?" My mother said in a puzzled tone.

"Aha!" Uncle Max said. "You're right. It's Rinso. And now," he said as he reached into the shopping bag, removed a strip of paper, placed it across the Rinso name on the box. There was rough printing on the strip of paper, it said ClinsO.

"ClinsO?" I said puzzled.

"Right," he said. "You're a smart boy." Then to the rest of the family, "ClinsO. Better than Rinso. Costs less to the grocery store so it sells for less. It works as good as Rinso. What am I saying? It's better." Pointing to the package he asked my mother, "Would you buy it if it was ten cents less than Rinso? Ten cents is a lot of money, yeah? You can buy a whole can of tomato herring for the family to eat for ten, eleven cents. That, with a slice of onion on a roll, a glass tea, you make a whole meal." He was referring to Del Monte herring in tomato sauce in the oval can that was a big seller in our community.

My mother stared at him then at the box. Puzzled, she asked him, "What do you mean?"

"I mean I will make ClinsO. I will sell it to the grocery stores. What I'm asking you is this, would you buy it if it's ten cents cheaper than Rinso?"

"Sure," my mother said. "Why not?" She stopped for a moment turned to Uncle Max and said, "It will clean the wash, you mean it?"

"Guaranteed. Absolutely," he said, his palm loudly slapping the table top. "One hundred per cent."

"The Rinso people, they won't mind?" my father asked.

"Why should they mind?" Uncle Max replied. "I don't call it
Rinso, do I? It's ClinsO. Is ClinsO Rinso, I ask you? What business is it of theirs so long I don't call it Rinso?" He waited for an
answer, there was silence. He said, "A big company like that minds
their own business, I mind mine. They can still make millions and
I make a living and—"

My father interrupted and said, "But I thought a company
like that, it don't like to have somebody take their name."

"*Ai*," Uncle Max said with a shrug. "Who's taking their name?
Who said ClinsO is Rinso? Did I say so? Don't you hear a difference,
hah?"

"I know, I hear," my father said. "But don't they care?"

"Care, shmare," Uncle Max replied. "It's not the same. They
say Rinso's the best laundry soap, I say ClinsO is. So what? I don't
care what they think, they shouldn't care what I think. This is
America where it says I can think and do what I want."

My father shook his head sadly. My mother was about to arise
from the table as she said, "You are making my head spin around.
I think I'll make the tea."

Uncle Max said quickly, "Wait. I got more."

"More soap?" I said.

"Aha! Who told you, *boychick?* Yes," he said as he removed
small rectangular red box from the shopping bag which contained
paper strip across its name.

It smelled like a hospital, biting hard into my nose as I said,
"It's Lifebuoy, that's the smelly soap."

"No, no," Uncle Max said as he passed the box to my father,
"It's Life Joy."

"What? Another one?" my father said.

"It smells like Lifebuoy," my sister said. "You can smell it a
mile away."

Uncle Max smiled. "That's the way it's supposed to be when
you make a soap like that. And people can buy it cheaper than
Lifebuoy. So I save them more money. Who doesn't need to save
money nowadays? Tell me."

I was about to say something, Uncle Max bent as he dipped his hand into the shopping bag and removed a paper-wrapped brick of soap. "You remember," he said to my mother, "you said last time you did the wash, other things, with Fels Naptha soap. Remember?" My mother nodded and he said with a quick point of his forefinger, "Well, here's Mel's Naptha, and sure, you guessed it, it's cheaper. And you're right, it's better than Fels Naptha. What could be better than that? Tell me," he said to my mother who stared as if hypnotized by his words and actions. Nobody said anything and Uncle Max suddenly asked, "Do we have a Melvin in the family, a *boychick* with that name? Maybe a cousin's cousin?"

My parents glanced at each other, shook their heads as my mother said, "No."

"No?" Max said. "Anyway, think about it and let me know if there is one."

"Well," my mother said removing the articles from the kitchen table, she placed them into the shopping bag. She turned to my sister and said, "Open the window so the smell can go." My sister went to the kitchen window, screeched it open, the fresh fall air rippled into the room, began to dissolve the odors. "Ah!" she said. "That's better." To Uncle Max she said, "I can tell you, it smells like Lifebuoy, like Fels Naptha, the box looks like Rinso. What do you want to do, with all those smells, make us not want to drink our tea?"

"You see?" Uncle Max said with a loud laugh, "the smell, it works. Right? And I'll tell you, only you, what I'll be doing next. There's that soap that you like, Lux. I'm working on that and I got my name for it, Lux-ur-ee. What do you think of that? And there's more than soap in this world. There's coffee, yes. The big seller is Maxwell House, yes?" He shook his forefinger at us for emphasis as he said," And I will make a Max's Swell House Coffee just as good, better, I guarantee it. And it will cost less." In my mind I could see the Maxwell House blue can emblazoned with its new name as Uncle Max went on with, "There's a hundred, a thousand things I could make. Like Roastum for Postum, like Hello for Jello. You wait and see what I can do."

"It's too much, too much," my mother said throwing up her hands.

Later, when he was gone, we sat at the table not knowing what to think. Finally my father said, "Is he crazy or am I crazy?"

"Who knows?" my mother said. "But crazy it could be."

"Lux-ur-ee Soap," my sister said with a laugh. "What's he talking about?"

We didn't see him again for over six months. He entered our flat carrying a shopping bag, a smile on his face, a glad hello to all of us. My mother, at the kitchen sink, wiped her wet hands on her apron. He went directly to the kitchen table, removed a box, ClinsO printed on it, all done professionally. Except for its name, ClinsO, and a few minor changes here and there, it was a Rinso box. He reached into the shopping bag once more, placed a small rectangular paper wrapped article on the table as well. Its perfumed smell spread across the kitchen.

He turned to face us as my sister said, "Lux-ur-ee Soap. And the label looks like Lux."

Uncle Max nodded emphatically. "I made it first," he said, "before Life Joy because it will sell faster." He beamed at us and said," Well?"

"I got to say," My father said shaking his head in wonderment. "You really made it."

"What do you think, I talk just to talk? Look at it," Uncle Max waved his hands at the two items. "I'm selling this already. To grocery stores, to the pushcarts on Orchard Street, to Jennings Street in the Bronx, to Bathgate Avenue, even to the *Talayner*, the Italians, on Arthur Avenue. I had to talk them into it at first, but after I got the first eight, ten stores and pushcarts selling it, other people heard about it, those two articles made a name for themselves and it all got a lot easier."

"You mean it?" my mother said sitting down slowly in a chair.

"Why should I lie to you?" Uncle Max said.

My mother served tea and some cookies, at intervals throwing glances at Uncle Max who said, "Here. Take the soap. Use them in good health."

"Are you working on those other things—Life Joy, Mel's Naptha?" I asked.

"Yeah. Sure. When I have the time. And don't forget the coffee and the Roastum. I'll make them too."

I could visualize Uncle Max as the USA king of soap and food. It seemed as if he could make anything once he set his mind to it. There was butter and cheeses, canned salmon and the herring in tomato sauce he had mentioned the other time he had been in our house.

It was almost unbelievable, but he had done it. We heard that he was selling to more and more outlets, that he had added Mel's Naptha soap to his line.

It must have been more than a half year later that he showed up again, nattily dressed as ever. When he sat down at the table and tea and sponge cake was served to him, my mother said, "*Nu,* well, Max, and so how is business?"

He sat silent for a moment or two staring into space, then he said, "The *momzerin,* the bastards, I fixed them, the Rinso people, all that. They went to court and I was supposed to stop selling my ClinsO, any of those items, but I showed them, the *momzerin,* I made more merchandise at night, I sold them to big customers I knew, I delivered at night, so those *momzerin* shouldn't know. I have the Rinso people *in dred,* buried. And I sold it for cash, cash only."

"You are not in business?" my mother said aghast.

"They closed me down," Uncle Max said.

"You lost it all?" my father said in a hushed whisper.

"All, shmall," Uncle Max said. "What they got from me was *bupkiss.* Nothing. I had no money—"

"No money?" my mother called out loudly. "How—?"

"Listen," Uncle Max said. "I'll tell you a little secret. Years ago when Belsky, the *momzer,* stole all that money, I had a good lawyer. Smart, oh, he was smart! He's cousin Morris' boy, Charlie, you know him. Smart, he went to college, to law school, he knows everything."

"So what did he do?" my mother asked eagerly.

"So he put everything in Mollie's name. Everything. The soap business we bought, that was the Brite White soap company. The ClinsO company that makes those other things I showed you, that was a separate company, that was my company. It was a company on paper, like Charlie said. I didn't make a profit, not in my books. I bought everything from Mollie's company and I paid her on the spot. Yeah, it's legal. All the profit was Mollie's. Sure, they closed down my company, but me, what could they get from me? I got no company, I got no money, no car, nothing. Mollie's got it all. So I have the Rinso company *in dred*, buried. When they told me to close down, I made the extra stuff at night. It's not on the books. They'll never find it. Never."

"*Ai*," my father said lifting his eyes to the ceiling. "Me too, I got no money, no job, no nothing. It should only happen to me, I should be so lucky."

Uncle Max smiled at that. "And something else," he said.

"More?" my mother said.

"We sold the Brite White company."

"You sold a company that makes you a good living?" my father said bewildered. "Why?"

"Because the soap chef began to ask for more money. On the books he worked for Mollie's company, not for me. He knew all about the court business but he thought he could hold me up for more money. But I'm not a fool, you give him once there's always more times. Who needs it? So he's the chef for the new people, let him ask them for more money. Let him see what they give him. Me, I already bought a dress business. I call it the Nu Design Dress Company. I bought it cheap, they were going bankrupt."

"What!" my father said. "In the *schmateh* business? I thought you always said it was not for you, there was too much competition, it was—"

"Who, me? I said that?" Uncle Max said his voice rising in disbelief. "Not me. Never. I never said anything like that. Not once, ever. I always said I wanted to go in business on Seventh Avenue, but in the right way. What are you talking about?"

There was no use in arguing with Uncle Max, he would not hear of anything else. The truth, his truth, was whatever he said at the time. And more, he was thinking of his new kingdom, he had lost the soap kingdom, that of ClinsO, the other soaps, the vision of Max's Swell House Coffee and Roastum had disappeared, but he was ready for the coming one.

Watch out, Seventh Avenue!

ALL THE MONEY
I NEVER DID MAKE

Those were the times when we had no money, none at all. Those were bad times, terrible times. We lived in a world that had gone crazy, people who desperately needed basic things, food, clothing, the barest minimums to make life bearable, yet could not afford to buy them, yet all the while surplus food rotted in warehouses, gluts of everything imaginable lay unbought in the stores.

We lived at that time in the Lower East Side, a huge mass of people compacted together, all with basic wants. And we dreamed dreams of escape from this, our world full of smashed hopes and of no substance.

That was the time we went to school, where we studied and for a time during the day we met our friends and forgot that outside world. I was thirteen then.

After school, an all-boys junior high school, after we had come home and done our homework, after we had eaten our supper, that was what we called it in those days, we would run downstairs from our tenement flats into the darkened street and four or five of us would meet under the corner street lamp. We would talk, of school, of handball, basketball, stickball games, lately of girls our own age who lived in the neighborhood. And we sang.

One of us, a bit more affluent than the rest, one who had a spare nickel, bought a colored song sheet, each issue printed on a different-colored paper, blue or orange or green or a pinkish-red. The song sheets contained the lyrics of the most popular songs— "Flying Down To Rio," or," The Carioca," or, "Brother Can You Spare A Dime."

And huddled together beneath the light of the street lamp, we read the words on the colored sheets and we sang, if we knew the tunes. If not we listened to those who did and followed their tune with a faltering echo of ours, our words and melody fusing together while the passersby would walk past, most of them ignoring us.

Once, a man, an old immigrant, walking by as we sang, called out to us, "It's your America. *Ai-yai-yai*, to be young!"

We talked and we sang. We schemed. How to make money to get out of the tenements.

"You make money with your brains," Goldie said one night.

His last name was Goldenberg but we called him Goldie. His hands were tremendous in size, he was the best handball player in school. On the outdoor playground court set against the huge wide wall of the ice factory, he could, almost on demand, smash a killer, the ball hitting the bottom end of the wall, sending it skittering on the floor of the court, impossible to return by his opponents.

"Yeah, sure," Max said in a scoffing tone. With a nod, "You make money by work, that's how."

"Oh, yeah," Izzy said. "Show me where there's work. Where?"

"I don't know," I said. "Nobody's got money. You can't make money without money."

Goldie laughed at us. Near us, on the opposite corner of the street, in the sudden heat of the early June night, the candy store had removed its portable windows leaving the top of the marble counter of the soda fountain open to the street. Some people were clustered there, a man ordered a two cents plain. Another was drinking a large five cents chocolate soda, his head held high, his throat extended as he drained the bubbly liquid.

. "Look at that," Goldie said. "What're they doing? Drinking sodas. And what does that mean, what do you think of?" He waited for our replies. We were puzzled by his question, we remained silent. "I think of thirsty people, right?" We nodded and he went on with, "And when I think of thirsty people, I think of egg cream. I think of Auster's egg cream."

"Ah," I said. "The best. Auster's egg cream."

"You bet," Goldie said. "The one, the only. Everybody knows Auster's egg cream. When they can, people go to his place, just for it. It's a couple cents more than a regular chocolate soda, but people want it, they pay it when they can. You know what?" he asked glancing around at us.

"What?" Max said.

Goldie's voice lowered. "See that candy store across the street?" he asked. "My older brother worked there last summer, remember? And people would ask him if they had an egg cream like Auster's. Sure, he said. But he lied. The man who owned the candy store don't know the formula of Auster's. Nobody does, Auster keeps it a secret. If we knew the secret," he whispered, "we could make a fortune. Auster's making money, just ask them at the candy store here," he said. "Ask anybody's got a candy store, any place in New York. They all try to make it like Auster's. They put eggs in the chocolate syrup, no dice. They even put Karo syrup in it, yeah, my brother's boss tried that once. No dice. They try everything. No dice. And Auster don't tell, he just goes along and makes his own syrup."

"So he's making a fortune," Max said. "So what?"

Goldie shook his head sadly as he said, "So if you knew the formula, you would make a fortune, right?"

Suddenly caught up with Goldie's idea, I said, "We could make it and sell it to all the candy stores."

"Right," Goldie said. "We make it, the candy stores do all the work when they sell it. They dish out the seltzer on top of the syrup, they mix the egg cream with the soda when the glass is filled, they take the money, put it in the cash register, they wipe up the counter, they wash the glasses. And we just make the stuff, sell it, and with the money we buy the stuff we need, we take some money for ourselves, the rest we put in the bank. How's that sound?"

"I don't know," Izzy said. "It ain't that easy. How do we get that formula? Auster ain't giving us that secret."

"We find out," Goldie whispered.

"How?" I asked in a whisper.

"We go to Auster's store after it's closed. We look around. He's got the stuff there he puts in when he makes the egg cream syrup. We'll find out what he uses."

Izzy spread his hands out in disbelief. "That's all we got to do," he said. "Just go into his store and steal the formula. That's all, huh?" he said with mock seriousness.

"That's not stealing," Goldie said. "We don't take anything, we just look around. If you don't take, you're not stealing."

"Hey, what're you talking about?" Max said to Goldie.

Some strollers were walking slowly by, the group became silent. We straightened up from our huddled scheming and we watched them closely as if they were spies sent to discover our plot. When they had gone by, we huddled once more, three of us staring at Goldie.

Goldie was saying, "Stealing is if you take what's somebody's. Right?"

"Right," the three of us said in unison.

"So it's simple," Goldie said. "We don't take anything. No take, no steal."

"But if the store's locked and we get into it, that's against the law," I said.

There was something about this plan that I wanted to like. Oh, how I wanted to make money and rise out of poverty. Oh, how I needed things. Each year, once a year, just before the Passover holiday, my family had bought me a new suit. And shoes. And a new shirt and a tie. New clothing for the entire family. That was in the good times, before the Depression, when my father earned some money. But now he didn't, and he hadn't for the past few years, and for four years I hadn't gotten a suit. I had had to wear my old worn suit, somewhat small for me now, my wrists and a part of each arm above them exposed. The cuffs of my pants had been let down by my mother and I had gone into the street ashamed' of how I looked crammed into that suit, my exposed wrists jammed as deeply as possible into my pockets. I tried to hide my shame, while a few of my friends, so very few, wore their new suits, and, oh, how I wanted that Passover suit now.

Listening to Goldie, I could see it in my mind, the smooth cloth full of newness, the sleeves long enough, just right, the pants long enough. And a new pair of shiny shoes. How I wanted all of that!

Goldie was saying, "So what if we get into the store. Who'll know? We get in, we get out. We got nothing on us, we got no hot goods, what're they going to do about it?"

"Yeah," Izzy said. "We don't do anything to the place, we don't break nothing, we're just looking around and—"

"How're we going to get in?" Max asked.

"There's a window there, high up over Auster's store kitchen in the back. We boost each other up, we open the window, we're in," Goldie said with a snap of his fingers. "We got us a searchlight, we look around. When we're finished, we leave."

"What about the cops?" I whispered as I looked up and down the street. Perhaps, just maybe, right now, the foot patrolman was walking his beat up this street.

"The cops? What cops? At night? Eleven o'clock? Nobody's around. They—"

"Eleven o'clock at night?" Max asked in astonishment. "It's too late."

"When else?" Goldie asked. "Auster's closed. At night, especially at eleven o'clock or so the cops are busy, they're doing all kinds of things. They're eating, they're sitting in the back room of somebody's place, maybe an all night restaurant, a place like that. They know where to go, they're getting paid off—"

"You've been seeing too many movies," I said. "What if the cops come?"

Goldie whacked his huge hands against his thighs. "So what if there's a cop? He's on his beat. We got one of us, he stays outside, he's the lookout. He sees the cop coming down the street, the lookout he can see him a mile away when the cop passes a street light. The lookout, he whistles, like this," Goldie chirped three short notes, "the lookout, he walks into the doorway and the hall of the building next door to the store, the cop doesn't see him, the cop goes down his beat. A few minutes later, he's gone. What're you getting all so worked up about?" he asked incredulously.

"What if the cops see us in the store?" Max asked, his words tip-toeing on one another.

"So he sees us," Goldie said loudly. Some of the soda customers across the street at the candy store heard his sharp voice, momentarily stopped their drinking and peered across the darkness to the cone of light where we stood under the street lamp. All of us said to Goldie, in soft sibilance, S-sh! He glanced across the street, his voice dropped to a whisper as he said, "So he sees us, so what? Maybe one in a million shot. If he catches us we tell him the window there in the back was open, we went in to see if Auster was being robbed. We say we wanted to help out, that's all. What's wrong with that?" We said nothing, we glanced at each other, looking for a hint of some sort from one another, either agreement or disagreement with the plan. I didn't know and I waited in silence. Hearing no objection from us Goldie said, "You're in?" We glanced at each other once more, nothing was said. Goldie said somewhat angrily, "Yes or no?"

Izzy gave a great audible sigh. "I'm in," he finally said.

Goldie began to smile. He looked at Max then at me. Max, silent, slowly began to nod his head. When Goldie stared at me, I, too, cautiously, began to nod. We all agreed to meet the following night. We would meet at ten o'clock, we would proceed to Auster's. We would do the job.

I went up to my house, it was late for me. Later than usual when I came up from the streets after meeting with the guys. My father was asleep in the bedroom. My mother said nothing to me but there were unspoken words on her tongue as she gave me a stern stare.

I told her there was a big, tough test coming up in school soon and I had been studying with Goldie. Tomorrow, I would also be home late, I had to study. Not too late, she said. I'll try, I replied, I'll do the best I can, I had to pass that test, I had to study. Get a good mark, an A, she said to me.

That was the first step, I told myself, to get her used to my coming home late tomorrow night. I hadn't wanted to lie to her, I fervently wished that I hadn't had to, but I knew that tomorrow night I would be coming home much later and I knew that she and my father would be asking pointed questions. Anyway, what could I do? I had planned my excuses with her as best as I could. The words, school, and, study, were magical words with my parents. Anything was allowed when the words were mentioned. Well, almost anything.

I slept poorly that night. Visions of cops crept into my mind and my mounting feeling that I didn't want to be caught. But I thought of Auster's egg cream, the best in the world, that made the palate salivate and sigh with blissful contentment. For when you wanted the very best.

And all that money, coming in if we knew the formula. If I got the money, I'd buy clothes for all the family, my parents, my brother and sister, and I'd order a case, weekly, of Good Health Seltzer from the seltzer man who carried up, on his shoulder, the long narrow wooden crate that contained the filled bottles with their metal siphons and carried down the empties. Without leaving the house, my family would use the magical formula egg cream any time we wanted. That was living.

But the cops, the cops... And I tossed and turned all night. Yet, I reassured myself, Goldie was confident, he was our leader. He knew, he wasn't afraid. Wasn't he the best handball player in school? So why should I be afraid?

The next night at ten o'clock, we met under the street lamp. Three of us were there, Max hadn't shown up. We waited impatiently for him for a few minutes and finally Goldie, in disgust, said, "He won't show. He's afraid. What's he got to be afraid of?" He paused, studied our faces, shrugged and said, "Forget Max, we're better off without him. If he's so scared, he'd only do something to make some trouble for us at Auster's. Let's go."

We walked down the darkened streets in deep silence. Now and then, when I felt that Goldie wouldn't notice it, I glanced wildly around me to see if there was a cop following us. Nothing. Darkness and the occasional black form of a walker, a lone automobile riding ghostly in the shadows.

We walked down the empty streets, my heart was pounding, I didn't want to be there, I wanted to be home, in my bed. I wanted to feel secure.

We walked slowly, Goldie had warned us not to do anything to arouse suspicion. "Talk a little," he said, but we had no words. "About school," he said. We didn't know what to say. "About girls," he hissed. "What about that girl you like?" he said to me. "You know, the tall one with the red hair that lives down the block from you."

"Yeah," Izzy said. "The good-looking one."

"You shut up! I don't want to hear that!" I whispered fiercely, struggling to keep myself from shouting. I stopped and turned to face Izzy and said, "You keep her out of this." And to Goldie, "You too. You hear?"

Goldie smiled, shrugged. "What did I say?" he asked spreading out his hands. "Okay, okay. At least you're talking."

"Not about her," I said sharply. "Both of you keep her out of this."

Izzy said, "Okay, okay."

For a brief moment I thought of her, she was a nice girl. I didn't want her talked about by anybody. Suddenly fear returned and barely listening to what Izzy was saying, I glanced around. Darkness, closed stores, a moving shadow, a stroller, nothing more.

We were two blocks from Auster's. We could begin to smell the place even there, the rich warm sweet smell of cooked chocolate, that magic smell that caught your nose and held it. The smell grew stronger as we approached the locked darkened store.

Izzy began to look around him apprehensively.

My head swiveled, my eyes became a periscope, searching for a dark uniformed approaching shadow. I was afraid, my throat felt dry, my tongue seemed swollen and useless, I couldn't talk. No, no, I told myself, I didn't want to be caught.

Goldie seemed unafraid and said in a normal tone of voice, "Auster's closed." Both Izzy and I, wordless, nodded dumbly in the darkness. "That's good," Goldie whispered. "Let's go." We followed him slowly with leaden steps, always looking around, peering into the blackness of the night. "Come on, a little faster," Goldie was saying.

Suddenly, in a strained whisper Izzy gasped out, "It's a cop! I can see him!"

He was running. Now I was running after him. The shadows of the night around me flickered and seemed to move. I thought I saw a cop. Suddenly I was running away from the law, away from crime, away from all of this. I could hear Goldie's speeding steps slapping the sidewalk, following me, all three of us racing away from Auster's, away from the sweet smell of chocolate, away from the money that I could have had, my dream gone.

THE LOSS OF INNOCENCE

The soapy water in the large tin laundry vat erupted and bubbled into soft popping sounds, smoke tendrils climbed curling into the air above the coal stove. Inside the vat laundry lay coiling and sliding slowly in the roiling water. Running from its both ends, the metal edges of the large container were parallel to each other, its two ends tapering to a curve, the center of each curve held a stained wooden handle set in a small metal projection.

In the heaving murmuring boil itself, propped against one of the sides of the vat was a length of rounded wood which the woman stirred listlessly round and round into the boiling vat.

Inside, in the tenement flat itself, even with the lone kitchen window open this late spring day, the air smelled damp, hot and soapy. In the kitchen, the woman's small, four-year-old daughter, Ida, sat at the porcelain-topped table, playing with an old rag doll. The mother, at the stove, stopped for a moment, wiped some strands of hair away from her damp brow, a small smile appeared on her face as she glanced at her daughter.

"*Mamaleh*," she said to her daughter. "You are such a good mother to your baby, you take such good care of your baby."

Her daughter looked up from playing with the doll and said, "She's a good baby, mama."

The mother nodded, turned back to the stove. Silently working at the vat, a faraway look in her eyes, mechanically pushing the round stick around and around, moving the *vesh*, the laundry, clumps of cloth sinking and appearing in the gray boil in the container, she thought of those years gone by when she had just married her husband, Mendel. That was the time before the Crash and the onset of the Depression, and they had rented a flat in another, an older building on the Lower East Side of New York. It had three rooms, and what they called the dining room they had furnished cheaply with a heavy oak table and chairs. The table sat beneath the light fixture with its gas mantles. On those rare occasions when they used the room, the gas mantles when lit, popped into a red-orange light, turned to yellow, then to a somewhat whitish brightness.

Later they had moved to another flat that had electrical lighting. In the kitchen, near the ceiling there had been a meter for the electricity, the meter had contained a slot where quarters were inserted when the lights began to dim and tremble. When the Depression came, when there were no quarters to feed the meter, when the electricity was cut off by the impersonal meter, they had used candles to light the flat at night. Every tenant in every flat had kept a reserve of candles for just those emergencies.

But that had once been, and since then had become different. The electric company operated differently, bills were sent out, and when she and her husband had no money available, there had been time to delay and stall. Most of the cooking was done on the coal stove, only occasionally, mostly during the summers, would she use the two-burner portable gas stove attached by a red rubber tube from one of the gas stove end-pipes to the main metal gas pipe that ran up the wall of the kitchen.

There had been those who took the gas pipe, as everybody called it, to commit suicide. *Ai*, poor, poor people, the woman thought shaking her head sadly. The times were terrible, terrible. Where was the *goldeneh medina*, the golden land?

Mechanically stirring the laundry in its soapy soup with round motions of the length of wood she thought of how she would like to buy a new pair of shoes for the little girl, but there was no money. They lived from hand to mouth, the shoes would have to wait. For a brief moment she looked at her daughter and sighed. Her body moved laboriously as she stirred the laundry in the vat. The Depression had been the beginning of real denial, of no quarters for electricity, of no payment for the gas bills until a collector came to visit them, the stalling of the payment of rent to the landlord, the use of the small book she clutched in which was entered her purchases whenever she shopped at the grocery store, the sporadic call to work for her husband in the garment center on Seventh Avenue, the squeezing of nickels, dimes and pennies, the eternal internal debate whenever something, anything, should be bought. Can we afford it? Do we have the money? Should we spend it on something else?

Yet sometimes there was a penny, two, a nickel, perhaps, to spare. When her husband, Mendel, miraculously had a little more work than usual and when his pay was a dollar or two more, she would spend an extra quarter, maybe a half dollar when the children's' birthdays came along. She had three of them, two older boys in school and Ida.

In good weather, there would be a wandering man in the back yard below who would look up at the windows and sing out loudly popular Yiddish songs. She would go to the kitchen window, open it, hold Ida up near her shoulder so that the little girl could see the singer down below.

After the man had finished with the song, he would remove his cap from his head and stare up at the windows above him. If she had some money, she felt she had to give him something, the man also needed money like everybody else did. He also had to live, to eat and pay rent and she would give a few coins to Ida who, with an awkward childish motion, hurled the money out into the air, both of them listening for the clink of the coins when they hit the pavement of the yard.

The man would scramble quickly to pick up the money, saying, Thank you, thank you, and would look up intently for the sight of other hands hurling some coins from windows.

The mother had said to her little daughter, "People are hungry, they have no eat and we must help them if we can. God should be good to us and give us some *parnusseh*, some money, so we can give some of it to a poor man like that."

Now an Old Clothes Man chanted out hoarsely from the yard below, "I cash clothes, I cash clothes."

And little Ida, listening to the chant said to her mother, "There's a man singing, mama. In the yard. Open the window."

Her mother, with a smile, said to her, "He's not a singer, *mamaleh*."

"Listen, he's singing, mama, I hear him."

"No, *mamaleh*, he's telling us he buys old clothes. Listen to him." And the mother chanted along with the man's words, and said, "See?"

"Is he poor?" the little girl asked. "Like the singer man?"

"Poor, we all are, *mamaleh*. But some are more poorer than others. Some have no eat." Quickly as if to ward off a spell, "God forbid, it shouldn't happen to us again."

"He sings a funny song. What does he do?" Ida asked as her eyes followed the man down below moving slowly across the yard, a large sack over his shoulder.

"He buys things, old clothes, something people don't wear no more, things they don't want," the mother said.

"People don't want no more?" Ida said wonderingly. "You wear the same thing, mama. Papa too."

"Yeah, yeah," the mother said as she brushed the child's hair back with a swift motion of her hand. "Some place, there's people who can't wear their clothes no more."

"They grow bigger like Heshy or Sammy?" the little girl asked speaking of her two brothers. "But when Sammy gets too big for something he gives it to Heshy. And you give some of Heshy's things to *Tanteh*, Aunt Simmeh, for the cousins."

"Yeah, yeah," the mother replied.

At the stove the mother used the stick to lift up a piece of dripping underwear from the cauldron. Dashing quickly to the sink nearby, she deposited the steaming articles there, ran back to the vat several times until the sink was filled with a pile of wet laundry. She rinsed and with great grunting effort wrung out each article until the vat was empty.

Carrying the twisted damp articles which she deposited on a chair near the window, she hung the laundry on the line that stretched from the kitchen to a huge pole in the yard as tall as the tenement itself. As she strung the laundry out on the line and pushed the line forward to make room for more of the *vesh*, the small rotating wheels at each end of the line squealed out loudly. When she secured the laundry to the line the clothespins growled softly as she forced their wooden fingers into damp cloth. The gusts of wind began to whip and sway into frantic movement the towels and sheets, several pillow cases, Mendel's BVD'S, bloomers, the boys' things.

The little girl played quietly at the kitchen table, mothering her doll, making conversations with herself. Her mother, finished with the hanging of the laundry, shut the kitchen window, stopped for a moment, heaved a great sigh of relief.

Yet she knew that when the laundry had dried, the next day or the day after that, she would have to iron it all, a task that took up all of a morning, heating the two black metal heavy irons on the stove, lifting one, testing its heat with one of her fingers wet with her saliva, hearing the hiss at her fingertip, knowing then that the iron was ready to be used. But that was another day. Today the washing was finished.

As she went to the sink she said to her daughter, "You must be hungry, *mein tyreh*, my dear one. Mama will make some eat."

The mother washed up at the sink, looked at her image in the small mirror above the sink, combed her hair. There were baked potatoes in the oven, but that was for supper. Later, after the boys had come home from school for their lunch, and the three children had eaten, she would prepare the *lungen* stew, the lung stew, for the family supper. She looked at the alarm clock on the small shelf above the sink, it was almost time for the boys to arrive. When they did, it was with a rush of noise, of a loud babble of talk awakening the previous quiet of the small flat.

Ida immediately asked them, "How was school?"

Her mother smiled, that was the question she, not her daughter, usually asked her sons. Heshy removed his plaid jacket, said, "It was okay."

Sammy, sitting down at the kitchen table said, "Yeah. Fine. Okay." Snapping his fingers he arose, hurried to the sink before his brother could, and washed his hands.

Both boys had finished with their washing and all the children were seated at the table. The mother had sliced bananas into three small dishes, added clumps of sour cream and a spray of sugar into each of them and brought the dishes to her children. She placed a bowl of three hard-crusted rolls in the center of the table.

The children had begun to eat hungrily, two rolls had disappeared, part of a third remained in the bowl. As they ate the boys bantered with each other and now and then they stopped momentarily to eat, or say something to their small sister and to their mother.

When they were finished the mother placed a glass of milk before each child saying, "Drink. It's good for you."

Each of the boys emptied his glass quickly. Ida was still sipping at the milk when the boys wiped their lips, and arose from the table. One of them said, "I got to go back to school."

Their mother nodded to them and Ida, the half-filled glass still in her hand said to them, "I will go to school. Next year when I'm a little bigger." And to her mother said, "Yeah, mama?"

"Yeah, mein tuchteril, my little daughter. Soon," the mother replied. Soon, she thought. It's too soon. To her sons she said, "Be careful. Be good in school, you hear?" The boys nodded and she turned to her daughter and said, "Finish the milk. We don't leave eat to throw out. Go, finish it."

The boys had gone, the house seemed strangely silent after the talk and joking the boys had brought with them. Ida picked up her doll and began playing with it as her mother removed the dishes from the table and washed them at the kitchen sink.

When she had finished drying the dishes, the mother prepared the banana and sour cream dish for herself, sat down at the table, picked up the uneaten half of the roll, slowly ate all of it. There was boiling water in the kettle on the stove, the small ceramic pot of tea essence near the kettle. She poured some essence into a thick glass, filled it with boiling water, carried it carefully to the table.

As she sipped her tea, there was a knock on the door. She looked up, startled, and asked, "Who is it, who?" There was a muffled reply, a man's voice, did he say his name was Max or Moishe or Muttie, it could have been anything, it was too garbled. "Who?" she called out again, arising from the table and going towards the door. "God forbid, there was no accident, hah?"

"No, no, no," the voice replied from behind the door. "No accident. It's Itzak." There was a short series of raps on the door. "I came to ask you something."

"Itzak? Itzak, who?" she asked looking at her daughter who had stopped playing and was now staring at the door.

"Itzak, from down the street," the man's voice said. "You know me, I was here a few times before, already."

The mother shrugged to herself, and as she unlocked the door her daughter came to her side. When the mother swung open the door there was a shabbily dressed man who said softly quickly in an imploring tone of voice, "Do you have something to give to a poor man? *A poor tzent?* A few cents, maybe? I need some money for my family to eat, for my wife and children." His hand was out, palm up, as he spoke.

Now the mother remembered him. Several times, some time ago, she had given him a few precious cents, but later, in discussion with some of the women who were her neighbors, one of them had said, "That one, that Itzak, he's a *goniff*, a thief. He lives someplace on the other side of the bridge, near Hester Street, and he comes here, to this side of the bridge, to *schnorr*, to beg. He goes around here, he makes believe he has no money, no job. He don't look for work like my husband, like your *menner*, your men. A *goniff*. When there's work, our husbands work, but that *goniff*, he works at being a *schnorrer*, he does that for a living."

Now, shutting the door as the man was saying something, the mother said, "No, mister. Not today. And don't come back."

Her little daughter was staring up at her in bewilderment, suddenly began to cry and she was saying, "But he's poor, mama, he has no eat. You always say to give something to a poor—"

"*Shah, shah*, don't cry, *mein kind*, my child," the mother said as she lifted up her daughter and kissed her face. "He don't need the money."

"But, why, mama, why?" the little girl mumbled into her mother's shoulder. "Why didn't you give him something?"

The mother heaved a great sigh and patted her daughter's back. "Don't cry," she said. "Don't. Someday you will understand."

THE TIME I WOULD BEAT
ARNOLD ROTHSTEIN

The school building was near the East River, its outdoor playground across the street from its red brick mass, one side of the playground ending at the wide brick wall of the adjoining ice factory. The handball courts followed each other the full width of the factory, its outer vertical wall was part of the courts. Some distance away were the basketball courts, so that there was a minimum of interference between players of each game.

During lunch hour, after we had eaten, we played there. Sometimes, when we delayed our studying at home, we played there after school. Handball, for the better players, was played with a Spalding rubber ball, when one of the players could afford the fifteen cents to buy the ball at Cheap Heshy's, the store that sold sports items as well as stationery and toys. The Spalding was a treasured object, it was expensive as well as the best and when it was lost it was a calamity.

The playground was a scene of constant movement, roller skaters with roaring metal wheels skimming around the courts. Shouts, arguments erupted constantly from the courts, You pushed me! No, I didn't! That was a foul! You're blind, I was safe! It was a killer! No, it wasn't, didn't you see it bounce before it hit the wall! You got in my way! You're blind! You're crazy!

A small group of the older boys who attended school stood huddled away from the courts, grouped around twosomes who played Underlegs, a penny gambling game in which one player spun a penny on the ground, stepped on the whirling coin, spun another penny, stamped on that with his other shoe. The other player, hoping to match the heads or tails of the hidden pennies, placed his coins in front of the shoes of his opponent. The first player would then step off his coins and if the second player had matched the pennies, the money was the opponent's. Otherwise the money was scooped up by the first player. The game went on until one of the players, the loser, would quit, and another take his place. Sometimes as much as fourteen cents was won or lost during those gambling bouts, a lot of money in those days for those older boys, the rough ones. They came to school because they had no jobs, they had no money, there was no other place to idle away the weekdays and so they came to school. I was not interested in their game, I was looking for Arnold Rothstein, for his game.

He had another name, his real name, but we all called him Arnold Rothstein because he was a gambler, not of the Underlegs type, he was not part of that gang, but still he was a gambler. There had been a real Arnold Rothstein, a big-time gambler who had been murdered and had been mentioned numerous times in the newspapers. We had given that name to our schoolmate because of his expertise.

Our Arnold Rothstein's game was something entirely different from any we had seen before. It too was played with a penny. You held your coin tightly between thumb and forefinger, your thumb spread over its minted date, to hide it while Arnold Rothstein would examine it. He would announce the minted year and if he was correct, the penny was his. In theory, if he lost, he gave you a penny. But he never lost. Never. I had lost a few pennies to him, but today I had my special pennies and I was looking for him.

At the playground, as the lunch hour was ending, I saw Goldie and asked him, "Have you seen Arnold Rothstein?" He shook his head. "Where is he?" I said. "I got to see him."

"Why?" Goldie asked as he walked alongside me towards the entrance to the school. "What's so special?"

"I'm going to beat him today," I said with a laugh. "I got it all figured out."

"You got it all figured out?" Goldie asked in amazement.

He had stopped, I along with him, and he stared at me while others pushed around us, on their way to the school.

Goldie was someone special. He was one of ours, the students of the school, those who came to learn. Although he was one of ours and although he didn't gamble with the Underlegs gang, they felt he was one of theirs too. Goldie with his huge hands, Goldie with his athletic ability, Goldie was by far was the best handball player in the school, he was probably the best basketball player too. He was unafraid, at ease in whatever game he played. The Underlegs gang respected him.

And I was saying to Goldie as we walked out of the playground, "You bet I got it figured out. I'll beat him today."

"I got to see that," Goldie said.

"When we find him, you'll see it," I said to Goldie.

We entered the school building, went to our classroom, Arnold Rothstein was seated there, two aisles away from me. I leaned over, whispered to him across the student who sat between us, "I got to see you. I want to play."

"Yeah. Sure. But we can't now. Later," he replied.

We were at the algebra class, Mr. Coolidge, the teacher, he was somewhat crazy, sometimes he threw things at his students when they didn't know the answers.

Anyway, Arnold Rothstein and I couldn't play in Mr. Coolidge's class, this was obviously one of those days when he was acting crazy.

The bell rang and the class gave a loud collective sigh of relief. We grabbed our books and papers and ran out of the room. We went on towards the gym class where, still in the corridor, I caught up with Arnold Rothstein.

"Come on," I said to him. "We've got to get going with our game."

He looked at me with an amused smile. "We'll have to see what happens in the gym class. I don't know, you know how Mr. Knight is. If we can't in the gym class, maybe someplace else. If we can't in school, I'll meet you in the playground after school. Okay?"

"Okay," I replied.

I wanted that game with him. Sooner than later. I had worked out a way to beat Arnold Rothstein and I wanted to do it now. Right away. Although I was a good student, one of the best in my grade, I forgot all about school work. I wanted that win, I wanted Arnold Rothstein's pennies.

I went to the gym class. There, Mr. Knight, our gym teacher, was standing at one end of the gymnasium. He gave us his faint smile and said, "Okay. It's Kill Me today. You know the game." All the basketballs and volley balls had been tossed towards the middle of the floor, the class had been arbitrarily divided in two, half on one side of the dividing line on the floor, the other half of the class on the other side. A whistle at his lips, Mr. Knight blew it into its sharp scream.

He walked out of range while each team scrambled for possession of the balls. When they were all scooped up, each side fell back to either end of the gym, all of us alert, all of us waiting. Those who had snatched up the balls waited for a propitious moment to hurl them at the opposing side.

The object of the game was for the ball to hit an opponent so hard that he would be unable to catch it. If he caught the ball and it bounced away from him, or if the ball hit him and he could not catch it without a bounce, he was out of the game. We had made of the game so much of a science that each team waited to secure possession of all the balls, then would advance to the center line while the defensive team would retreat to its end of the room and there each player dropped quickly to the floor while an orchestrated volley zoomed over them, or hit them, or someone would manage to catch the ball in mid-air.

Goldie, tall for his age and with those huge hands, was always the captain of our team. He could clutch a basketball in his hand like a grapefruit, he could lead us to victory. When his team had possession of all the balls, he assumed command as he advanced towards the center line, his small army trooping behind him, all coming to a halt at the line as Goldie called out to his cannoneers, "Okay! Let's go! Fire!"

Arnold Rothstein had somehow always managed to be on Goldie's team. When the game was in play he would stand directly in back of Goldie who became his shield. When the opposing team, in possession of all the balls, heaved a barrage, Arnold Rothstein would drop down to floor behind Goldie who usually remained standing, with those hands ready to catch a rocketing ball directed at him.

There were times when his opponents directed all the balls only at Goldie, he would then drop to the floor. And Arnold Rothstein was always behind him, always one of the last to be hit and go out of the game.

I was not so lucky. Once, only once, did I remain the lone survivor and that was because Goldie and I were on the same team. Goldie, in hurrying back as he watched the opposing team march up to the dividing line, had tripped over Arnold Rothstein's prone body and been hit by a barrage and had been disqualified. I had gone on to win the game.

Mr. Knight, as the game progressed, watched it with great interest, sometimes unconsciously twirling the ends of his waxed mustache, always the little smile on his face. When at last, one player remained, Mr. Knight blew his whistle and ordered us into the showers.

We undressed in the locker room, went into the communal showers and although we had hot and cold faucets for each shower, Mr. Knight operated the master control. The water came on, warm, just right, we washed ourselves, then suddenly the spray would turn icy cold and we knew that Mr. Knight had manipulated the master control.

We pranced about, yelling to him, although we knew it was useless, It's cold! It's cold! and one by one we fled from those frigid streams of water and ran out into the drafty, chilly locker room, shivering, our teeth chattering. Mr. Knight, that smile of amusement still on his face watched us go shivering by.

As I dressed I looked for Arnold Rothstein. He was nearby and as I buttoning my shirt, I approached him and asked, "Well, what about it?"

"Not here, not now. We can't," he replied as he laced his shoes. "Knight's here. You know what'll happen if he catches us. They'll send us to the assistant principal, he'll take away our money, he'll whack us on our hands with that big ruler of his. Later, later," he said.

We couldn't get the game going in school, something always made it impossible, always one thing or another. We had a test, or it was this, or it was that.

Goldie came up to me and asked, "You play with Arnold Rothstein yet?"

"No. We couldn't do it yet, it didn't work out."

"Let me know," Goldie said. "I've got to see that. You sure you're going to beat him?" I nodded. "How?"

"I'll tell you later," I replied. "Goldie, I promise I will."

Finally, finally, our classes for the day had ended.

I rushed out to the playground looking for Arnold Rothstein, Goldie had run out, following me. My hand in my pants pocket clutched the two shiny pennies. Where was Arnold Rothstein? Now I saw him approach, an air of confidence about him.

We'll see who's so confident after the game's over, I said to him silently in my mind. We'll see.

Without a word the three of us went to the farthest corner of the playground. Arnold Rothstein was smiling and I smiled back at him, he didn't know what I knew. I had polished two pennies with Bon Ami, shining them up to such a copper brightness they appeared new. They were new to me, they had to appear new to Arnold Rothstein. They had to.

"Okay," I said to him. "I'm ready."

"So am I," he replied.

I grasped one shiny coin as tightly as I could, my thumb hid the mint date. This time I would beat him, I could feel it. Near me Goldie was watching it all intently, staring at the two of us.

Arnold Rothstein bent forward and studied the coin for a few seconds. "Nineteen-twenty," he said.

I looked at him in amazement. It was impossible! Hadn't I polished the coin with Bon Ami? It didn't scratch. I looked up uncomprehendingly at Goldie, I mumbled to Arnold Rothstein, "Yeah." I handed him the coin and I reached into my pocket for the other penny and said, "Wait a minute. I got another one."

We played the game again and once more I lost. How was it possible? How did he do it? I asked myself. Those coins had looked new to me. What did he know? As I handed him the penny I said, "How do you do it?"

He grinned and said, "It's a secret."

Goldie tapped me on the shoulder to indicate that he was leaving. I looked up questioningly at him as he shrugged and walked away.

I turned to Arnold Rothstein and said, "But how—?"

"I can't tell you."

"Look," I said. "I'll even give you a dollar if you tell me." I didn't have the money, I didn't know how I would be able to get it, but I didn't care, this was a secret worth having. I had to have it. With a wry smile Arnold Rothstein was shaking his head and I said, "Two dollars. That's a whole lot of money." He shook his head once more as he began to walk away.

I caught up with him and I offered him five dollars, ten, and he shook his head and said to me, "Nah. I won't do it. Why should I? You think I'm crazy? They don't call me Arnold Rothstein for nothing."

GIRL OF HIS DREAMS

Danny stood outside the candy store, he had a little time to spend before he would have to go back to his house in the tenement and finish his homework. He glanced across the street at the fruit and vegetable store, she, Frieda, was not there. Only her parents and one customer were visible through the grimy store window. Danny would have liked to have seen Frieda, a glance of her would have been sufficient for him.

He had watched her over the many months, been drawn to her, at times seen her standing on the stoop of her tenement house, staring out into space. What was she thinking of? Who was she thinking of? It had alarmed him, it still did now, that she would be thinking of another young man. Danny wanted to be her boyfriend, he wanted to talk to her, be with her.

He told himself he would ask her for a date. Yes, he would, the next time he saw her. He would get the money somehow, two dollars would be sufficient, more than enough. Seventy cents for the movies for the two of them, seats in the orchestra, not the fifteen cents second balcony seat that he always purchased for himself, climbing up and up still higher, up the stairs of the Loew's Delancey that seemed endless. Then after the movie maybe forty or fifty cents for ice cream sodas for the both of them at a really nice ice cream parlor. That made a total of a dollar and twenty cents, well, a dollar and a half would do for the date.

He really hadn't had a talk with her, just a polite hello to her when he entered her parents' store to buy five cents soup greens his mother needed, which Frieda wrapped in cylindrical fashion in newspaper. She had replied with an almost automatic echo of his word. He didn't know whether or not she knew his name, but she would, oh, yes, she would, he told himself.

He glanced at the empty stoop to her house. He was thinking of what he would say to her, what she would reply to him. They would be walking down Delancey Street smiling to each other, he was holding her arm, the scenario forming in his mind when he heard the voice of the candy store owner.

"Danny," the candy store man said. "Go up and get Frieda, you know, from the vegetable store , go up to her house and tell her she got a telephone call. You hear?" Danny nodded. "Apartment 3D."

Nobody Danny knew had a telephone, well, almost nobody. Maybe his Uncle Sol who had been a dress cutter and now was a partner with three others in his Bon Ton Frocks, a dress factory on Seventh Avenue, yes, Uncle Sol had one. But everybody else he could think of, those countless people in the tenements around him relied on the system of calling the neighborhood candy store, ask for someone to be called to one of the store's telephone booths. Calls within the city limits cost five cents, the caller almost always would be telephoning from the pay phone of another candy store.

"I'm going," Danny said. He looked up at the third floor of the tenement opposite where he stood. Dark was falling, he could see glass windows painted yellow by the setting sun.

The candy store owner said, "*Gay schoin!* Go already! Go!"

"I'm going, I'm going," Danny said.

As he raced across the street, entered the dark hallway of the tenement and bounded up its worn steps he was thinking of his friend Izzy, who had told Danny that he had been the messenger for two separate telephone calls for Frieda.

"A guy?" Danny had asked attempting to sound casual.

"A guy," Izzy had said. "I was inside the candy store when he called and I answered the telephone. He had a deep voice, like this," Izzy had forced his voice to its lowest pitch and had croaked out, "Call Frieda. Apartment 3D." Izzy's voice cracked and he had stopped.

Another guy? Danny thought sadly. Older, maybe. Maybe. No, Danny couldn't let it happen, he would ask Frieda out for a date, now, tonight. It wasn't fair.

And Izzy had said, "—the crazy things you see when you go upstairs to tell somebody there's a telephone call. Like that time with Mrs. Klein—". Danny was blotting out the words, still thinking, another guy, no, it can't be. Izzy had gone on, "—like sometimes a man comes to the door in his underwear, sticks his head out, like that. And Mrs. Klein, once I came up there to tell her about a telephone call, I was in her house while she was looking in her bag for the nickel to give to me. You know she's got a crazy thing hanging on her wall, crazy. A big cardboard target on one of her walls, you know a big bull's eye. Clean, no marks on it, like those things you throw at it, you know—"

"Darts," Danny had said almost unconsciously.

Over the years he had gone from reading Edgar Rice Burroughs' Tarzan series as well as his science fiction books. Having finished those, Danny had gone to mysteries, to Sherlock Holmes, Philo Vance, Charlie Chan, a host of others, all he could find in the public library. When he had graduated to more serious fiction, he had read about the game of darts being played in English pubs.

"Yeah, darts," Izzy had said. "But you sure see and hear crazy things, don't you?"

And Danny had thought, A boyfriend calling Frieda? No. What would she be doing with a boyfriend? Danny had never seen her with one, nobody in the neighborhood had even mentioned there was one. Danny desperately did not want to think about that, as he groped about for another answer.

Waiting expectantly for the reply Danny had asked Izzy, "Was it somebody from her family maybe?"

"How should I know?" Izzy had replied. And Danny had asked whether Izzy had overheard any of Frieda's conversation when she had been in the telephone booth and Izzy had replied, incredulously, "I don't listen in to girls when they talk. What for? When they talk to their girlfriends, to hear about dresses and shoes, things to wear, things like that? Or when they're talking to their boyfriends, listen to that mush? You think I'm crazy, or what?"

Well, maybe it had been from someone from the family, someone, an aunt or maybe an uncle or Frieda's *zaydeh*, grandfather, maybe was sick. Yes, maybe that was it.

He found himself in front of the door to the flat marked 3D. Puffing with exertion, he had raced up the staircase, why he didn't know but he had and now he stood outside in the hallway as his breathing began to return to normal.

He knocked on the door. "Who is it?" Frieda's voice called out. "Me. Danny." The door opened. There she was. He couldn't take his eyes off her. He found himself saying, "There's a telephone call for you down at the candy store." Her face brightened with a smile.

She said, "Thanks. Wait, wait a minute." She turned, went into the kitchen, returned with a coin in her hand, said, "Here, thanks."

Danny stared down at the nickel in his palm. He didn't want her money. No, what he wanted was to be with her. Not this. Not to be treated like Izzy, or the others, those who had been merely messengers, instruments to inform her that there was a call for her. They didn't care for her like he, Danny, did. Nobody could care for her like he did.

As she went to shut the door of the flat he moved away and accidentally brushed up against her. He wanted desperately to touch her hand, to hold it, to tell her, No, don't go. And if it was a boyfriend he would say to her, I'm here, you don't need anybody else.

She was running down the stairs, the heels of her shoes making sharp staccato sounds, he raced after her. Down into the street, across to the candy store, to the telephone booth where the ear piece hung dangling from its heavy wire.

She shut the door of the booth, picked up the hanging piece and began to talk into the mouthpiece. Danny loitered in the candy store attempting to listen, but all there was for him was the heavy glass of the folded door of the booth muting and muffling her words, her words that he could not understand.

Something seemed to have gone out of him. He tried to reassure himself, No, it wasn't a boyfriend, it couldn't be, she had no boyfriend. But there were those doubts, they would not leave him, he was besieged by them.

Finally she was done. At last, Danny sighed to himself. She opened the booth door, was out into the store. Danny followed her into the street, across to the stoop of her tenement house where she stopped when he called out her name.

"Yes?" she asked. He mumbled something, her name. He found himself feeling childish, acting childish, the words that had sounded so good in his mind had vanished. Other, disconnected words came from his mouth. What was the matter with him? She was looking at him, a small smile on her face. She said, in an understanding tone of voice, "It's okay. I've got a few minutes to spare."

He had been staring at her, at her face, her figure. She was a nice girl, he would treat her tenderly. Suddenly embarrassed, Danny looked away from her face.

Stumbling over the words he said, "I don't want your nickel. Here." He put out his hand, the metal of the coin was damp with sweat from his tight hold.

"No," she said shaking her head. "It's yours. You earned it." No, no, no, he was saying and she said, "Yes. I want you to have it."

He stared down at the coin in his hand, and as his gaze returned to her, he said, "Will you—Will you go out with me? I mean, about a date."

She began to laugh softly. "I can't," she said. "I don't have the time." The sound of her laughter made him feel as if she had struck him.

His face reddened with embarrassment, he wished it hadn't, but he couldn't control himself. He said, "Okay, okay. If that's the way you want it."

She quickly said, "I'm not laughing at you, Danny. Honest."

He felt better. He felt the hot flush ebb from his cheeks. "Then go out with me," he said.

"I can't. I've got things to do." She gazed at him for a moment, and with a rush of breath said, "Danny, you know, I'll be getting busy with Party work—"

Party work? he thought. What party? Whose party? And it suddenly came to him as he said incredulously, "The Communist Party?"

She was nodding vigorously. "The Party. Yes, someone just called me and said I've been accepted. You know how it is on the phone, you can't say a lot, he just said I was in." She was laughing softly as she came closer to him. "What do you believe in? Do you believe in the Party?" she asked.

He didn't know what to say. Over and over again he had heard the words, bourgeoisie, petit bourgeoisie, capitalists, the masses, workers, the proletariat, fellow workers. He had heard the phrase, Religion is the opium of the people.

He had heard all those words and more, the arguments, the words flung in heat from family member to family member, the party-line words from his Uncle Moe and his wife, the rebuttal, if it could be called that, mainly by his Uncle Sol whom everybody in the family called the rich Uncle Sol, but who could not compete with Moe in argument, not that Uncle Moe's words had any validity with Danny, they hadn't. But Uncle Sol was incapable of original thought, he didn't read, what he did was bury himself in his business. That was his life. And all Uncle Moe did was parrot words that had been supplied by the radical newspaper, the Daily Worker.

He remembered the family gatherings at Zaydeh's house held every few months which the four sons and three daughters, all married, had attended, the, grandchildren running pell mell through the railroad flat, the rooms of which ran in a straight line from the front to the back of the building. The entire place smelled of that delicious aroma of stewing meat simmering with carrots and onions. Danny's seven aunts and uncles had brought food along with them, cakes, apple strudel, bread, rolls, a carton of tea, fruit. The women had brought chopped liver, *latkes*, pancakes, a sweet carrot dish, *tzimmes.* There, before they ate, each uncle had approached Zaydeh, and had pressed money into Zaydeh's gnarled hand.

The rich Uncle Sol and his family always arrived last. They entered the flat, Uncle Sol kissed Bubbeh, his mother, and as he said hello to Zaydeh, Uncle Sol palmed folded money bills to his father.

The women began to bring the food to the table in the dining room where the adults were to eat. The children ate in the kitchen, their noise spilled out to the rest of the flat. A child began to cry and its mother hastened to its side. Those at the table, the first adult shift, ate quickly, not many words were exchanged in the hurry to make room for the second shift.

At the table Uncle Sol said to Uncle Moe, "Well, *vee gates,* how's it going?"

Uncle Moe said, "How can it go in this stinking country? You tell me."

"A-agh!" Uncle Sol said. "Again with the Communist talk?"

"What do you mean, you capitalist, you! You got a business, the *schmateh* trade, you and your rags, you're bleeding the workers white while you sit back with your fat cigar—"

"What cigar? What bleeding the workers, what sitting back, I work eighteen, twenty hours a day. What're you talking about?"

"And how do you live and how do your workers live, hah?" Uncle Moe said.

My Aunt Ruth said, "Will you both shut up? The same old story, like a victrola." She had graduated high school before the Crash, had taken piano lessons. She had read the best of literature, Shakespeare, Dostoievsky, Dickens, Tolstoi.

"Ruthie," Uncle Sol said, "*farmacht der pisk,* shut your mouth. I'm talking."

And she said, "All noise, sound, that's what it is. Just both of you be quiet. Let's have a nice gathering today. For once."

Uncle Moe said to her, "You. You abandoned the class struggle, how can you live with that?"

"Oh, come on," she replied. "You, Moe, you parrot the Worker. Blah-blah-blah-blah. It says stand on your head, you stand on your head. It says black is white, then for you black is white. When are you going to think for yourself?"

Uncle Sol jumped in with, "Yeah. That's what I say. Think for yourself."

"You," Aunt Ruth said to him. "That's what I say to you too, when will you think for yourself?"

"Listen, Ruthie," Uncle Sol said angrily to her. "I don't like the way you talk to me. You understand?"

"So you don't like it," Aunt Ruth replied. "What do you know, Sol, except the *schmateh* trade? How to cut dresses? Do you read anything but the comics in the newspaper, I don't mean the Worker. Do you read a book, any kind beside your checkbook? Do you talk about anything but your business?"

"Ah!" Uncle Moe said. "You're right about that last thing. A pearl of wisdom, that's it."

"Enough!" Zaydeh finally shouted out. "No more! It's enough!" He shook his head and said, "Eat up, keep quiet! Then you'll play your poykair," referring to the penny poker game they usually played after the meal.

As the old scenes momentarily flashed through his mind and had gone, Danny looked up at Frieda. Remembering her last question, he said, "What do I believe? I believe in the individual. I believe in me and in you. I believe—" Frieda began to shake her head in disbelief. "Why?" he asked. "Why can't I believe in that?"

"Because it's false, it's a lie," she answered. "It's something the capitalists want you to believe. Individuals can do nothing. The proletariat," Ah! That word! Danny said to himself as he shut his eyes as if that could eliminate sound of it, and she was saying, "move things, the individual does nothing. Look around you," she said. "Do you like this?" she asked pointing to tenements. "Do you? Me, I detest it, I hate it! I'm getting out. Don't you want to get out of this ghetto, this hell hole? This place where they've caged us?"

Danny stared up at the tenement buildings, their tops mantled in black by the falling night. A few early stars shone and shimmered up there in the sky, a sliver of a moon, a slice of yellow slowly sailing in a dark blue sea. He hated those buildings, how he hated them! They stood there like rotting teeth biting into the sky, he wished the Navy would bring their destroyers into the East River, empty the buildings of all their inhabitants, empty the Lower East Side, not one person remaining, and shell and demolish those buildings, all of them.

"I hate this goddammed place," he said to her.

"Then do something about it," she said. "Join with us, make the capitalists afraid of us, make the revolution happen."

"The revolution?" he said in amazement. "What revolution?"

"The proletarian revolution. Like it happened in Russia and the Soviet Union came about. It'll happen here, I can tell you that," she said.

He stared at her, uncomprehending. Was this the Frieda, the girl that had so occupied his mind?

"There'll be no revolution, no," he said shaking his head.

"No?" she asked. "Look around. No jobs, no food, no clothes, evictions, the capitalists getting richer and fatter, the proletariat getting nothing, less than nothing. Do you know something?" she asked somewhat belligerently.

He said nothing, what could he say to her now? And she said, "Do you know Mrs. Klein?" she pointed to a nearby tenement building, "up there, in 4D?"

"Yeah," he said wearily. "The widow. She's got a daughter."

"Right," she said. "You know what she does, Mrs. Klein?" Without waiting for his reply she said, "She practices. With a gun."

"A gun?" he whispered slowly as if he couldn't believe the words. "A gun? Mrs. Klein with a gun?"

"Yes," she said. "Not a real gun but the kind with a spring in it, a toy gun, you push the wooden shaft into it, the end of the shaft that hits the target, that's got a suction cap on it so when it hits it sticks to the target that she's got tacked on the wall. She's preparing for when the revolution comes."

It was too much for him, it was senseless, impossible, something even a child would have difficulty in believing. Confused, angered, he said, "There'll be no revolution, you'll see. And Mrs. Klein, she's out of her mind. You believe in that crazy practice? You really believe in it? What are you thinking about? Does it make any sense? Mrs. Klein wouldn't know what to do if you got your revolution, you wouldn't know what to do. What would you do? Would you kill?"

"Me?" she said. "Sure. You bet I would."

Danny couldn't believe it. This wasn't Frieda at all, this was somebody else, a crazy imposter gone mad posing as Frieda. He shut his eyes, he wished he could shut his ears, those words were insane. She would kill? And for what? For what?

He said, "Your mother, your father, your aunt or uncle? Whoever? You would kill them?"

"If I had to, if they stood in the way. Yes, to move the revolution forward. To get a better life for the proletariat."

He laughed harshly. "You'd kill," he said angrily. "You'd kill people to give people a good life? Holy God!" he exploded. "What're you saying? Do you hear what you're saying? Toy pistols? Killing to live?"

She tensed in great anger now. Somebody, a tenant, went by them, said a passing hello to Frieda. Frieda looked up to the windows of the Klein apartment. Someone was at the window, it was the Klein daughter who called out to Frieda, "Well? Is it yes?"

"Yes!" Frieda shouted up to her.

"Come on up," the daughter called out.

"Okay. In a minute," Frieda said to her. And to Danny, in a tone of derision, "So tell me what big thing you're doing to make the world better."

"I'm going to be a doctor," he said.

He didn't know how he would do it, how his family would manage it. Where would the money come from? But somehow it would happen, he hoped. They would do piecework, all the family, they would work at home. His mother and father would work when she had finished with her housework, his father when he came home from work at his shop, if there was work. They would work at making leather belts, braiding loops of leather one into another, pulling at the leather, the brown or black colors staining their fingers, the stress of the constant pulling causing their fingers to ache. During the summer he would be a waiter in a resort.

"You've got the money to do it?" Frieda asked derisively.

"We'll get it. I'll go to City College," he said. "Then to medical school. I'll better my world, I'll better my family's world, I'll better other people's worlds, that's how I'll do it. You can't better a world by killing, you better it by healing."

He had seen Paul Muni in a movie about the life of Louis Pasteur. It had moved Danny tremendously, Pasteur working against all odds to benefit mankind. You did it by ridding the world of disease, of hunger, of pestilence. And little by little you raised up the world.

"You can't better the world by making the capitalists fatter," Frieda said.

He shrugged at the stranger in front of him. The Frieda he had conjured up in his mind was gone, had never been. This was someone he didn't know at all. Because he was angry with himself and with her he said caustically, "And what will you be doing to better the world? You, personally?"

She smiled derisively at him as she said, "I'm asking to be assigned to selling the Worker at the entrance to the subway station. I'll help educate the masses, we'll be the vanguard. You'll see." And in a normal tone of voice, "Come join with us."

He shook his head, more to himself. It was all useless. How had it come to this? "You'll do what they tell you to do?" he said dully. She nodded. "You call that freedom? They decide, you don't have a say about it, and you do the donkey work? That's freedom?"

"When you have enough to eat, a nice place to live in, a steady job, when everybody can educate their children, that's freedom."

"You're dreaming," he said. "A pipe dream. It won't happen under a dictatorship."

"A-agh!" she said angrily. "Who can talk to you? I tell you something, Danny," she said, her eyes blazing. "I don't ever intend to go out with you. Never. It's you, people like you who stand in our way. What made you ever think I'd go out with you?"

He wanted to harm her then, his rage was boiling, there were ready words in his mind to wound her but with great effort he held himself in check. Instead he said, "I was wrong, yes, I was wrong. And you were wrong. It would've been a terrible mistake." But now his anger exploded and without realizing it he hurled the nickel still held in his hand to the ground and said, "Take your damned money! Who needs it?"

She moved away from her parents' house soon afterward, he heard that she went to live with a cousin in a cheap apartment outside of the East Side, in Chelsea somewhere. He didn't see her anymore. Once in a great while he momentarily thought of her, but now he was too busy with his school work at City College.

Months later, after he had finished with his classes for the day at the college, when he was exiting from the subway, he saw her, she was hawking the Daily Worker, chanting to everybody nearby, "Learn the truth. Read it in the Worker. Don't be fooled by the capitalist press! Work for your interests, not the capitalists!"

She stopped a young man and began speaking earnestly to him. He was drawn to her by her looks and her figure, he appeared to be listening, he was staring intently at her face. He nodded automatically now and then, seemed to be in agreement with her.

Danny stopped, stared at her, she now lived in a world that was alien to him, somewhere else light years away. And before, in his dream world, how he had wanted to be with her, to protect her from the world she had run to, from the jackals and the sharks, the predators, the liars, the users of people.

But it had all come to nothing. He would no longer dream longingly of her, that was finished, he knew it. She noticed Danny and approached, a smile on her face. "Danny," she said as if they had not had angry words that time long ago, months and months before. She glanced down at the books he carried in his hands. "City College, huh?" He nodded. "You're saving the world?"

There was the barb. She couldn't hold back, could she? With a smile on his face, he replied, "I'm saving the world the best way I know how. And you? You're saving the world with the Worker?"

"The truth will set you free," she said glancing over his shoulder to see whether a likely prospect had come into view.

"That's Biblical," Danny said. "That doesn't come from your gods Marx or Lenin or your comrades."

"Why don't you find out?" she asked. "Buy a Worker."

"I've got enough truths," he replied. "Truth up to here." He placed the side of his hand up to his throat. "I don't need any more."

Frieda saw a woman emerge from the subway exit. Abruptly, Frieda left Danny, ran over to the woman, was talking to her, moving along with her, cajoling her, waving The Daily Worker in front of the woman.

Shaking his head sadly, Danny turned and walked away. It didn't matter anymore.

MRS. 3B

She stood alone, silent, on the stoop of the wide tenement building, gazing out over the heads of the women who were her neighbors, looking for someone. It was a sunny afternoon, the other women had already cleaned their flats, had planned their evening meals, now all of them were seated on folding chairs in front of the tenement, all clustered near their baby carriages, some still rocking their babies to sleep, others talking to each other in muted voices, their other young children scampering on the sidewalk near their mothers. All except the lonely woman, Mrs. 3B. Everybody called her by that designation since that was the number of her flat.

They were on a street at right angles to the main thoroughfare, Delancey Street, where the Williamsburgh Bridge rose in a steady climb of massive horizontal riveted steel, spun metal cables, all rising higher and higher, spanning the East River a distance away, joining the Lower East Side with the area in Brooklyn known as Williamsburgh.

"A *koorveh*, a prostitute, that one," one of the women whispered to her seated neighbor, thrusting her head in the direction of the lone woman.

"Yeh, yeh," the other woman said as she rocked her carriage in slow tempo, saying, sh! sh! mechanically to her stirring infant. And to the other woman she said, "And, my God, a Jew yet!"

"They shouldn't allow such people here, a *nafkeh*, a whore," another neighbor, Mrs. Levine said. "She has no shame, nothing. And her husband . . ." she shut her eyes as her voice rose with each of her last words.

"A pimp," another woman, Mrs. Rafsky, said. "A *koorveh* with a pimp yet, a husband and a wife yet, and they let them live in this building? The landlord, he should throw them out in the street, it's a shame for the children, what do they think when they see those two doing those things? It's a shame for all the neighbors, we shouldn't allow it, a shame for our husbands, they look at the *koorveh*, what do they think?"

"A shame, a shame," Mrs. Levine said. "We should all talk to the landlord, he should do something."

"Nah, it won't help," another woman, Mrs. Berkowitz said. "My husband, he talked to the landlord already, and the landlord acts like he's deaf. All he wants is his rent money, he don't care what his tenants do."

The tenants, especially those who lived on the same floor as the *koorveh*, as well as the floors above and below it, all of them heard her cries from her flat when her husband beat her because she hadn't earned enough money.

"The pimp, he should get hit by a truck," Mrs. Rafsky said. "To live with such an animal, *ai-yai-yai*." Her head rocked from side to side.

"She married him, didn't she?" Mrs. Berkowitz said. "Why did she do it?"

"Yeh, yeh," Mrs. Levine said. "But she could get a *gett*, a divorce, no? The rabbi would give her a *gett*, one, two, three. She's a Jewish woman, she shouldn't be doing what she's doing."

"A divorce, it's a *shandeh*, a shame," one of the other women who had been listening said. "Who gets divorced?"

"*Shandeh, schmandeh*," Mrs. Rafsky said. "It's a shame but it's better than living with that animal husband."

There was a silence. Finally Mrs. Levine said, "And we have to live together with that *koorveh*? That's the shame."

The lone woman stared out over the other women. She saw her husband turn the corner from Delancey Street, another man walked beside him. As they approached the tenement, Mrs. 3B sighed to herself, turned, entered the tenement building and began to trudge upstairs to her apartment.

"A-ha! She's going," Mrs. Levine said. She looked up into the street, saw the *koorveh's* husband, and the other man, and with a violent shake of her head said, "A-ha! Here he comes, the no-good husband, the pimp. And with a customer yet."

The other women turned their heads to stare at the approaching men. The husband disregarded the women, the other man, in embarrassment, attempted to look above their stares. The two men passed the group of women, entered the building. One of the woman spit loudly after them.

"He should drop dead, he should break a leg," Mrs. Rafsky said vehemently. Her infant began to cry, she bent over the carriage, closer to the child and said in a soft and caring tone, "*Shah, mein kind, shah*, don't cry, my child."

The women stared into the dark empty hallway of the tenement. In a short while the husband emerged from the building, alone, walked past them, his pace undiminished. The women stared at his receding figure, he finally disappeared as he turned the corner into Delancey Street.

The women stirred, shook their heads sadly, turned their attention once more to their children. A small boy of four ran up to his mother, and hopping back and forth on his legs said, "I got to pee. Quick." Some of the women lived three, four, five flights up in the tenements, and since there was no time to leave their babies and accompany their boys upstairs to the toilet, it had become usual for a woman to take her small son to the edge of the sidewalk where she quickly unbuttoned the fly of his pants.

He began to shoot a stream into the street. Immediately other young boys joined him and all lined up on the edge of the sidewalk, they stood in concert, their streams arc-ing high and out. It had become a contest to see whose stream went out the farthest, and now little girls, their heads at an angle stopped to stare at the boys' fleshy protuberances. Finished, one of the boys whose stream had gone out the farthest into the street shouted out gleefully as he returned to his mother to have his fly buttoned, "I won! I won!"

"Yeh, yeh," his mother said, her fingers worked at the buttons, closed the fly. The other women whose sons had joined in the competition did the same. The little girls resumed their play, the boys returned to their shouting and running, all was normal once more.

One of the women in the group asked, "So what are you making for sopper?"

"Tomato herring," Mrs. Berkowitz said.

Earlier in the day at the neighborhood grocery store, she had bought a ten cent flat oval can of Del Monte sardines in tomato sauce, a staple food among all of the women. She would serve the fish with vinegar poured over them along with slices of raw onion and fresh rye bread. The family liked it, along with the fish there would be a dish of boiled potatoes and sour cream, followed by tea. It served her family of four. Anyway it was filling, it was cheap, this was the Depression and pennies counted.

"And you?" someone asked Mrs. Levine.

Mrs. Levine managed a smile and said, "A little meat, *gedempt*, potted meat, you know my Harry likes meat for his sopper." Her husband was a blacksmith, his shop was on Division Street, there were still a sizeable number of horse-drawn wagons in use although their number was dwindling. Dwindling too was the number of blacksmiths on the Lower East Side, gasoline-powered vehicles were taking over. Now there remained two blacksmiths in the area. Harry was a *shtarker*, a strong one, banging his heavy hammer on the white-heated metal, beating his strong metallic tattoo on his anvil.

"Ah-h-h!" Mrs. Berkowitz said with a slight touch of envy in her voice as she shook her carriage. "Everybody should be able to afforda it."

"*Ach!* What are you talking about?" Mrs. Levine said. "You think we're millionaires? Harry makes just a living. The horses, they're less and less. See. Look in the streets. How many horses do you see now? Cars and trucks you see, yes? We make a living, that's all."

Before any of the women could say anything the man who had gone up to the *koorveh* emerged from the building. He moved quickly, averting the women's stares as he went past them, their eyes following him, their heads shaking in disapproval. He turned the corner and was gone.

"*Ai, de nafkeh*," Mrs. Rafsky said. "She'll come down now and look for another one."

"Such a life, such a life," Mrs. Levine said sadly.

"Only for my enemies," Mrs. Rafsky said with a heavy sigh.

The other children were playing on the sidewalk, their voices high and shrill filled the air. A horse dragging a wagon filled with red ripe tomatoes went clopping down the street. The wagon came to a slow stop near the women. Its driver, a middle-aged man wearing a cap shouted out, "To-may-toes! Two cents a pound! The best to-may-toes! Two cents!"

Mrs. Rafsky left her carriage, went up to the man and ordered two pounds. As the man weighed the tomatoes on his hanging scale, she fished carefully into her small clasp purse and removed four pennies. Other women approached the wagon and made their small purchases. The horse stood still, only its tail whisking and flicking against the flies on its rump.

Now it was time. As if on a signal, the women began to prepare to leave, calling to their children, gathering them, while the children asked for another few minutes of play, Just one more minute, ma, and finally, one by one, all except Mrs. 3B, they trooped into the tenement building leaving their carriages garaged under the staircase. Going up the stairs, the chattering children tagging after them, the hallway filled with smells of food, they said goodbyes to each other and entered their flats.

Upstairs, Mrs. Levine tended to the meat on her stove and set the kitchen table. Her husband would be home soon and although business had slowed up somewhat he still worked hard, shoeing those horses was not an easy job and when he came home, after his hello to her, he would wash up and remove that stable smell from himself. He would sit down and read the Jewish newspaper, the "Forward," while she finished up with her cooking chores.

Now at the table, as they ate, Mrs. Levine said to him, "Harry, it's that woman, that *nafkeh* . . ."

He looked up from his plate and said, "Again? That *koorveh*? What is it now?"

"*Koorveh, schmoorveh*," Mrs. Levine said. "What about her husband, the pimp? He goes out looking for men, for customers for her. What should she do? She's afraid of him. He beats her."

Mr. Levine said, "She should leave him."

"Who leaves a husband?" Mrs. Levine asked. "What kind of a thing is that to do?"

"It's better than doing what she's doing, isn't it?" Mr. Levine said. He tapped his forefinger on the porcelain top of the kitchen table, a small drumming sound. "Would you do it, hah?"

"No, Harry. How can you say that to me?" She glared angrily at her husband who put up his hands defensively in front of his face. "Would you be a pimp for your wife, God forbid?"

"No," he replied.

"Well, there," Mrs. Levine said. "I wouldn't do what that women does, never. And you wouldn't do what her pimp husband does." They settled into silence, eating slowly and finally she said, "Maybe they don't have the money. Maybe she has to do it, maybe—"

"Maybe, maybe, maybe," her husband said as he took a sip of hot tea from the glass he held gently between his fingers. "The Rafskys, do they have money, hah? They took in a roomer so they could make the rent, yes? Who's got money? But those women aren't *koorvehs*. One way or another, they live, they eat, they don't do what she does."

"That woman," Mrs. Levine said as she arose from the table and began to clear the dishes. "She's living a terrible life, just terrible. I wouldn't wish it on a dog."

Mr. Levine shrugged. Those two, they did what they did, nothing he could do could change it, she would still be a *koorveh*, her husband would still be a pimp.

Mr. Levine would worry about things if he could do something about it, but there was nothing he could do for those two. Anyway, he had enough worries of his own, he had just heard that one of his big customers, a bread company, would be mechanizing its store deliveries, converting from horse and wagon to trucks. He wouldn't tell his wife about it, no need to worry her, this wouldn't be fatal to his blacksmith shop, but it would hurt. Anyway, both of them would live, they wouldn't starve, they would remain in this flat, things would somehow go on. *Ach!* What a world! What a world!

Pretending, he smiled up at his wife as she busied herself washing the dishes at the sink, her hands mechanically going through the cleaning motions. As she wiped each plate she was thinking, A terrible thing, that pimp, he forces her, his wife yet. What kind of animal is he? It was forbidden, a terrible sin. And yet the wife, why didn't she do something? Why didn't she say, no, I won't, I won't be a *koorveh*. Why didn't she go to the district attorney and tell them her husband was beating her? And yet... and yet... The man didn't have a job, everybody knew jobs were impossible to get, who could get a job in this terrible Depression? They had to do something to live, didn't they? But not that. Never. God forbid, any woman should have to do it.

Finished at the sink, Mrs. Levine dried her hands on the damp dish towel, removed her apron and picked up an article of clothing she was mending. She sat down on a chair in the kitchen. Her husband across the table went through the newspaper, grunting in approval at something he had just read.

"Harry," she said, her arm thrusting out as needle in hand she pulled the long thread taut. "How is the business? All right?"

"Yeh. Sure," he replied without looking up.

"Thank God," she said. "I thank God every day we got something."

Mr. Levine said nothing. Soon he arose and went towards the bedroom. His wife followed him and they went to bed. They slept, occasionally there was a far noise from the bridge, the muted clatter of a vehicle, a cry from an awakening infant, the cries subsiding gradually. Silence came, the building slept.

Suddenly she heard it, the high sharp scream, like nothing she had heard before. Mrs. Levine awoke to its piercing noise, she now heard the woman cry out so sharply, so terribly. Oh, my God, he's killing her, that poor woman! Mrs. 3B! she thought.

She nudged her husband awake shouting, "Wake up, Harry! Quick! Quick!"

Her husband, rubbed his eyes, became awake. "What is it?" he asked.

"He's killing her, don't you hear?"

Mrs. Levine jumped out of bed, grabbed her bathrobe, shoved her feet into her shoes. Now her husband was up, jamming his legs into his pants. They ran out of their flat, out into the hallway, rushing to where the screams, louder and louder, were emanating.

The woman was howling, once more, again, the sounds tearing out of that woman's throat. A small crowd had gathered in front of the woman's flat, with Mrs. Levine in front, her husband behind her. Mrs. Levine had only one thought, A Jewish woman, he's killing her! The screams tore out louder from behind the door.

"Call the police!" Someone was shouting.

The screams continued, there were thuds behind the closed door. Gathered before the flat they heard the thuds, the battering, the awful cries. "No! Don't! Please! No, no, no!"

Mrs. Levine banged on the door. "Open up!" she shouted hoarsely. The screaming and noises from the apartment continued. "Open up!" She turned to her husband and screamed, *"Gutt in himmel,* God in heaven! Do something, Harry! You can't let him kill her!"

"Open up!" he began to shout. He banged on the door, it shook, trembled under his fists, a drum-like noise booming out. There was a sudden silence, the noise inside the apartment stopped. They could hear the woman inside whimpering terribly, animal noises. "Open up!" Mr. Levine ordered.

"Go away!" the husband shouted through the door.

"Open this door or I'll open it for you!" Mr. Levine roared out as he banged furiously on its wooden panels. "I'm coming in, you hear? You better open up!"

The door shook under his hammering, a wood panel began to groan, a small split appeared in the wood. The banging continued,

Mr. Levine was shouting, his face red, a chorus of voices swelled up from the people behind him. Finally the door opened, there was the woman, blood streaming from her nose, a blotch from a hard slap across one cheek, she stood sobbing uncontrollably before them. Behind her, in the apartment, chairs were scattered, broken glass and china lay strewn on the floor. Her husband stood with clenched fists at his side glaring wildly at the crowd.

Mr. Levine entered, followed by two other men. As they approached the woman's husband, Mrs. Levine and some of the other women entered the flat and crowded around the beaten woman.

Mr. Levine, in a controlled dangerous voice was saying to the man in the apartment, "Who do you think you are, hah? You wake up the whole place, you think—"

"Who do you think you are! Get out of my house!" the man hissed.

"You—you—" Mr. Levine said menacingly as he came closer to the man. "You open up your mouth once more and I'll show you who I am. They'll carry you out of this house, you hear me?"

A heavy silence fell. Behind them Mrs. Levine was saying to the battered woman, "You got a towel?" The woman nodded dumbly. Mrs. Levine said to one of her neighbors, "Go get a towel from the kitchen, we got to wipe away the blood. Go quick!" The woman scurried into the kitchen, found a towel near the sink, grabbed it, ran water into it, wrung it out and hurried back to the battered woman. Gently she dabbed at the blood on the woman's face while Mrs. Levine, her voice uncontrollable now, screamed out to the man, "*Merderer!* Murderer! Animal!" Turning to the woman she said, "Is this what he does, this? Unbelievable! You can't stay with him." The woman, sobbing, shook her head in silence, moaned lightly. Mrs. Levine said, "Oh, my God! Will you look at that!"

A neighbor was saying to the woman, "*Shah, shah,* don't worry. We won't let him do it to you." Gently, gently, she cleaned up the woman's face. "Come," she said. "Don't go back in there."

The woman's eyes widened. "What? What?" she mumbled between groans.

"You can't go back there. You can't live this way. He'll kill you. What kind of a life is this for a Jewish woman?" Mrs. Levine said.

The woman was shook her head dumbly. A neighbor leaned towards Mrs. Levine, whispered, "Where can she go?"

Mrs. Levine, her arm around the woman's shoulder, said, "So she'll come to my house, she'll sleep there. I'll make room."

Mr. Levine was saying to the man, "You're lucky, this time." The man was about to say something, he glanced fearfully at Mr. Levine's physique, said nothing. Mr. Levine shouted "You listen, you! Next time," he said slowly and deliberately, "I'll come in and I'll break your arms and your legs, you hear?" The man, his fists clenched tightly at his sides, stared at Mr. Levine who said, "I'll come in and I'll put you in the hospital." Shaking his fist in front of the man's face, Mr. Levine said in a menacing whisper, "Don't fool with me, mister, you understand? I'll teach you to be a *mensch*, a human being."

THE DAY AT CONEY ISLAND

Squeezed, compressed on all sides by the other standing human beings in the BMT subway car, its seats all grabbed long before, the warm sour smell of sweating flesh all around him, Danny managed to turn his head and said to Goldie standing beside him, "It's goddammed hot. When is this ride going to end?"

On that steaming summer Sunday morning they were on the Sea Beach line to Coney Island, desperately seeking relief from the oppressive heat wave that had enveloped the city for over three days. With temperatures near a hundred degrees during the days, along with humidity near record heights, the nights not cooling down, Danny and his younger brother had attempted to sleep on the tarred roof of the tenement they lived in on the Lower East Side of New York. But it had been impossible, the oppressive heat had been inescapable. The remainder of his family had attempted to sleep on the metal fire escape that jutted out of the aged building, whose entry was a window from their flat.

They called the roof of the tenement Tar Beach, the young people came there to sunbathe during the bright sunlit days of late spring and summer. Under the heat, the tar turned to a semi-liquid glue which spread and squished under their shoes as they walked to find an empty space. During those broiling nights, the roof had been crowded with tossing and turning tenement tenants all trying desperately to pull sleep to them.

Below, all the fire escapes of the building had been filled with people, some staring up at the sky, others moving, all seeking to find a comfortable spot in which to relax, a spot that eluded them.

On the street below, on and near the stoop of the building, in the darkness of the heavy night lit only by the street lamps, people sat dumbly on folding chairs, some had nodded off, some snored, some spoke softly to one another, some sat staring out at the blackness.

The scorching heat had come over the city, a hot heavy felt denseness which had flowed in and around everything. It had seemed that the heat would never go away. Outdoor metal burned to the touch, the sidewalks were frying pans, people sweated in steady streams.

Saturday night, when they usually met on the street corner near the candy store, Danny and Goldie and Max had agreed to go to Coney Island. They would meet early Sunday morning, go to the BMT subway station on Essex and Delancey Streets, take the subway, change for the Sea Beach express train whose last stop was Coney Island.

Danny would have liked to take the special bus that stood on Delancey Street, but the bus ride cost twenty-five cents, it was more than they could afford, while the subway cost a nickel. The bus would have been delightful, Danny thought, it was a special vehicle with no sides, only rows of benches, a floor and a roof for the riders, the roof held up by intermittent vertical narrow beams. The front of the vehicle contained the usual cab for the driver. Danny had also thought of taking the trolley from the Brooklyn end of the Williamsburgh Bride. The special summer trolley too had no sides, but the trolley took forever, it turned and curved all through Brooklyn, it made innumerable stops, it was too hot, Danny had no time to spend on that trolley, he wanted the cool ocean, the sooner the better.

Now jammed in tight in the subway, human flesh pressed to human flesh, Goldie stood nearby gazing out unseeingly across the car, his eyes glazed. Max, the smallest of the three of them, was lost somewhere in the mass of jammed humans in that car. At each stop, in some inexplicable fashion, more passengers were being added to the train, shoved in by subway employees who were called pushers.

Danny held on tightly to his rubberized canvas bag which contained his underwear, a brown paper bag which held his lunch of two hardboiled egg sandwiches and an apple, a towel, a thin blanket with a jagged rip at one of its ends. He was wearing his bathing suit under his clothing. The blanket would serve to stake out his territory once they were on the beach. Later, after he had spent the day swimming, he would get dressed under it..

The train swerved, its wheels screeched, filled the underground with its howl that knifed the eardrums. The massed crowd, as one, swayed into the turn, corrected itself when the train came out of the curve. The underground darkness suddenly became bright sunlight, the train was outdoors now, roaring and clattering along the rails. The car in which Danny stood was still hot but now seemed different, it still smelled of heat and sweat but somehow seemed fresher. The clack of the train over its railroad ties beneath beat a rhythm into Danny's brain. And he waited, waited, yet wanted it all to be over, for it to be the end of the line, Stillwell Avenue.

At last it was. They poured out of the cars of the train, a flood of humans, all of them running except for the aged. The parents of small children, some carrying babies, moved faster, rushed for the exit and rushed for the street.

Out in the street now, lit brilliantly by the merciless sun, they heard the roar of the ocean's surf, loud then soft, repeating itself endlessly. The throng began to slow somewhat, Coney Island was under their feet. The beach lay not too far away, just a few blocks and they would finish their long trek.

Max called out from somewhere, "Hey, fellers, wait for me!" Goldie raised his hand so that Max could see them in the crowd. Danny and Goldie stopped, a flood of humans streamed around them. Now Max was there with them, and they walked on.

They were walking up Surf Avenue, past the booths selling ice cream, frozen custard, hot dogs, sodas, knishes, waffles, others selling spun sugar candy. The sidewalks were jammed with stationary people lifting uncapped soda bottles to their lips.

There were some restaurants for these for those who were still affluent in this Depression, but Danny knew nobody who could afford to eat there. There were several stores that sold items for the beach, articles for swimming, thin rubber bathing shoes, bathing caps in many colors, water wings purchased by non-swimmers or by parents for their very young children, which were blown up by mouth then tied to the non-swimmer, the filled off-white bladders seemed like a pair of wings. There were stores which sold salt water taffy, the machines in their windows were bright metal spindles mixing and curling the wide strands of taffy into skeins.

Here and there were small side shows, with canvas banners depicting freaks, Siamese twins, a tremendously fat lady with her immense girth, a bearded lady, someone called a half-man half-woman, a dog-faced boy, dwarves, the misshapen usually hidden human parts of human life.

Danny and his two friends walked quickly past all of this, there were open-fronted places where barkers urged passersby into rides. One of them was shouting out, "Come on in, folks! Ride the autos!" Small metal ovoid cars all in different bright colors which seated two people, all heavily bumpered with wide deep rubber set above their wheels, a single antenna rod in each rear, which touched against the heavy grilled electrified ceiling which sizzled when the cars moved. From somewhere a roller coaster clacked metallic chatter as it roared down its steep incline.

Danny and his friends hurried on, there was The Whip, passengers screaming and laughing with delight and terror. Crowds filled the sidewalks spilling into the streets themselves. There was noise, shouting, confusion, the flow of the throng towards the beach. They passed Steeplechase Park with its multitude of rides. A calliope brayed out a tune, the melody blasted out into the streets. A race with carousel-like horses, their bellies set upon metal tracks roared by, their riders hunched and laughing.

"Let's hurry it up," Goldie said. "It's hot. Let's get to the beach."

Danny was sweating, his body clammy and steaming, his clothing glued to himself. The sweat rolled down his forehead, drops trickled into his eyes, the scene became blurry. The sun blazed fire. They turned into Twenty-third Street, up ahead several blocks away, at the intersection, was a portion of the wide boardwalk, the shaded beach beneath it.

Clutching his canvas bag tightly Danny began to hurry towards the beach, the other two beside him. Sweating heavily, they were under the boardwalk, they stopped for a brief moment to feel the coolness of its shadowed depths.

Cool, cool, cool, Danny had forgotten what cool was, now it felt so good. They were walking on sand now and in this dim space ceilinged by the bottom of the boardwalk some people sat escaping the heat.

They stopped to remove their outer clothing, carried their shoes and socks, as they went hurriedly on and entered the exploding sunlight of the beach. There was a mass of people so cramped together that no sand seemed visible.

The heat once again beat down upon them, frying them as they threaded their way down the sand. Young people, old people, teenagers, children, all had already staked out their beach claims for the day. Food was being eaten, children were crying, laughing, babies' diapers were being changed, young people were laughing, frolicking, others were singing. Beach purveyors were hurrying through the throng shouting out their wares, Popsicles, Eskimo Pies. The Eskimo Pie vendor carried his large round orange metal canister harnessed over his shoulder. When he made a sale and lifted the lid of the canister, white mist, the gas of dry ice, escaped in a small eruption into the air. The Popsicle vendor carried a rectangular insulated container which also contained dry ice. The soda vendor, bottles crammed in a large bucket filled with cracked ice now and then stopped to uncap a soda and sell it to a thirsty buyer.

The hot sand burned fire on the soles of Danny's feet. He pranced fast and high down the beach. People shoved, pushed, ran, collided with each other. Danny ran on, the soles of his feet more and more had become furnaces. He was at the water's edge, the roll of the surf had stained the sand a dark brown tint. Danny stood on the damp sand, cooling the soles of his feet as he scanned the beach.

"I can't find a place," Goldie said looking around at the mass of humanity. "I don't see an inch of sand around."

Out in the surf, near the edge of the beach, wide-bodied women bobbed up and down in the water, never dipping lower than their throats. Men, also flabby and fat, non-swimmers, splashed awkwardly in the water, their arms flailing, and all around were children, some wore water wings and pretended to swim.

Farther out, in the gleaming rolling waves, swimmers were stroking, some of them swimming seriously. On the beach, the lifeguard perched in his chair in a wooden tower, squinted into the sun, watched the swimmers far out, sometimes blowing his whistle and calling out to someone who had gone out too far, asking the swimmer to return.

Danny was saying, "There's no room now. Look, the tide's going out, there'll be more beach later."

"That's later," Goldie said. "But right now we need a place to put our stuff down."

"I'm looking," Danny said as he searched the beach. He shook his head and said, "What the hell, let's find somebody who'll hold our things for us." Nearby, surrounded by young teenage boys, was a group of five girls sitting on a blanket. Danny pointed them out to Goldie and said, "Let's go ask them to mind our stuff."

The three of them pushed their way towards the girls. As they approached, Goldie said to them, "Hi. How're you doing?"

The girls looked up, turned to look at each other. One of them said to Goldie, "We're doing fine," and laughed as she asked Goldie, "And how're you doing?"

"We're just fine," Danny said. "Do you mind if we just left our things here for a while we took a swim? We'll be back soon."

"We don't mind it at all," another girl said, "I was just thinking of going in for a dip myself." She turned to one of her friends and asked, "You're coming in, right?" Her friend nodded, the two girls began to rise.

Danny placed his bundle of clothing and his canvas bag on the edge of the girls' blanket. Max, Goldie and Danny joined the two girls, all of them ran towards the surf, their feet splashing in the water as they ran wading and slogging sending up gleaming splashes and beads of water.

Danny dived into a large roaring roller, the water closed around him, dark and salty, stinging his open eyes as he stroked in the greenness, dimly seeing the lower parts of bodies of those nearby. When Danny surfaced, he looked around. Goldie had just surfaced, Max now bobbed up, his mouth open, taking in great gulps of air. One of the girls rose up from the water, the other one, her friend, was stroking expertly towards them.

"Hey! You're good!" Max said to the girl who was the true swimmer.

"Why not?" she said with a laugh. "You think only you can swim?" She turned to her friend and said, "You're doing all right, Evelyn. Coming right along." Evelyn rose from the water and joined her friend.

"What's your name?" Danny asked the girl who was the swimmer. There was a momentary silence. The surf rolled in, curled, turned white at its crest, tumbled and fell in a roar, ebbed slowly back. Danny said, "Your friend's name is Evelyn. What's yours?"

"What's yours?" the girl asked.

"Danny. And these are my friends Goldie and Max. Now, come on, what's your name?"

"Clara," the girl said. The surf boomed, some swimmers, heads in water, collided with them, then went on. "Where do you live?" she asked.

"In a house," Max said laughing as he glanced at his two friends. "How about you?" The girl said nothing.

"Come on, let's swim," Danny said to break the silence. "Why don't we have some fun and enjoy ourselves? It's too hot to stand here and ask questions. We can do that afterwards."

He liked how the girls looked, they were so well-formed, thin, tanned but the memory of that terrible heat still lingered in his mind and more water, this water, could drive that memory away. That was more important than where a girl lived.

Clara was saying, "But you sure asked a question when you asked me what my name was, didn't you?"

"What'd you want him to do?" Goldie asked. "Say to you, hey, you? You wouldn't like that, would you?"

Danny didn't wait for a reply, he dove deep almost to the water's bottom, cool, other-worldly, the dim roar of its liquid movement sounded in his ears, the outside turbulence of the ocean above now gone. There was only quiet water with a slight swell, a dark green world. He stroked and stroked, gliding through the water, coming for air into the bright blinding sunlight.

Two more girls from the group had joined them. All of them, Danny, his friends, the girls, all seven of them swam, and Danny who swam well wanted to go farther out, out where the real swimmers were. He could see their arms moving fluidly and methodically, appearing and disappearing into the water. But the girls were all here, they were fun, they laughed, they told secret jokes to each other.

Now and then Danny would submerge, glide through the water, grab one of the girl's legs and as she laughed and screamed, lift her and spill her into the ocean. Max and Goldie had also been at it, now all of them, all seven played the game, the girls protesting loudly as they laughed and screamed, the boys pursuing their sneak attacks.

Clara was Danny's favorite victim. He didn't know why he was attracted to her, maybe because she swam so well, maybe because she was unafraid, maybe because she screamed so little and laughed so much when she was up-ended. And maybe because she looked so good in her bathing suit, so well-proportioned, maybe because he felt so good when swimming underwater, he tackled her. It was fun, he liked swimming with her, he liked the game they were playing.

They emerged from the ocean, the girls removed their colored rubber bathing caps. Clara, with her long hair down her back, looked even better to Danny. Goldie busied himself with Evelyn, Max selected one of the other girls. Danny and his friends sat down on the edge of the girls' blanket and one of the girls said it was time for lunch.

"You got your lunch, I hope," she said to Goldie. He nodded. "Good," she said. "What've you got? I got a baloney sandwich."

Goldie reached into his canvas bag, removed out a sandwich, lifted the upper lid of white bread, said he had lettuce and tomato, Max said he had a salami sandwich, Danny said he had a hard-boiled egg sandwich.

"Me, I got a ham sandwich," Clara said.

Danny glanced sharply at Goldie and Max. He had never knowingly eaten ham, he never would he told himself. Clara, held up a sandwich, called out, "I got two sandwiches, I can only eat one. Anybody like an extra ham sandwich?" Turning to Danny she asked, "Would you like it?" Danny shook his head and she said, "What's the matter?" Smiling, glancing at her friends, she turned back to him and asked, "You kosher?"

"We don't eat ham," Danny said.

"Why not? What's wrong with it?" Clara asked. "It's food, right? Kosher is for the old country, this is America, our families came here to get away from the old country, didn't they?"

Danny didn't know why he had become involved in this discussion but he could not help saying, "They came from the old country, yes. But they're still Jews."

"Who said they're not?" Clara said lifting her eyes. "But what has that got to do with eating ham?"

"Ham's not good for you," Max said.

Goldie and Max were talking to the other girls, Evelyn sat silent. Clara said, "What's wrong with you guys? They inspect ham here, ham's just as good as anything else." She leaned towards Danny and asked in a teasing tone of voice, "You eat milk after you eat meat? Cheese maybe, or a milk shake, a malted, a glass of milk, after you eat meat?"

"Yeah," Danny said. "Sometimes."

"That's supposed to be forbidden too, you know that?" Evelyn said.

"I'll do that but I won't eat ham," Danny said.

Clara glanced around at her friends. Some of them were smiling, Clara grinned at them, turned and said to Danny, "Oh, what do you know, a rabbi. We got us a rabbi. And where do you live? You promised to tell us before, before we went into the water."

He didn't like what she was doing, she was toying with him now, he wouldn't play along with her, he would not show her his growing anger. He said with forced pleasantness, "On the East Side."

Goldie now said to Evelyn, "Why? Now you tell us where you live."

"Brooklyn," Evelyn said. "Bensonhurst."

"Wouldn't you know," Danny said. "One of those."

"One of what?" Evelyn asked. Danny remained silent, she demanded, "One of what?"

Danny sighed. Now it had all become impossible. She lived in another world. Depression or no, if she lived in Bensonhurst, her family was one of those relatively few who were living well. Bensonhurst was one of the places where wealthier Jews lived.

He said to Evelyn, "One of those who don't have to worry about getting enough to eat, about living pushed into a goddammed tenement, about not having money for anything, that's what."

"Shouldn't I be glad that I'm not?" Evelyn said.

"I'm glad you're not," Danny replied. "I wouldn't wish it on you."

He felt that he couldn't be friends with any of the girls, that was impossible. Anyhow, you didn't see girls from Brooklyn, not from the part of Brooklyn in which she lived. The Bronx boys didn't, the East Side boys didn't. You didn't take a Brooklyn girl out, because when you did, you had to see her home, and late on a Saturday night or really early on a Sunday morning, after all the subways had stopped running express trains, you took a local train home. The train stopped at all the stations along the route all while you had fallen asleep on that subway seat for those two hours or more that it took to get to the East Side. Somewhat magically you awoke at your station and you staggered sleepily home.

It didn't pay. Not for that different world, not for that interminable ride, not to be condescended to. Not that. Anyway, he didn't have the money for a real date.

He would make the best of what he had for today and he said, "What the hell are we getting so hot and bothered for? You girls have your sandwiches, I'll have mine, we'll all have ours. What's all the fuss about?"

And now Evelyn said shaking her head, "Clara has chicken sandwiches, not ham," Clara began to laugh softly and Evelyn said, "She was just kidding." And to Clara, "Weren't you?"

"Yeah," Clara said with a grin.

"She loves to kid," Evelyn said.

"Yeah, so do I," Danny said in a flat tone of voice.

There was a silence, finally they began to eat. Max told a joke he had heard on the radio, he knew how to tell a joke. They laughed. The quick-moving feet of several boys running by sent up sprays of sand.

Someone, a jokester, had dug a hole in the sand, covered it with several flat sheets of newspaper, and had carefully topped it with a layer of sand so that the newspaper was no longer visible. They watched from a distance as an unsuspecting walker's leg tore through the paper, down to the hole's bottom. The victim, a man, began to shout curses as he slowly hobbled away. Danny looked back at his friends.

The group finished with their food, the three boys collected all the garbage, deposited it in a trash can nearby. When they returned to the girls Max said he was going in for a swim. Danny and Goldie followed him in, two of the girls trailed after them.

Into the surf once more and swimming, Danny couldn't help but think of Clara, Why should she have acted towards him the way she did? He wouldn't have done it to her. Angry with himself he thought, Why should he be bothered with her? He wouldn't ever see her again.

Finished with their swim, they returned to the blanket. Clara asked Danny, "You going to any of the rides?"

Danny said, "Nah. We'll spend all the time here, then we'll go home."

"The East Side," Clara said.

"Yeah," Goldie said. "The East Side. That's where we live."

Evelyn said, "I guess that's where most of our families came from. My parents used to live there when they first came over from the old country. It's just a place to live, that's all."

Danny smiled at her, she wasn't anything like Clara. Yet to him she too was still an outsider, one of those lucky people who didn't know what the East Side meant. Danny wished that Clara had to try to sleep through those terrible nights on the fire escapes of tenements. Or on a blistering tar roof. Or sweat a forever damp-ness that soaked your clothing, or go one day without eating.

It was now late afternoon. Some people, especially those families with small children, were leaving. Some space on the beach had become available, space littered with newspapers, bits of sandwiches, pieces of fruit, peach pits, wrappers from popsicles, empty soda bottles.

Danny noticed a spot not too far away. He nudged Goldie. "Let's go there," he said. "There's room now. Okay?"

Goldie shrugged and whispered, "Okay. These girls are nothing special."

"What're you talking about?" Evelyn asked.

"I was telling Goldie," Danny said, "that we have to be leaving soon, we're going back, we have to study."

"Study? What for? It's summertime, there's no school," Clara said.

"To be a rabbi," Danny said wanting to play with her. He winked at Max, who began to smile. "There's no summer vacation when you want to be a rabbi." Clara stared at him as Danny turned and said to Max, "Come on, let's go. We got a spot over there." He smiled and nodded to the other girls, the three boys picked up their canvas bags and clothing and said their goodbyes.

Seated on their own blanket, they looked back at the girls. Evelyn had arisen and was picking up her towel, the other girls stood up, gathering their things.

As the girls were leaving Clara called out to Danny and his friends, "Give my regards to Delancey Street."

"Sure," Danny replied putting on a huge smile for her.

Evelyn shrugged, the girls walked away, slowly disappeared in the milling crowd. The beach was still crowded, the ocean at its lower depths remained thronged. On the beach was a profusion of colors, of bathing suits, towels, blankets. People's skins ranged from pink to dark, dark ebony.

Goldie said, "I bet there's a million people out here today."

"More," Danny said. "Anyway, we'll see what the "Daily News" says it is tomorrow."

"A million and a half, I bet," Max said.

They swam once more. In the surf they met some girls with whom they went through the ritual of water-tackling. Everybody laughed, the girls screamed without terror as they were lifted up and heaved into the sea. It was all passing fun.

Time passed quickly, a river of humans, a flood, was now leaving the beach. Sadly it was time to go home. Danny said with a heavy sigh, "Well... we've got to go."

Max wanted one more dip in the ocean, it would be the last one. Running through the more open spaces on the beach they plunged into a high wave rolling towards shore, wishing desperately for the day not to end, yet knowing that it was ending, that nothing they could do would make time stop, make the earth stop revolving, make something happen so that they could swim there forever.

And soon, dripping wet, suddenly feeling tired and tight-skinned, prickling heat from their fresh sunburns, they plodded towards their blankets. They picked up their belongings, packed most of it in a roll, picked up their canvas bags and walked slowly towards the boardwalk.

There, under the boardwalk, in its cool dim shade, under their blankets, they slipped into their underwear and pants. When they were fully dressed, they went out into the late sunlight of the street.

Walking slowly towards the subway, they stopped for a five-cent cone of frozen custard. Savoring it slowly, they stood staring down the avenue. Finished with the custard, they plodded slowly on, the crowd streaming in from all the side streets, all converging on the subway station. They shoved their way through the turnstiles. The subway station was a din of noise, voices, shouts, the cries of babies. Danny pushed his way through to the station platform where he and his friends waited for the Sea Beach express train.

The train finally arrived. At this late afternoon hour it was no longer crowded with those coming to the beach, the train quickly disgorged its few passengers. There was a mad scramble by those returning home, a rush inside the cars, seats were immediately grabbed. Standees became pressed against one another, the subway pusher outside on the platform heaved and shoved a few more bodies into the cars. The doors hissed shut, the train began to move, the steel vertical beams of the station whooshed by and became a blur, they were out in the open, the local stations went whizzing by.

A sort of stupor came over Danny, he stood jammed between people, he could not fall if the train came to a sudden stop or turn, nobody could fall, each subway car was solid with jammed humanity. He could feel the heat rising under his shirt where his body had been exposed earlier to the sun.

Goldie was near him and he knew that Max was somewhere close by in that car. Danny felt tired, his energy used up, he felt the day was over, the sand gone, the ocean gone, the frolicking, the coolness, all gone. Now, in spite of the whirring subway fans, there was a solid heat in the car. He stared unseeingly through a grimy window of the car, there was a constant blur, everything was a dreamlike blur.

The subway went underground, the blackness clattered and echoed. It was almost night, the day was over. Only the heat was real, only the crush of humans was real, he was back at the beginning of the day with everything close, hot, clammy. But now he was going in the other direction, back to sleeping on fire escapes, of Tar Beach, that was becoming more and more a reality. Suddenly all that was real now, too real. Even on that train now still in Brooklyn, the East Side had become real, Coney Island a fading memory.

He said to Goldie, "We'll come back next Sunday again, right?" Knowing that next Sunday, seven days away, seemed like a year away.

A MATTER OF LANGUAGE

During those early Depression years, Marty had been accepted by the tuition-free College of the City of New York, CCNY, as it was called. From the beginning the students had been told that all of them had been the cream, the elite of studentdom, large numbers had been turned away to seek, if they could, entrance at other colleges. But everybody knew that the number of free colleges were exceedingly few. The weeding out had come and gone and now, here he was, at the uptown campus.

He had taken the subway from the Lower East Side, changed trains for the Broadway IRT line and had become lost in his studies while he sat on the woven straw seat of the train and had arrived at the 137th Street station. From there, which was Broadway, he had trudged up the hill to the campus with its gray stone Gothic buildings, its Lewisohn Stadium near Townsend Harris Hall.

Almost without thinking, moving from building to building to where his classes were located, he had entered this world, become a part of it. In the warm weather he ate the lunch his mother had made for him which he carried from home, stuffed in his imitation leather briefcase. Each morning, at his locker, he had deposited the filled brown paper bag into the locker and had returned to remove it when he had a free period sometime around noon.

Sometimes he ate alone, sitting outside on the campus, watching the stream of students flowing in all directions, to the gymnasium, to the Engineering Building, to the Main Building where the Great Hall was located. Other times in the alcoves near the cafeteria he ate along with some of his schoolmates, Danny, George, a few others. During lunch hours the alcoves were a huge babble of noise, of argumentations. Here the political ones, the

Socialists and the Communists held sway, preaching to the non-aligned.

That day, after his English class, outside on the campus bisected by a street running through it, Marty looked for one of his friends, but there was none, anyway, not yet. Near Townsend Harris Hall, he saw Earl, sitting alone, beginning to eat his lunch gazing vacantly into space. Marty, still looking for his other friends, approached, said Hi, Earl lost his glazed stare, looked up at Marty and smiled, his teeth white against his brown-black skin.

"Hey, Marty, how's it going?" Earl said speaking with a broad Southern accent.

"Not bad, Earl, not bad at all," Marty replied.

Danny appeared at Marty's side, then along came George, both of them said hello to Earl. George said, "Let's go to the alcoves to eat, see what's going on."

Earl began to shake his head. "Not me," he said. "Too many speeches, too much buddy-buddy there. Jesus, like they were some kind of insurance agents trying like all hell to sell you an insurance policy. I've had my fill of that. Too much." He bit into his sandwich.

"Come on, Earl," George said. "Don't you like to listen? Sometimes I think I can learn something."

"Unh-unh," Earl replied. "I don't like sloganeering, not at all."

Marty liked the soft sound of his speech, its slow rounded rhythms. Hell, he knew why Earl didn't want to go, it was obvious. Earl's skin was a magnet, he would be a prize to those political recruiters in the alcoves if they could sign him up in the Party. Shaking his head Earl said, "I like it right here, nice and quiet-like. No fussing, no speeches, nothing like that. You guys want to go there, go right ahead. I'm staying right here."

Marty looked down at the small pile of books that lay near Earl. There was the Spanish book containing the lesson that he and Earl could be called on to read and translate in the Spanish class scheduled the hour after this lunch hour.

"I'm going," George said. "You guys coming?"

"Yeah," Marty replied. Before leaving he said to Earl, "I'll be back soon. You'll be here? We'll go over the Spanish together."

"*Si, si,*" Earl said with a wan smile, his soft accent flavoring the words. "*La leccion. La* bitching *leccion.*"

"*La leccion,*" Marty said with a laugh. "*Con El Profesor* Garcia. The one, the only."

"The same," Earl said shaking his head sadly. "See you."

"To the alcoves, men," George said. "Let's go, guys."

They said their goodbyes to Earl and joined a ragged stream leading to the Main Building. Inside, still clutching their brownpaper lunch bags stained with blots of oily seep from their sandwiches, they entered one of the alcoves.

Italy had invaded Ethiopia and its emperor, Haile Selassie, had beseeched the world for help against the invader. To no avail. In the alcove they had just entered, one dominated by Communists, a speaker was reading aloud Count Ciano's, Mussolini's son-in-law's, lyrical account of the air bombing of Ethiopian villages, the bomb bursts erupting and forming petals like flowers, he had said. The speaker was telling the others there that Fascism was an evil to be fought and eradicated. And what were you doing about it?

Danny, munching on his sandwich said loudly, "Sure, that's bad. I don't like the bombing and killing of any people, I don't like dictatorships of any kind, and I'd go along with you," pointing to the speaker, "if I heard something about what's going on in Russia."

"Trotskyite!" several of the Party people said angrily, their eyes glaring coldly at him.

"The Soviet Union is the bastion of democracy!" someone else said loudly. The crowd in the alcove stirred, looked from Danny to the speaker who said, "There is true democracy in the Soviet Union, there is no discrimination—"

"That's not what I hear," Danny said. "My family came from Russia. Once in a while they still hear about what's going on."

"Malcontents," the speaker said. He gave a false smile to Danny as he glanced out at the crowd. "Did your family like it so much under the Czar, huh? Why in hell did they run to America if it was good there then?"

"They ran like your family ran," George said. "They didn't like the pogroms, the forced conscriptions into the army that discriminated against them, they didn't like being in those *shtetl* ghettoes, they didn't like being treated like sub-humans. You know that and I know that. But your family also ran to America. Then why do you say or give the impression that this is such a bad place?" The speaker had attempted to interrupt George but the crowd had shouted him down and George had taken over for the moment.

Marty said, "What you just said about people running here away from the Czar, if you think it's so bad here, why don't you go there?"

A few listeners said, Yeah, Why? Others, backing the speaker, hurled taunting questions at Marty, All you know is personal attack, is that it? What do you know, talking like that? Argue the question, you're an ignoramus, there were loud voices everywhere.

Marty wondered why he had come to this alcove, Why hadn't he remained outside in the sunlight and eaten his lunch there? Was it information he wanted? he asked himself. No, not really. He knew about Italy and Ethiopia, what he wanted were answers to what was going on in the world, a world seeming to go out of control. He wanted a simple answer, yet the world was complex, simplicity had vanished a long time ago. But there had to be an answer, a remedy for what was going on.

The speaker to whom he had directed his question was now saying, "I'm here because I'm an American, that's why."

Marty said nothing, it was no use. He shrugged, said to the speaker, "And so are we."

"So don't talk about why our families came over here," Danny said.

"I'm talking about Fascism," the speaker said. "I'm talking about the illegal invasion of a country by Mussolini. I'm talking about the Fascists killing the Ethiopians, that's what I'm talking about."

The friends of the speaker nodded their heads. One of them said, "Down with Fascism!"

Marty turned and said quickly to his friends, "Let's get out of here." He crumpled the top of his lunch bag, inside there remained an apple and a slice of sponge cake still to be eaten.

"The same old Party line," George said. "Over and over again. I get tired hearing it all the time."

As they began to leave Danny said to them, "I'm staying. I just want to know what they have to say."

Marty shrugged, he and George left the alcove, joined the flow of students out into the street. As they emerged into the sunlight, more students were now clustered in groups, some still eating their lunches, others discussing class assignments, talking about forthcoming tests, some reading lines from books in half-aloud mumbles. Here and there, a lone student sat reading or slowly eating his lunch.

The two of them stopped near the large bust of Abraham Lincoln sitting on its pedestal, its face blotched with green paint that someone had hurled on it in an act of political defiance. Marty said to nobody in particular, "Yeah, it's true, the same old Party line. But it's also true, they've invaded Ethiopia, they're killing people. It could mean the spread of war."

"No," George said. "It's something that's contained, a sort of private war, something between Mussolini and Haile Selassie. Things'll settle down, everything'll become quiet soon, you'll see."

"Maybe," Marty said. "I hope so. There's enough trouble in this world without adding to it."

They stood in silence for a moment. George left to go to one of the other buildings where his next class was to be held. Marty looked across the campus, he saw Earl still sitting in the same spot, deep in thought. Marty approached, said Hi, Earl looked up at him and smiled.

"Back so soon?" Earl said with a grin.

"Yeah. Can't stand the talk, talk, talk," Marty said.

"I know how it is," Earl said.

As he sat down beside Earl, Marty reached into his paper bag, grasped the apple and said, "I get tired of their constant recruiting tactics, you know?" He bit into the apple with a liquid crackling sound.

"Oh, I know, I sure do know," Earl said. "You don't know what it's like—" He was about to say more but he suddenly became silent.

Marty glanced at him. Yes, Marty knew, it had been so obvious. All the recruiters had to see was a black face, and it became a crusade, they had to have that person a member of the Party. They discussed among themselves, they planned and campaigned for that prospective member, they never let up. Marty bit into the apple once more.

The apple finished, the slice of cake now in his hand, Marty said to Earl, "Want a piece of cake?"

"No, no," Earl said in his slow drawl. "Thanks. I've had mine. Apple pie, no less. Not blueberry, but apple." Laughing now, he deliberately pronounced the bee as a cross between a vee and a bee. Marty began to laugh loudly.

Early in the semester Professor Garcia who was on staff at the college for over twenty years and had originally come from Spain over thirty years earlier, had lectured the class on Spanish pronunciation. He would deliberately ask one of the students to read a passage in Spanish containing the word, *vivir*. As the student pronounced the word, the professor stopped the reading and said in his still heavily-accented English, "What is that word? I did not hear it. Again." The student said the word once more and Professor Garcia said emphatically, almost angrily, "No, no, no! It is *vivir*," pronouncing the vee as a cross between a bee and a vee. "*Vivir*. You hear it? Say it," he said to the student. The student pronounced the word with great deliberation and Professor Garcia said to the class, "Say it!" Almost in unison the other students pronounced the word. "That is much better," Professor Garcia said.

"But our teachers never told us, we always pronounced it as a vee," one of the students said.

"I cannod be responsible for the lazy teachers," Professor Garcia said. "*Porque* they do not know, what do American teachers know? Americans, know one thing good, to make apple pie, that is what they know."

Marty had finished his piece of cake, brushed the crumbs from his clothing, wadded the brown paper bag into a wrinkled ball. He said to Earl, "How's it going? About Spanish, I mean."

Earl remained silent for a moment then said, "One thing I learned in Garcia's class. No zmoking. My friend," he said with mock seriousness, "I do no zmoke."

Marty nodded. It was a passion with the professor, his campaign about not zmoking. All that was necessary was for a student to mention the word, smoking, and the professor was off, the entire class would be spent on the evils of smoking. At each class, if he could, one of the students would attempt to bring up the subject to divert that hour to Professor Garcia's oration instead of the lesson for the day.

"Somebody'll give it a try at class today," Marty said.

"Anyway, you'll do okay, Earl. Don't let him ride you, just take it easy."

Earl stared at Marty, finally said, "Yeah. Yeah."

Finally Marty asked, "You do the reading for today?" Earl nodded and Marty said, "Well, that's all you need." Marty knew it sounded false, perhaps patronizing, although he hadn't meant it to be so, but what could he say to Earl, what was there to say to him?

Earl began to pick up his books. "Got to go," he said. "See you."

As Earl began to walk away Marty said to him, "See you in Spanish class."

Without slowing his pace Earl replied, "Yeah."

Marty saw Earl disappear into Townsend Harris Hall. There was still a little time before the next class and he glanced at his Spanish book and began to read hearing in his mind Professor Garcia's accented voice saying, I cannot be responsible for the lazy teachers.

Later, in the Spanish class, before Marty or anybody else could mention something about smoking, Professor Garcia began the recitation by calling on one of the students to begin reading the assignment. It was evident that there would be no discussion on no zmoking today. The Spanish lesson was on in earnest, it could not be derailed. The first student finished with his reading and translation, the professor called on another student, then another. The fourth student to be called on was Earl.

Earl, tense, nervous, began reading slowly and deliberately. As hard as he tried he could not remove his Southern drawl, it seeped into the Spanish words he uttered.

Suddenly furious Professor Garcia shouted out, "No, no, no! It is enough! *Por dios*, what is wrong with you, eh? You cannod pronounce the words like they should!" Earl stopped, frozen, his face rigid, his eyes almost closed, the jaw muscles of his face knotting and moving. And Professor Garcia, anger spread on his face, his clenched fist banging on his desk, that anger now in his speech making his English even more accented, said, "I cannod onnerstan' how you have this terrible accend in Es-panish. What is wrong with you, eh?"

Marty couldn't bear to look at Earl's face any longer, it was too much. Filled with anger he turned away, stared hard at Professor Garcia, hating him now, hearing those damned mispronounced English words beating on Earl.

GYPSY

It was a mistake, she knew it. She shouldn't have said it, she knew too well that it would begin the argument, the words would become louder and louder, the exchanges more hurting. It had been just a few words but it would end in a war.

I don't like that name, she had said looking away from her father as he sat across the kitchen table. He, as he always had, had called her by her Hebrew name, Itteh.

What do you mean? he had said suddenly looking up from his supper plate, his voice rising in anger, his face setting in steely fury, his eyes narrowing. Itteh, Itteh, that's, your name. That's what it is. Itteh in Hebrew, Yetta in English. And Zuckerman after that, the last name. Tzuckermann he had said, pronouncing it the Old Country way. She had not been able to stop it, the words had erupted from her mouth and she had thought bitterly, I hate that name, do you understand? And now, wishing she hadn't said that simple phrase, the argument had become joined, her father's face had become even more rigid. It had taken on its cast of retribution, those eyes of his now becoming larger and larger. Her mother at the stove holding a plate of boiled chicken that was to be her own serving, had now become a statue there except for her eyes rolling then momentarily staring up at the ceiling of the room.

She turned her glance away from her mother and said, "I don't like the name, Yetta Zuckerman," the words were uncontrollable, surging up within her in a tide that her mouth couldn't stop. "It's from the Old Country, it's—"

"Shut up!" her father shouted slamming his fist down on the porcelain top of the kitchen table. "You must be crazy! Yes!" He turned to his wife near him now at the table, she mechanically placed her half-filled plate on the table as she glanced hurriedly at her husband then her daughter. "You hear that, hah?" Yetta's father was saying. "You hear that from a daughter? She's ashamed. Of her name, Itteh, that was her great grandmother's name, she's ashamed of our name, Zuckerman. Our name, you hear that?"

Yetta's mother stared at her daughter as she said, "You should be ashamed. To say a thing like that."

"It's nineteen thirty-five. The twentieth century. It's not like the Old Country, a hundred years ago. Here it's different. You don't need the old names, the old customs."

"You need the new, hah?" her father said to her in a barely controlled tone of voice. "You're going to be the new person. Free. Yeah?" He turned towards his wife and said to her, "You hear that? Free. Hah?" He turned once more to his daughter and said, "Free to do what? Free to live how? Tell me. You know so much, tell me."

His face jutted across the table, she could hear his heavy breathing, could see the muscles of his jaw tensed and knotted.

Yetta shut her eyes and said wearily, "You don't understand."

Why had she started all of this? It was all useless, the words, the anger, going round and round in tighter and tighter coils, nothing resolved, it never was. What came out of it all was her anguish which she couldn't stand, this living on the Lower East Side in this tenement which she couldn't bear, always being forced to be, to do what she didn't want.

I don't want it! her mind silently shouted out to her. I can't stand it! I won't have it! I can't, I can't!

And her father clean-shaven except for his small Van Dyke beard, a man who should know better, he had run from Russia to escape the hated life there, the pogroms, the forced conscription into the army, the Russian Pale, the anti-Semitism. He had run from Russia to America, had gone to night school, had totally mastered the English language, had found work as a writer for the Jewish newspaper, the "Forward," who spoke English well except for that lingering foreign accent, a man who seemed liberated to everybody around them but as far as she was concerned was still shackled to the old ways and would forever remain chained to the ghetto mentality.

And her mother... With that thought Yetta had shrugged to herself. Her mother, a housekeeper, that was her life. That and to bear children although she had had only Yetta. There was more to life than that, than washing clothes, preparing meals, being a drudge.

Her father said mimicking her words, "I don't understand, hah?" He gave a humorless laugh. "You, you don't understand. Nothing, you hear? Not one single thing." He shook his head in disbelief, turned to his silent wife who still stood motionless at the table and said to her, "Eighteen years old and she knows everything. I don't know, her mother doesn't know. I don't understand, her mother doesn't understand. Only she knows." He turned to his daughter and said bitterly, "You know nothing. You're an idiot." And audibly, to himself, "To have a daughter like that."

This time Yetta remained silent, there was no sense in arguing, it led nowhere. She would have to get out, get her own place, make her own world, be her own person, not a puppet worked by the whims of her parents.

She shut her eyes momentarily and said fiercely to herself, I can't stay. It's hell. I must leave.

Previously, over two years ago, Edie Romany had moved from her other apartment in Greenwich Village to a new place on Bank Street which she shared with two other women. The new apartment was small, it had two bedrooms, but it was all they could afford, they managed, one of them sleeping on the day bed in the living room. They were friends, they seemed to understand one another and they understood that when one of them wanted the sole use of the apartment for a night, the others would find a place to sleep somewhere else, at a friend's. And there were times when the three of them went out together to somewhere in the Village, just to sit and talk, have something to eat and drink.

They spoke of literature, one of them wanted to be a writer; they spoke of art, the other woman wanted to be an artist. They spoke of current news topics, one of the women was radical, speaking mainly of the class struggle, of the bourgeoisie, of capitalist imperialism. But in spite of that woman's radical speeches, she seemed to be a nice person and she fit in well with Edie and the third woman who was less radical although she was caught up in social issues, the problems of the poor, of the Negro, in the necessity of having a union for all workers.

That was all well and good. But while she, Edie, was interested in social issues too, she was a Gypsy. With her dark skin, her black hair, her dark eyes like two large olives, wearing her two large hoop earrings which danced down upon her cheeks when she moved, her skirt with its many colors, a vividly-hued blouse, black espadrilles laced above her ankles, she knew that she was different from the other two. They never called her Gypsy to her face, only Edie. But when others spoke of her, she was called the Gypsy.

She had moved many times and had shared many apartments in the Village. Often it was the incompatibility of those she had lived with, other times because the places had been too small and too cramped. Once she had lived alone in a single small room but it had been a sort of a prison for her, a place to run from.

Before the war she had worked in several factories, one of them at a machine sewing men's ties, another in a small place that manufactured cosmetics. She had gone from that to being a waitress in the Village Barn on Eighth Street, the money was better, it wasn't bad, but it wasn't good either, you lived on tips, the hours were terrible, you started in the evening and worked till the place stopped serving late at night. Edie wanted the night hours for herself, to be able to date, to go out somewhere with a man and enjoy herself. She didn't want to be tied to that night job, to have to work weekends, it was not for her. She had waitressed in one place after another during the war, but still not satisfied, she had looked around and finally found a job she now held in the Village, selling costume jewelry at Frankie Tomaselli's shop.

Frankie was a wild one, working bare-chested at his bench, an acetylene torch in his hand, welding his designs together, the flare of the torch lighting up his skin. Visible to all who entered his shop, he would glance up momentarily when someone entered and if it was a pretty woman he would stop his work, and torch still held in his hand would survey the woman closely. If the visitor met his expectations he would give her a great smile, nod his head in appreciation and slowly return to his work.

He was an easy boss, he allowed Edie to wear his jewelry on loan, whenever she felt she wanted to wear new earrings or a pin or a ring. He loved to joke, telling stories as he worked, making Edie laugh.

He went out with many women during those first few months when Edie was working at the shop. But one day he asked her to go out with him the coming Saturday night to Cafe Society Downtown, a nightclub, to hear Josh White sing his songs while that guitar, Josh's guitar, would thrum out those unbelievable chords that was Josh's trademark.

At the nightclub, Josh, an unlit cigarette tucked at an angle over one ear, sang one folksong after another, his high warm voice fused with the guitar chords which sang to her. After the show, at their table, Edie and Frankie watched as Josh moved onto the floor of the nightclub, expertly weaving between the small tables crowded near one another, making his stops here and there, bending slightly to speak to someone, laughing, his laughter loud and deep.

"He sure is something" Frankie said to Edie. "You can't help noticing him, can you?" Frankie turned his face away from Josh and stared at Edie as he said, "You know, I like being with you. You enjoy everything so much, you really do.

She smiled at him and said, "You do too, Frank." She had never called him Frankie although that was his name in her mind.

"It's Frankie, Frankie," he said.

"You too, Frankie," she said with a bright laugh. "You know," she said, "it's different being here with you than it is when were both in the store together, isn't it?"

"Yeah," he said. "Lots." He puffed on his cigarette, exhaled, and said, the white smoke coming from his mouth, "We got to change that somewhat, okay?"

Josh stopped at their table. He knew Frankie who insisted that Josh sit down at their table and have a drink with them. Frankie introduced Edie to Josh, caught the waiter who was passing by and ordered drinks for all of them.

"A Gypsy?" Josh said staring at her. "You mean, a real one?"

Sure," Frankie replied. "I pick the good ones, don't I? The different ones. She's a Gypsy princess too. No run-of-the-mill ones for me."

"A Gypsy princess," Josh said.

Edie said, "And no run-of-the-mill ones for me either." Turning to Josh she said, "I know what they call him, Wild Frankie. They don't call him that for nothing. He sure isn't your average guy, is he?"

"It's a tough world," Frankie said. "You got to be wild to bear all those troubles that hit you. Right, Josh?"

"Right," Josh replied. He lifted his glass, nodded to them in a silent toast and downed the drink. "Got to go," Josh said with a laugh. "I got some friends out there I got to say hello to. You know how it is." And to Edie, "Glad to meet you." Tilting his head he said, "A real Gypsy. What do you know. A princess too." He arose from his chair, moved on to another table nearby, bent to talk to someone there, laughed loud and long.

At their table Edie and Frankie watched as Josh moved on, snaking between tables, making his stops, laughing, touring the room.

Frankie and Edie had a good time the remainder of the evening. Talking, smoking, having something to eat, watching the show. To Edie it was a wonderful first date.

Before her second date with Frankie a few weeks later, she attempted to compartmentalize her role with Frankie and her feelings towards him. While she was in the store, she worked for Frankie. He was her boss. Period. And when he had taken her out to Cafe Society, that had been something else. To her he was another

Frankie, a date unencumbered by who he was at the store. On a date he's someone else, no boss.

He asked her for another date. They went to the Village Vanguard, they pushed their way through the crowd at the door. Frankie approached the head waiter and said to him as he shook his hand, "I love you, pal. Get a nice table for me."

"Hey," the head waiter replied with a laugh. "Who don't love me? They all love me on Saturday night, they want that good table. And they all love Frankie. Right?"

They were given a table near the small stage. Soon the Iron Duke appeared singing his Calypso songs, taking topics shouted out by the crowd, instantly forming and rhyming the lyrics. Edie found herself caught up in the atmosphere, she loved the Iron Duke, she loved his singing, she loved the nightclub, she loved being there with Frankie.

They danced after the show, Frankie became wilder and wilder, snapping his fingers loudly to the beat of the music, spinning and moving quickly so that slowly at first, some of the other couples on the floor stood on the side of the dance floor and watched Frankie and Edie glide and gyrate. When the music was over, there was wild applause from the onlookers. Frankie bowed several times to the grinning audience.

"I liked that," he said when they were at their table once more. "Didn't you?"

Edie said with a laugh, "It's crazy. You're crazy. And I love it."

"'Yeah," he replied. "I love it too. And I am crazy. And you're a little crazy too. We make a good pair, don't we?"

"How do you mean?" she replied.

"We ought to be together, living together. Right?" He stared into her face and said, "Why not?"

"Well . . ." she said. Well ... she thought, why not? Why not enjoy life while I can? And I will with Frankie. What am I waiting for?

She would move into his three-room apartment on Morton Street, she would still work for him of course, work would be work, it was understood that their true personal lives would not intrude upon the functioning of the store.

Despite the admonitions of her two women friends who shared the apartment, who warned her to be cautious, everybody in the Village knew Frankie was wild, that he was a notorious womanizer, she would only bring grief to herself, Edie moved out of their shared apartment and went to live with Frankie.

She was behind the counter of the store arranging a display of newly-designed pins, Frankie was at his workbench, at work on a pair of earrings, when the man entered. She barely noticed him, she was busy arranging the display and still looking down at the pins had said mechanically, "Yes? Can I help you?"

When she glanced up the man was staring at her. He stood stock-still, his stare never wavering. There was something... No, now she suddenly knew it, it was impossible! How could it be? It was her father. After all these years, how could he have found her? After fifteen years, how? How?

Staring grimly at her, he approached the counter, she noticed that his black Van Dyke beard was now totally gray. His eyes were puffed, deep circles of flesh beneath them. His face was the face of before, of long ago, only older, lined and creased.

Now at the counter he said, "Itteh, Itteh, it's you?"

She couldn't bear it. It wasn't true. Why this? Why to her? "I can't talk to you," she whispered hoarsely to him. "Please go. Please."

"I go nowhere. I stay here," he said his voice beginning to rise. "I want to talk to you."

"Something wrong?" Frankie, bare-chested, called out from his bench. "Is everything all right?"

Edie glanced wildly at him. "It's nothing. Nothing's wrong," she said in a rush of words attempting to control herself. And to her father in a whisper, "I can't talk to you."

"You talk to me here," he replied, his words deliberate. "Or you talk to me someplace else, I don't care. But you will talk to me, you hear? I'm not going away."

"S-sh!" she whispered crazily. Glancing quickly at Frankie who was staring at them she called out to him in a false cheery voice, "Frankie, I'm going out for a few minutes. Be right back."

Without waiting for a reply, she hurried from behind the counter, went to the door, was out in the street, her father following her. She wished him gone, she didn't want him beside her, she didn't want him to talk to her, especially on the street where people might see them together. She began to run to a nearby coffee shop, entered, hurried to a table lost in a far corner. When she sat down she saw her father at the door of the shop, breathing heavily.

Staring at her, he approached the table and sat down. There was a heavy silence. She didn't know how to begin, what to say. This was an inconceivable meeting, how could she force time to fly by so that all this would be over with, how to make this nightmare disappear?

The waitress appeared, Edie said mechanically to her, "Coffee." Without looking up her father nodded to the waitress.

The waitress was gone, the terrible leaden silence between Edie and her father remained. Shifting his chair so that he was now closer to the table he cleared his throat and said to her, "So this is who you are. So this is what you do. So this is what you are."

Edie made no reply. Long long ago when she had been a member of the family she had learned to armor herself against the fear of them, both her mother and her father, but especially her father. She had vowed to herself never to show them her pain, she would never never react to their barbs, she had sworn she would never cry, at least when they were present. Not show them anything, not fall into the trap of saying what they wanted to hear or see. She would live her own life, in her own way, according to her own wishes, not the one they had designed for her.

"Why are you here?" she finally heard herself say in a strange foreign voice.

"Why shouldn't I be here?" she heard him say. "I'm your father. I have a right to talk to my daughter. Is there a law against it?"

The waitress arrived, placed the cups of coffee in front of them. When she was gone, Edie forced herself to look at him, attempted to make her voice seem calm and normal, said, "There's no law against it. What do you want?"

Her father gave a great quivering sigh. "I want to find my daughter," he said at last. "It's fifteen years, Itteh."

"I'm not Itteh," she snapped angrily looking squarely into her father's face. "Itteh's dead, do you hear me?"

He shut his eyes tightly, "So Itteh's dead," he said flatly. "So who is my daughter now? Tell me."

She could almost feel the bottled anger behind his words. Shaking her head she stared down at the brown liquid in her coffee cup, forced herself to look at him once more and she said, "I'm Edie. That's my name. Do you understand?"

"Ah!" he whispered, laughing scornfully. "So now I have no daughter, hah?"

"You should've had no children," she said turning away from his stare.

"We should've had children," her father said. "And we should've had a daughter who wasn't ashamed of herself, either. Or ashamed of her parents, maybe how they looked, how they acted, of how they spoke. Someone not be ashamed of what she was." She attempted to interrupt him but his words trampled on angrily. "What are you now? A Gypsy?" He began to laugh bitterly. "Oh, my God, my God," he said. And finally his face close to hers he asked, "Why that? Why not something else? Why not Irish? Or Italian? Or Greek? Why a Gypsy?"

"You would've complained if I had chosen anything," she said angrily.

She stared hard at him and he nodded. "Yeah. Sure," he replied. "I certainly would've. But, why? Why choose anything? Why not just be what you are?"

"I did it," she said deliberately, "because I wanted to."

"Because I wanted to," he mimicked Edie's voice. His eyes slitted in anger, said, "Like a three-year-old wanting everything, wanting nothing, just wanting. Like a baby throwing a tantrum," talking now in a childlike voice, "because I want, because I want."

There was an intolerable silence and finally she said angrily, "You want what you want, I'll want what I want."

"Ah!" he said shutting his eyes, shaking his head sadly.

Edie looked away, stared into the mirror above the counter of the shop. They sat angled so that she could see their images in that long mirror. She could see her father's face as he spoke, his mouth moving, the words coming from a different direction than that from that mirror. Staring at the mirror she felt it was totally unreal, it was not her father speaking but a flat picture that pretended to be her father and she heard him say, "—-exotic, you wanted something exotic, something new. But nothing is new forever, it becomes the usual, a habit, the exotic becomes commonplace. Then what? Another passage to another thing? And then one after that? Never thinking about what you are, who you are." He shook his head and mumbled, "*A-a-i.*" He stared down at his hands and said softly, "To have it come to this. To this."

"I didn't ask to be born," she said in a furious whisper. "Who asked you to have me? You wanted to do that—that thing with her. That's why you had me."

"That's enough!" her father shouted. Across the room of the shop, the waitress, startled, stared at them. Edie shrunk within herself, she had never been able to withstand his anger, had always been afraid of it. As she was now. "Who do you think you're talking to?" her father roared out. "To one of your friends, hah? I'm—"

"Get out! Get out of here, you hear me?" she began to shout, not looking at him. She half-arose but her father was out of his chair, his back to her, he was striding furiously out of the coffee shop. The door was now closing, he was gone. She sat down in her chair once more, stared out at the room seeing nothing, telling herself not to cry, she would not cry, she would never cry. Go! Go! And don't come back, ever, she said silently to the door of the shop, to the emptiness there. Slowly she ran the back of her hand across her nose.

It had been almost two years since she had last seen her father. She had wondered how he had come to find her that day he had appeared at the store. And she had suddenly remembered. A Saturday night before his appearance when the store had been busy and some couples, obviously visitors to the Village, had entered. The women had approached the counter, the men stood in a small huddle near the door, and Edie had looked up at the men, there was something vaguely familiar about one of the faces. It was a fleeting thought to her then.

Later, when she had asked herself over and over again, how had her father known where she was, it had come to her. One of the men was her cousin, yes, Norman, it must've been Norman, and although she had known him when he had been ten or twelve, the face was almost the same, only older. She had noticed his fixed glance on her, but the store had been so busy, there was a constant flow in and out, and almost an hour later, when the customers had thinned out, she had looked up and they were gone.

So it had been Norman, possibly indecisive in his discovery of her, probably later he had come to realize who she was and had gone to her father and told him. It was funny, funny in a sort of crazy way, that for fifteen years her father hadn't been able to find her although they had been no more that a half hour away from each other. You could bury yourself in the city and not be found. Why had Norman come along and spoiled it all?

Now and then she thought of her mother and father, those thoughts cruelly creeping into her mind. She would battle silently to erase them, to exile them to some deep remoteness, bury them in a deep crevasse of her mind, a place that would be lost to her forever. But there was no such place. The thoughts came, and when they did, she occupied herself with useless things to do, anything, to dispel them.

And they triggered off other thoughts, of the time at a party with Frankie and some of their friends when one of the men speaking of a recent business transaction, in conversation with Frankie, had said, So I jewed him down, got a better price, saved myself a nice little bundle, not bad, eh? She had involuntarily stiffened at that phrase, the usage of that word. And Frankie hadn't said anything.

he didn't know its meaning to her, he would never know. It was nothing to him. Yet why hadn't she let it slip by, why remember it, it was only a word. Damn him! Damn that word! Damn everything that made her react in this way!

At the shop she had allowed herself to take notice of Frankie's reactions when some pretty women entered the store, his quick admiring glances at them as he surveyed their figures and faces. She told herself that he worked bare-chested at his bench to attract the women who came into the shop. Maybe, she told herself, she was imagining things, maybe she was making something out of nothing. Maybe. Maybe not.

She worked in the shop. She was still the Gypsy princess except for that brief painful interlude with her father. But that had been almost two years earlier. She probably wouldn't see him again. And those other things that had plagued her since his visit, of who she really was, of what she had been before she had become a Gypsy, of what would happen to her in the future, all these thoughts had slowly begun to fade away. She was Edie Romany, that was who she was, what she always would be. That was all. And that was that.

That night she was alone in the apartment. Things were slow at the shop, Frankie was scheduled to attend a meeting of some sort, she had decided to come home earlier than usual to work on the bills of the business while he remained at the shop until it was time to close. There was a knock on the door. She looked up from the ledger she was working on. "Who is it?" she asked.

"Me," the voice said faintly.

She arose, went to the door. "Who?" she asked.

"Me. Me," the suddenly familiar voice said.

"Go away!" she said quickly. "Just go away!"

From behind the door her father's voice said, "Open the door, you hear? I won't go away. Open up!" There was the heavy banging of his fist on the door. "Open up! Open up!" his voice shouted out.

The door shuddered under the pounding of his fist. She thought of the neighbors, it was impossible for them not to hear the clamorous banging on the door. There was no alternative. She was defeated.

"Stop!" she called out. "I'm opening the door. Just stop!"

The banging ceased. With a great sigh of despair she opened the door. And there he stood, her father, he looked much older than that other time two years before when she had last seen him. Without a word he entered the apartment, went up the hallway to where the light shone over the table Edie had been working on in the living room. She glanced quickly out into the hallway to see whether any of the neighbors had opened their doors to see what had been going on. No, all was quiet, and quickly Edie closed her door, locked it, stood for a moment as she invisibly armored herself against what was to come.

When she entered the living room he stood there and said to her, "This is how it is, eh? That I must bang on the door and yell, to be let in by my daughter, the Gypsy, yeah?"

He glared at her and she approached the table. He sat down in one of the easy chairs and she, still standing, said, "What do you want?"

"Ah!" he whispered looking up at her. "Such a gracious welcome—"

"No, no, no," she said. "I won't listen to that. What do you want?"

"I want my daughter back," he said as he sat down.

She shut her eyes against the scene, she wished she had some way to plug her ears against those words. She said in a dead tone of voice, "You're looking for a small child. I'm a grown woman. What you're looking for is gone, doesn't exist. Why can't you understand that?"

"Oh, I understand. I understand very well. Lots of things. I see my daughter wasting her life, that I understand. I see her pretend to be what she isn't, that I can see." He looked up at her once more and asked, "Are you married? I see on the letter box downstairs a different name for this apartment." She shook her head. "Are there children?" She shook her head once more. "Then what do you have? Tell me." Something in Edie had gone out of her, that steel she had forged internally whenever she had faced him. And now she waited, afraid of his words, knowing that more would come. And her father said, "You have no children. Who will remember you when you are gone, hah? Who will say, My mother, my father, or my grandmother, my grand-father, used to say this, do that, play special games with us, call us by special pet names? Who? What is the value of a life if it is not in remembrance by children, grandchildren? Without that, when you are gone, it is as if you never were there, that a shadow had come and gone," he snapped his fingers, "Like that."

"I don't want to hear it," she finally said grasping the back of a chair.

"I want it said. I must say it." He looked across the table, stared at his clenched fist. She glanced across the room, into the night-blackened windows, into the outer night. Her father's voice went on, "You are living a life of pretense, of fraud. You live with that bare-chested one—that man—" She began to interrupt but his words went on relentlessly, "that man who will leave you some day." She turned to walk away and her father said wearily to her, "Let me talk. I can see it. Why can't you? When that happens what will you do? Live with another man? And then? And then?" He paused, she said nothing. "Life is nothing without commitment. When you live together, there is nothing, no commitment because you can live together and one of you can decide to leave. When you marry there is commitment, with the other person, with the families, with society."

She felt her anger rising now. Once again grasping the back of the chair she leaned forward towards her father and said, "I'll live with somebody if I want to, I'll get married to somebody if I want to. Or I won't. I don't have to ask anybody, you hear me?"

"Yeah. Sure, sure," her father replied, his words full of disbe-lief, of disapproval. "And children?"

"Children? What for?" she said. "Who wants children in a crazy world like this?"

"It's the only world we have. It can be a terrible world, Itteh, terrible. But we must try to make it better, however we can—"

Oh, my God! she thought. He's preaching now. She couldn't stand it, she wished Frankie was there, he would be able to manage her father, Frankie would argue for her. But no, she suddenly thought. There will be a fight, an argument, it would have to come to that between them. She knew there were other, still unspoken issues between them, and that would come out into the open. She looked at the clock ticking on the small table in of a narrow vertical mirror on the wall above it. Frankie might be coming home soon, just to change before the meeting. Stay away, Frankie, she silently prayed. Don't come. Let him leave here, first. Just let him leave. Please.

"It's enough," she heard herself say to her father. "You've had your say. Enough."

"No, Itteh—" he began.

"I'm not Itteh!" she shouted out. "Itteh's gone, finished, dead."

"Yes!" he shouted in return. "Itteh is dead. There was another Itteh, a cousin of yours, another named after your great grandmother, she remained in the Old Country. They killed her. That Itteh went up in smoke and ashes with most of the family. Maybe all, I don't know. I just now found out about her and some of the others. That's why I came to see you, to make you realize you have an obligation—"

"What obligation?" Edie asked, startled now, bewildered, furious at her father for telling her all this. "What did I, what do I owe her? Did I ask her to stay in the Old Country? Did I force her to stay, what did I do to her?"

"You forgot about her," her father said slowly. "You abandoned her and the others too by disowning all of them. In a way you did to yourself what Hitler did to them. You murdered yourself, one less Jew in the world, without even the use of the camps and the ovens. You should be proud of that, Itteh, Edie, Gypsy, whatever you are. You did Hitler's work. You should get a medal for that from him."

Furious now, the room around her a swirl, she screamed at her father, "Get out of here! Don't come back! I don't want to see you, I don't to hear you! Get out!"

Silence. Heavy. Unbearable. Her father had risen from the chair and now stood motionless. As he stared at her, she noticed his controlled anger showing only in his clenched fists banging against his thighs. She stared at the slow metronome of the movement of his fists smiting himself. Then without another word he turned and left the apartment.

She stared at the closed door, hearing her heavy breathing, inhale, exhale, inhale, exhale, the tick of the clock keeping pace with the sounds coming from within her. She looked around the room, empty, empty at last, silent, silent at last. No more words, no more reproaches, no more anything. At last that was all over. Finished. Done with. She began to stare out into space, hearing within her, Itteh, Itteh, the name she wanted lost and forgotten. But this other thing crept into her mind, remained there, would not leave, there had been another Itteh, someone she had never known but someone who had, in some fashion, been a part of her, their names had been attached, Siamese-twinlike. And that Itteh was gone. Smoke and ashes, her father had said, his voice still rumbling in her mind.

No, she wouldn't cry, she couldn't cry, she had welded that armor to herself too well. And she thought, A whole family, gone? Destroyed?

It wasn't a definite thought, it was as if she had become a marionette moving to invisible manipulations. Slowly, almost trancelike, she walked to a closet in the kitchen, removed a small dish, a book of matches, a small white candle which she had put there as a reserve should the electricity fail, returned to the living room, went to the small table in front of the narrow mirror. She lit a match, it hissed into flame and with the lit end heated the bottom of the candle, saw it begin to soften and melt, stood it upright in the cooling wax adhering to the plate, lit the wick of the candle, saw its flame sputter, come alive as she blew out the fire of the match.

She returned to the large table, sat down, and fascinated by the candle's flame, stared at it. Now and then she looked into the mirror, watched its flame flicker and twist, jump and curl, soon saw its melted wax in slow small trickles, like tears, roll slowly down its sides. Suddenly, she emerged from her trance, saw the flickering flame, and realized that in the old tradition, she had lit a candle for the dead.